MW01449778

coolness to the wind

the publishing CIRCLE™

Text copyright © 2024 Candace Cox
All rights reserved.

Without in any way limiting the author's and publisher's exclusive rights under copyright, any use of this publication to "train" generative artificial intelligence (AI) technologies to generate text is expressly prohibited.

No part of this publication may be reproduced or transmitted form or by any means, mechanical or electronic, including photocopying and recording, or by any information storage and retrieval system without permissions and writing from the publisher (except by a reviewer, who may quote brief passages and/or short brief video clips in a review.)

Send permission requests to the publisher at:
admin@thepublishingcircle.com.
Attention: Permissions Coordinator
Regarding Skylar Slate

This is a work of fiction. Names, characters, organizations, places, events, and incidents are either products of the author's imagination or are used fictitiously. Any resemblance to actual persons, living or dead, or actual events is purely coincidental.

Published by The Publishing Circle
www.thepublishingcircle.com

COOLNESS TO THE WIND
FIRST EDITION
ISBN 978-1-955018-68-5 (eBOOK)
ISBN 978-1-955018-58-6 (SOFTCOVER)
ISBN 978-1-955018-64-7 (HARDCOVER)
ISBN 978-1-955018-67-8 (LARGE PRINT)

Cover and book design by Michele Uplinger

*Mary,
Always keep your cool!
Skylar Slate*

coolness to the wind

a novel

skylar slate

the publishing CIRCLE

*For everyone
who has ever been fifteen.*

coolness to the wind

a novel

skylar slate

chapter 1

LIZZIE TRIED TO FIND A DRY SPOT ON HER PILLOW. She flipped it over, then stripped the damp case off altogether. The part of her brain that urged for comfort warred with the true reason she couldn't sleep: guilt and humiliation. She flung the pillow across the room.

I don't deserve a pillow. I don't deserve comfort of any kind. I don't deserve the relief of sleep. I didn't realize I was such a horrible person. Stop, she told herself. *Think about something else—maybe the good times with Shelly. Yes, the good times. That rainy January afternoon when we'd gone crazy with the makeup in front of the mirror in my bedroom. Laughing. Shouldering each other aside in my bedroom mirror. My bedroom at home. Home.*

Before. Before I became so despicable that I can't sleep.

Before.

chapter 2

"I DON'T SEE WHY I HAVE TO GO," LIZZIE SPOUTED AS SHE swung her suitcase onto the bed.

"I'm not leaving you here alone. Besides, you love Mimi. You'll have a good time," her mother said with the slight singsong cadence that grated on Lizzie as if she were a kid being told to brush her teeth or eat her peas.

Lizzie grabbed handfuls of underwear, threw them into the suitcase, and slammed the dresser drawer shut. *State the obvious, why don't you, Jane? Of course, I love Mimi.* "You know, Jane, you're not making this any easier by talking to me like a three-year-old. You're just compounding the humiliation of shipping me off because you think I need babysitting for one lousy weekend."

"Feeling left out that you're not coming with your father and me?" her mother replied with annoying perkiness. "I asked you if you wanted to come with us and you said no."

"Oh, come on! Do you really think I'd want to get into the back seat of a car to drive how many miles to some hotel for a rubber chicken dinner? Right."

Her mother stood with her hands on her hips and glanced into Lizzie's half-filled suitcase. "You know this is a business event for your father. You should be proud." She removed one of Lizzie's tee shirts, folded it more neatly, and replaced it the suitcase. "And stop calling me Jane. You may call me Mom, Mother, or Mama. You know, like when you were three years old." Her mother smiled as she said this.

"I'm fifteen, not three, Jane." Lizzie let out a loud sigh of exasperation. Her mother actually sounded like she thought she'd have a great time. Look at her, just gliding over toward her bedroom. And me? I'm stuck spending the weekend with Mimi, at Wren Haven, "A Continuing Care Retirement Community", as the entry sign proudly declares in gold lettering. This plan is *so* uncool.

The importance of the coolness factor couldn't be underestimated. It had taken her a couple of months to recover from the indignity of being cut from the cheerleader tryouts, ever since which she had kept a low profile. Her luck and status had turned unexpectedly when she'd defended Shelly from an attack by Paige Pressman, class bully. Okay, *defended* might be a bit of a strong word for what had happened.

Paige had been laying into Shelly in the middle of the C corridor after home room one Monday morning. By chance, Lizzie had been wearing the new boots with heels that gave her a good two-and-a-half inches of height. She strode up and posed behind Shelly's shoulder, right hip thrust forward, left arm with books on her left hip, and glared down at Paige. Two seconds later, the steam went out of Paige. All she could manage was a purposeful swing of her shoulder, a condescending sniff, and a stamp down the hall. Subsequently, Lizzie seemed to get her choice of tables in the cafeteria, and both she and Shelly had been on the guest list for Maggie Wilson's famous Halloween party. Shelly put up a sign on Lizzie's locker that said, *Miss Coolness*. That's what makes a Best

Friend Forever, Lizzie would reflect more than once. Obviously, such status must be closely guarded and could easily be put at risk if word got out of a weekend spent at Wren Haven instead of hanging out at the pizza place, the mall, or just plain hanging out.

What added to the weirdness of the weekend plans was that her mother had been flitting around the house for the past three weeks as if she'd won an around-the-world cruise. She'd bought a chic navy-blue dress, unwrapped it with a flourish, slipped it on and danced around in front of the full-length mirror, asking, "Do you like it?" Lizzie, lounging on the bedroom floor with her back propped against the wall, had only grunted, returned to her texting, and did her best to blatantly ignore the euphoria, ignore the dress, and ignore the dancing in a continuing effort to express her indifference.

Lizzie crammed more clothing than she'd need for just a couple of days into the suitcase, then dumped everything out. Just because she'd be incarcerated at Wren Haven didn't mean she didn't need to dress well.

Her mother reappeared at the doorway, still seemingly unperturbed by Lizzie's provocations. "Why don't you bring your bathing suit? You said you wanted to go out for swim team next season and there's a pool where Mimi lives. Get some practice time in."

Lizzie rolled her eyes and pretended not to notice when her mother tossed her bathing suit, cap, and goggles into the suitcase. For spite, Lizzie packed her trendy, black, hip-hugger skirt that was so short that her mother had deemed it inappropriate for school—inappropriate for anyplace, actually—and the black top that skimmed the waistband of the skirt, designed, of course, to give a peek at her belly button when she walked. That might be the only perk of staying with Mimi—her mother wouldn't know what she'd be wearing on Monday.

* * *

With an unnecessary *umph!* Lizzie tossed the suitcase into the back seat of the car, then slumped into the front passenger seat and jerked her door shut.

"All set?" her mother inquired with such unflagging buoyancy that it annoyed Lizzie even more, if that was possible. The motor turned over and the car backed out of the driveway.

"Mmm," Lizzie mumbled, trying to make the syllable sound bored. She put her earbuds in, tilted her head back against the headrest, and closed her eyes. This'll shut her out, she thought. Keep me from barfing from hearing more of her cheerful chirpings.

The acquiescence that would get Lizzie through the weekend kicked in. She told herself it would just be a weekend. Well, a weekend and a day, but she'd be in school on Monday. She'd survive.

Three-quarters of an hour later, Lizzie looked over at her mother as they drew closer to the sprawling complex that was Wren Haven. Her mother still beamed. Lizzie yanked her earbuds out. "What's so special about this weekend? Some lousy dinner with boring speeches doesn't sound that exciting to me."

Her mother's shoulders dropped and her smile faded. She put her blinker on to turn, sighed, and hesitated as if wondering what, or how much to say. "It's just that your father and I never seem to get away."

Something other than her usual directness came through in the way she spoke. Resignation? Sadness? Lizzie sensed the undercurrent but said nothing.

"It's always something. Your father and I wanted to take a vacation last summer, but then his car died, so we had to buy a new car instead. And the year before, we booked that cabin up in the mountains and it rained all week." The nearly imperceptible hum of the tires on the road beneath them was the only audible sensation. Her mother seemed lost in her own thoughts for a moment before she inhaled deeply, her shoulders rising a bit and then falling. She gave a quick side nod of her head. "It wasn't much of a vacation. I spent most of the time doing things I always do—cooking, laundry—just doing them in a different place." She paused, then gave a small sigh. It was almost as if she was speaking to herself, half-hypnotized by the roadway ahead. "Even the weekends don't seem like downtime—grocery shopping, bill-paying, errands."

Lizzie noticed a fine vertical line near her mother's mouth that she hadn't seen before. An inexplicable wave of guilt washed over her, settling in her belly like a load of coals. Lizzie told herself she shouldn't feel bad. She hadn't caused the car to break down or had any part in renting the cabin. But something in her depths percolated to the surface and told her why she was uncomfortable. Her mother had never spoken to her this way before—as if she was someone who could be trusted with private thoughts, adult thoughts, not the usual pleasantries or rote parental instructions for a child. And the coals scorched her belly because she was repaying Jane's trust by giving her a hard time for no other reason than it was just so much more self-righteous to act like a jerk.

What a realization. Lizzie felt the urge to reach out and touch her mother. Touch her shoulder, touch her forearm. She wanted to say, "You and Dad go. Have a good time." But it was too uncomfortable to toss away the coolness that just an hour ago had her arguing over why she had to go to Mimi's. Lizzie fiddled with her playlist, uncomfortable with the idea she could act like an adult. Somehow her coolness felt less cool, undermined by that keen feeling of guilt or shame or sadness or whatever it was. Maybe all those things.

A gust of wind nearly slammed the car door back on Lizzie as she opened it in the Wren Haven parking lot, making hauling her suitcase out of the car that much more difficult. Mimi waited on the sidewalk with open arms. Lizzie let her enfold her in her generous size 14 girth. Mimi had a bit more silver in her hair, but the same clear blue eyes sparkled, and she voiced a welcome full of pure love. Leaving Mimi's embrace and accepting a kiss, Lizzie headed inside to Mimi's apartment to stow her gear in the den-with-pull-out sofa room that would be her bedroom for the weekend. She could hear Mimi and her mother following behind her as they came inside, her mother muttering something about borrowing the soft-sided tote bag.

". . . the new dress…

". . . oh, and it's a deep blue silk, with a wide sash . . ."

"But you didn't bring it? I would love to have seen it."

The two were positively animated. Lizzie rolled her eyes. She might have known the two of them would find the dress worthy of a half-hour discussion.

Lizzie wandered back out to the living room, where the two still prattled on. She let Mimi put her large, soft arms around her thin shoulders and leaned back into her grandmother's warm bosom. On an impulse to send another jab at her mother, she let herself droop, rag-doll style, in Mimi's arms, crossed her eyes, and let her tongue hang out of the corner of her mouth. Then she straightened up, broke free of Mimi's hug, and announced, "I've got homework."

Her mother slung the tote bag over her shoulder and turned to Lizzie. "I'm going to be leaving, sweetie." When Lizzie had been younger, her mother would have followed with, "and you be good for Mimi." But today it was just a tacit warning silently given with the simple firming of her lips and a barely perceptible rise of her left eyebrow.

chapter 3

ARRIVING TO DINNER IN WREN HAVEN'S LARGE, elegant, communal dining hall, Mimi and Lizzie joined Charlie, a slender, white-haired gentleman with a full, trim mustache. Lizzie's thought of, *He must be what is meant by 'distinguished'*, was interrupted by a tickle at her left ankle, causing her to give an involuntary kick. With a sharp yelp, a blur of white fluff jumped up into Charlie's lap.

"Hold on there." Charlie fussed as he cradled the dog. "This is Snowball. He won't hurt you. He's just curious to meet someone new."

Lizzie reached out to pet Snowball's silky white fur and scratched him under the chin. Wasn't there some law about dogs in dining facilities?

"Do you have any pets?" Charlie asked.

"No," Lizzie answered, then added, "I had a goldfish once. My father brought it home for me when I was in grade school. It died the next day."

Snowball wasn't the only one curious to meet someone new. One by one, the table filled up and Lizzie soon realized she held Celebrity of the Day status.

"Hey, Mimi! Got a new friend?" The question came from a spry, balding fellow of medium build who placed both hands on Mimi's shoulders. Mimi patted one of his hands as he took the seat next to her.

Lizzie used to think Mimi was her family's honorific for the grandmother. In the case of Lizzie's grandmother, her given name was Miriam, but family and everyone else had always called her Mimi, and it seemed to suit all purposes.

"Lizzie, meet Herb," Mimi said. Lizzie felt privileged by her grandmother introducing each person on a first name basis. Having the ability to address someone in the elder generation by their first name instead of having to call them Mr. So-And-So or Mrs. So-And-So felt good. Grown up. Lizzie nodded at Herb.

"Herb is a special friend of mine." As Mimi squeezed Herb's hand, Lizzie felt an instant of self-conscious surprise, then managed a too cute, "Nice to meet you."

"You play any sports?" Herb asked, seeming unfazed.

"Sports? No." Ugh, this is going to be a long dinner, she thought. "But I'm thinking of going out for the swim team."

"Swimming! Is that right?" This piqued Herb's interest. "I love to swim."

Charlie interrupted. "Snowball can swim. Came in third in the dog races last summer. Won a yellow ribbon."

"Yes!" Mimi perked up. "Quite a good turnout this year. There were all kinds of dogs splashing around in the pool."

Swimming dog races. This is something new.

Charlie asked, "You have any pets?"

Lizzie blinked. "I had a goldfish once . . ."

Mimi leaned over with her napkin to her lips and whispered, "Charlie is forgetful." Charlie fed Snowball a biscuit, apparently

coolness to the wind

having forgotten he asked the question.

Lizzie leaned toward her grandmother and, in a voice low enough to be discreet, asked, "Isn't there some sort of law about animals?"

Having since joined the table and seating himself next to Lizzie, a man with fluffy white hair and gentle eyes leaned toward her and quietly said, "Snowball will always get Charlie back to their apartment, so everyone looks the other way. It's fine." He extended his hand, and in a more normal voice said, "I'm Mac. You must be Mimi's granddaughter. We've been hearing about your plans to visit us for the last three weeks. We've been looking forward to meeting you."

Another woman arrived and Mimi introduced her as Greta. With Greta's arrival, everyone began to order. Greta wore a black sweater with long sleeves she tugged at as soon as she sat down. She had a heavy accent and an irrepressible cheeriness about her, commenting on everything from a new traffic light at a nearby intersection to the upcoming election for the Wren Haven residents' council. Lizzie refrained from sighing. It's just one weekend, she reminded herself. Her thinking shifted as the server placed their plates before them. *Well, table service is certainly a notch up from having mom call to me to set the table, tell me to clear the table, nudge me to load the dishwasher. Why was I so resentful about spending the weekend here?* This thought produced an imbalance of logic. A half minute later it dawned on her: none of her supposed friends had expressed half as much interest in her in the last three months as these people had in the last thirty minutes. Too bad they don't count, she thought.

Finishing dessert, Herb circled back to talk about sports.

"You play pool?"

Lizzie looked up. The question had been directed at her. "Me? No."

"Doesn't matter. Mac and I'll teach you. Come along with us." He and Mac excused themselves from the table and gestured at her to follow them.

12

Mimi gave Lizzie a nod and a smile and somehow the mountain of homework became less pressing. It seemed that even at Wren Haven Saturday night called for some latitude.

"Great. Just in time," Herb said as they entered a spacious area with three new-looking tables, two of which were already in use. "You have to get here right after dinner or there's a long wait."

Herb undertook guiding Lizzie through the rules of the game and Mac showed her how to hold the cue and line up the shot.

I could get the hang of this, Lizzie thought mid-way into their second game, then gave herself a silent pat on the back as she sank one into the corner pocket.

Later, as they headed down the long corridor of apartment doors, Herb said, "This is where I get off. Mac, you're closer to Mimi's apartment. You'll see Lizzie back, won't you?"

With a wave, Mac kept his pace and said over his shoulder, "I won't let her get lost."

Ordinarily, Lizzie might have bristled at the implication that she couldn't make her way from one end of the old folks' home to the other, but with a thousand apartment doors distinguished only by a mysterious color-coding that she had no intention of trying to learn, she wasn't too proud to have a guide.

With just the two of them walking together now, Lizzie reached for conversation. Although nice to have been taught to play pool, what could they talk about? She settled on, "How long have you lived here, Mac?"

"Just a couple of years. Almost since I retired, actually."

"What did you do before you retired?"

"Finance." He said it in the same way her father would say he was in sales. Enough information, true information, but said in a way that did not invite further inquiry.

"Do you have a family?"

Mac's expression faded and his voice dropped a note, the crispness shown during the pool tutorial gone. "I lost my wife not long after I retired." Mac's step slowed. He looked down at the carpet as he put one foot in front of the other, hands in his pockets. "It was a real blow. We had planned to do so many things together. There were so many places we were going to travel to. We were going to try folk dancing!" He gave a rueful smile.

Just let me drop through the floor this minute, she thought.

"Of course, all that changed when Jean went. I quickly got tired of eating dinner alone, so I came here. It worked out well. Plenty of nice people. A lot of them quite fascinating once you get to know them. And Herb's a great guy to shoot a couple of games with."

She realized Mac was talking *to* her, not *at* her. Walking the quiet corridors, it seemed neither of them needed to impress the other. They were just taking a walk, having a talk.

"You have any brothers or sisters?" Mac asked.

"No, it's just the three of us. Mom, Dad, and me. Oh, and Mimi, of course." She definitely wasn't going to count the creepy uncle she'd only met a couple of times.

More silence. But now the silence felt comfortable, something of a relief after a string of discomfitures. For the second time that day, Lizzie had the new experience of having someone speak to her as if she was worth having a serious conversation with. Someone other than her best friend, Shelly, anyway.

chapter 4

Lizzie awoke to Mimi's touch, brushing the longish strands of blonde from her forehead.

"Wake up, sleepy head!" She brushed another strand from Lizzie's cheek. "Do you always sleep this late on a Sunday morning? You've missed Sunday services."

Mimi's pearls fell across her chest.

"The pearls are real," her mother once told her in hushed tones that suggested they were valuable enough to belong in a museum. That was a few years ago, before Lizzie became too aloof to be impressed by such things.

Mimi's dress sort of rustled as she leaned toward Lizzie. The beautiful scent of Mimi's lily of the valley perfume wafted toward Lizzie in the warm room.

Lizzie squinted as the sun struck her through the venetian blinds. She propped herself up on one elbow and looked around, re-orienting herself.

"You've been to church already? Where?"

"Over in the auditorium. Every Sunday."

Lizzie flopped back on the pillow. She reached up and fingered Mimi's pearls, trying to discern what was so valuable about them. The heaviness of them weighed in her palm.

"They're an heirloom," Mimi said. "They'll be your mother's one day and someday yours, I expect."

Lizzie and Mimi stayed like that for another minute. Quiet. Sunny. Lizzie squinted and Mimi brushed another stray strand of hair from Lizzie's face. Lizzie smiled in warm contentment.

"Up now!" Mimi said with a lift in her voice and a playful slap to Lizzie's thigh. "It's time for brunch!"

In a different dining hall, in a different building, brunch at Wren Haven had a festive atmosphere. If not quite carnivalesque, it was certainly an indulgent, shoulder-to-shoulder, inspiring-the-taste-buds-after-inspiring-the-spirit ambiance. There was a huge buffet with a bright mosaic of fresh fruit. Enticing aromas of warm yeast and sugar and cinnamon floated up from baskets of breads and pastries of every description. Giant silver chafing dishes with their globe-like lids turned back displayed spicy sausages, perfectly grilled bacon, and scrambled eggs. A large Black man with a broad grin played food magician to the cluster of Wren Haven residents who watched him flip up the omelets of their imagination. "Peppers and onions!" one called out as the vegetables scattered and smattered in the fry pan, flipped moments later by the magician behind the table. How does he do that, Lizzie wondered, tossing food eight inches in the air? With each flip, tantalizing aromas wafted over to the side of the table where Lizzie and others leaned slightly toward the omelet circus. Working four pans at a time, his skill truly offered something to behold. The monotony of weekday cornflakes and doctors' cholesterol concerns were thrown to the winds of Lipitor, and magic seemed to spin in the air, thrown there by the chef with a wide grin who wore a pristine white toque.

Lizzie had just decided to forego her usual chocolate milk for what smelled like a tempting French vanilla coffee when she ran into Greta at the apple strudel board.

"You sit with me," said Greta. "Mimi will find us."

Halfway through their mountainous plates, Mimi approached with a robust-looking woman in tow.

"Lizzie," Mimi said, "this is Virginia. She holds the Wren Haven record. She's got a swing like you wouldn't believe."

Lizzie leaned forward, the ambient noise of the huge dining hall making it easy to miss a word here and there. "Record?"

"Great job snagging this table, Greta," Virginia complimented her.

"Swing?" Lizzie tried again, her question lost. What was Virginia champion of? Maybe tennis? Then it struck her: it didn't matter. They were all here, chatting away, enjoying their magical omelets, and feeling pretty in their Sunday dresses, their colorful taffeta, dressy dresses, and it didn't matter who held the record for what. It jarred Lizzie's context of grades and team scores and degrees of coolness. Involuntarily, Lizzie conjured a phrase, *Wren Haven—a Parallel Universe Community*. She surprised herself as she thought this with less cynicism and more of an affectionate wonder.

chapter 5

Another day at school over, Lizzie scanned Washington Street, then looked up and down Pierce. She couldn't help being annoyed, thinking, come on, Mimi, you know you're supposed to pick me up, and I'm freezing out here. The plan had been that Mimi would pick her up after school and later that evening her parents would pick her up from Wren Haven on their way home. But now, no Mimi. Thankfully, she wasn't getting wet. Ominous gray clouds hung in the sky and the wind bit through her jacket. A heavy dampness hung in the air from the morning deluge that lasted through lunchtime and the sky looked like it might have more in store. Or would it be snow next? The dropping temperature suggested the roads could be getting slippery.

Lizzie had one of those small builds that guaranteed that even when grown, she would feel February in her bones. Just as she reached for her cell phone, not especially wanting to know what time it was getting to be, she heard her name called. On the opposite corner an older woman waved broadly and called her name.

Lizzie bounded across the street, her leg muscles making her wish she had kept up with gymnastics classes. The face looked familiar, but it wasn't Mimi. Lizzie reached mentally for a name. From the brunch table yesterday . . . not Greta, the other one—right, Virginia!

"Hey, Lizzie. Surprised to see me?"

"Hi, Virginia. I was just waiting . . ." Lizzie craned her neck to look down Pierce Street again. "Mimi was supposed to pick me up."

"Yeah, I know. She had an errand she needed to see to and asked me if I'd fetch you. Hop in."

Virginia slid in behind the wheel. Lizzie, feeling a bit stunned, stood hugging her books. From inside the car, Virginia swung the passenger door open and looked out at her. "Well, come on. You'll freeze out there and I've got the heater on."

All those childhood warnings about not accepting rides from strangers rushed back to her in a split. They were scenarios just like this one: your daddy sent me to bring you home; I have candy for you; want to see my new puppy? She stood there. Was Virginia a stranger? She'd only met her once. It had, however, been a genuine introduction by her grandmother. Lizzie looked at the reddening fingers of her left hand clutching her books and felt a fresh shiver as a gust of wind smacked her cheek and snuck under her collar. She made a calculated assessment: tennis champ or not, if necessary, she could take Virginia. She bounded into the passenger seat with gratitude.

chapter 6

LIZZIE THREW HER COAT OVER THE BACK OF A CHAIR SO she could grab it and dash as soon as her parents came to pick her up. She settled into her homework at Mimi's dining room table. Life at Wren Haven had been entertaining, but she needed to get back to real life.

A couple of hours later, Mimi's landline rang. Great, she thought. It's Dad, and he's calling to tell me they'll be here in a half hour.

"Lizzie, it's Virginia Grant. I've got this computer and I can't seem to get into my email. Could you come by my apartment and see if you can figure out what I'm doing wrong?"

"Sure."

"I'm in unit 245, just down the hall and around the corner."

"I'll find it," Lizzie answered, clipping the words. She hung up the phone with a slight slam. Not that Virginia wasn't nice, she just needed to get out of this place.

Lizzie entered Virginia's apartment. It sported a different layout than Mimi's, with one corner of the living room allocated to a sleek office set-up, including the latest laptop and printer. Lizzie seated herself at the desk in front of the computer screen. Above were some bookshelves, laden with a variety of titles.

"Would you like a soda, dear?" Virginia called, halfway to the kitchen.

"No, thank you."

"How about some cookies? Lizzie heard her bustling toward the kitchen again.

"No, thank you." She was willing to come to Virginia's apartment to get her email problem sorted out, but she wasn't here for a tea party.

Several minutes later, Lizzie had delved well into Virginia's email, trying to find a problem, or a potential problem, or something that could be perceived as a problem. She heard Virginia buzzing around like a speed freak.

"Virginia, why don't you tell me what you were trying to do and how you were doing it?" She pulled a chair close to her, indicating that Virginia should sit down, pay attention, and give her what she needed to get her email problem solved.

Beyond a few cryptic responses, Virginia seemed given to nervous chatter. "My son gave me this computer for Christmas. He's in charge of the technology department where he works . . ."

Lizzie remained quiet, subject to her running thoughts. Okay. I can be nice, and I can be polite. And I can get this email glitch fixed and be out of here in another couple of minutes.

"And his two sons, my grandsons . . ."

Great, she thought. We're now getting into the family tree.

"It's so nice to get their emails. They tell me about their hockey games. Do you play hockey?"

"Uh, no," Lizzie said, a little confused at this change in subject. Computers, cookies, hockey. Okay. Not much in the inbox. Some spam. "You want me to block this junk mail for you?"

"Would you? Oh, that would be very nice. Are you sure I can't get you some cookies? A soda?"

Again with the cookies. "No, thank you." Lizzie thought she might find a clue in the delete box. Interesting. Virginia had read and deleted a message from the older grandson just an hour ago. She soon discovered Virginia got her bank statements online. And had an order confirmation from an online site. While it wasn't any of her business how much money Virginia had in her bank account, it did take some doing to get this stuff up and running and order your senior citizen apparel online.

"You say your son gave you this computer at Christmas?"

"Yes!" Virginia answered with a smile and shoulder straightening, the global body language for maternal pride. "Of course, he lives a couple of hours away, so I don't see him as often as I'd like. I haven't seen him since Christmas. After we opened all the presents, he wired this whole contraption up for me in a matter of minutes." Another smile. Another squaring of shoulders.

Lizzie leaned back in the chair with her hands loosely clasped in her lap, tilting her head toward Virginia. "What did you do after that?"

"Oh, we had Christmas dinner, of course. I made a nice turkey. And, of course, my cranberry relish—"

So, the son didn't set up all these online connections, she did that herself. Cookies? This cookie is sharper than she lets on. "There's nothing wrong with your email, Virginia. You just didn't use the right icon."

"Is that right? How clever of you! Now I'm a tad confused by this book." She reached for *Computers for Seniors for Dummies*. "I couldn't make sense of this chapter. Now, where is it?" Virginia fanned through pages haphazardly.

Lizzie took in more of the immediate space. To her left sat a new printer which held ivory-colored paper. The day's mail had been tossed into the wastebasket, but also a half-crumpled sheet of ivory paper on which was printed some sort of letter, likely a letter off one of Virginia's computer files.

Virginia continued rifling through the book, a little too randomly, it seemed. "Here it is. This chapter on saving."

Leaning against the back of her chair, Lizzie suppressed a sigh and took the book from her at the opened page. She deliberately flattened her voice, saying, "Saving is for when you are creating documents."

"Documents?"

"Yes. Like if you're using your computer to write letters." Why didn't she believe Virginia's confused expression? "Or make lists. Do you do that, or do you just read email?" Lizzie glanced at the computer clock.

"Just email."

"Then don't worry about saving." Why would she lie about such a stupid thing? Lizzie didn't have a clue, but it didn't matter. In another minute she would be out of there and wouldn't care one way or another about Virginia's email, computer, or clever son.

Virginia grabbed the book back and shoved it onto a bookshelf. "Now I've got another question. I was reading about the D drive. What's that used for?"

At that, Lizzie's antennae went up even further. From supposedly not being able to find the email icon to being interested in the distinctions among drives, didn't compute. Did she or didn't she have a computer issue? She began to suspect this supposed computer problem was just a ruse to keep her here. She stared at Virginia but didn't respond.

Curiously, Virginia chose to ignore Lizzie's unresponsiveness. Instead, she took a new tact with, "Gracious! Look at the time! We'd best be getting to dinner," and sprang from her chair.

"Thanks, Virginia, but no. My parents will be here any minute and they'll be looking for me."

"Oh, but surely at this hour they will expect you to have had dinner."

She'd had enough. Lizzie stood and took a step to confront Virginia. "Where's Mimi?" Lizzie felt the vehemence in her request but refused to apologize.

For a half second Virginia looked caught, then she recovered. "Like I told you earlier, she needed to run an errand."

"What errand?" Lizzie demanded.

"I don't know. I don't interrogate someone who asks a favor. She asked me to pick you up this afternoon and I did. That's what we do here at Wren Haven. We do for each other."

"She should have been back by now." Lizzie's voice held an intentional hard edge.

"She's been delayed is all. She called earlier and asked me to pick you up and to see to your dinner. Now let's go. We're celebrating a birthday tonight," she finished with a little melody in her voice, a toothsome grin, and balled hands at her chest.

Lizzie gritted her teeth behind her lips. She wasn't interested in a birthday party at Wren Haven. On the other hand, how could she be annoyed with someone trying to feed her a good dinner? And, she realized, suddenly feeling hungry, the food here is quite excellent, far better than the fast-food stop her parents probably had in mind—whenever they finally arrived. She consciously brought her temper down a notch, tried for a genuine nice-girl smile, and said, "Yes, of course. Thank you, Virginia."

Herb beckoned to them as they entered the dining hall. "Hello, Lizzie. Nice to see you again. Decide to stay with us a little longer?"

"No, I thought my parents would be here by now, but they're not, so Virginia talked me into eating."

"Well, you just sit down here and join us. Do you know these fine folks?"

"No, just you and Virginia." Lizzie glanced around the table, thinking, this is as bad as being the new kid in a class where I have to learn everyone's name. No, it's worse, because I probably won't ever see these people again.

"Well, let's get you introduced around," said Herb.

"I'm Greg," said a man with wire-rimmed glasses, "and this is my wife, Beth, and Edith and Marv and Alice." One by one, they nodded or raised a hand in greeting.

Marv had already opened several birthday cards and half-tucked them under his plate. Lizzie said simply, "Happy birthday, Marv."

Alice had something different in mind. She reached for a plastic bag hanging on the rear of her chair as the server approached. "Here, bring us some wine glasses, won't you?" She handed him a heavy-looking vinyl sack. "Careful. Don't break them."

"Wait a minute," Beth spoke up. "I brought one, too." She handed the server a colorfully wrapped parcel in the shape of a bottle.

When they returned from helping themselves to the salad bar, each glass was three-quarters full of white wine. Lizzie took a sip, half expecting to have her hand slapped or suffer some other embarrassing scene, but no one took note of Lizzie sipping her wine with everyone else.

Finding herself still the semi-celebrity, Lizzie fielded another question. "And you spent the entire weekend with Mimi?" asked Marv.

She sighed inwardly. It couldn't hurt to be polite; she'd be gone soon. "Yes. It's very nice here. My parents went away for the weekend. I expected them to pick me up by now." Where the heck were they? And Mimi? Where had she disappeared to? Did they all just abandon me here at Wren Haven? This seemed like leaving the baby on the church steps, except they'd left her at the old folks' home.

"Maybe they decided to stay an extra day," Edith suggested.

Actually, Lizzie thought, this idea was not totally outside the realm of reason. Unusual, perhaps, but not implausible. Mental snapshots of her mother's elation at the prospect of a weekend at a fancy hotel flitted through her head.

"Maybe," Lizzie said, as a new thought occurred to her. Could they have planned it this way? Staying an extra day? Just as a private celebration of her father's success? It fit with why Jane had borrowed the extra tote bag.

"Where were they coming from?" Marv asked.

"I'm not sure. I think they were heading south when they left on Saturday."

Alice leaned forward, trying to catch the eye of one or another of her tablemates. "Did anyone see the 5:00 news? That thunderstorm that came through here earlier today hit pretty hard a little further south. I didn't hear it all. I was folding the laundry when it came on, but I think they mentioned flooding. And detouring traffic. There may have been something about a bridge, too."

"Lizzie, you may be with us a little longer than you expected," Greg said, "if the normal roads aren't open."

Great. Another night here in the old folks' home. However, she felt somewhat relieved. If Alice was right, that would explain everything. If they were being detoured onto some of those rural backroads, the cell coverage could be spotty. Not such a mystery. Lizzie yawned.

Virginia refilled the wine glasses from the bottle the server had left in the cooler. Lizzie concentrated on her Beef Wellington, but half-picked up Alice's whispering, "Ginny, do you really think . . .?"

Virginia, unmoved, responded under her breath, "Trust me."

Lizzie took no interest in their side conversation. She yawned. She felt so drowsy. She reasoned it must be because they kept the place a little overheated.

The din of the dining room declined and the wait staff's clink of silverware grew more perceptible as the dinner hour wound down. Theirs was one of the few tables still finishing up. The server looked impatient. Lizzie yawned again.

"Lizzie, I'll walk you back to Mimi's," Virginia offered. "She's probably back by now."

Lizzie entered a silent apartment. Strange, she thought, that Mimi hadn't returned. But Mimi was a grown woman and she certainly didn't have to answer to anybody, least of all her. She yawned again. She could literally feel her eyelids drooping. Very uncool. She would just curl up and get a nap before her parents arrived. She shuffled into the pull-out sofa-bed room and saw that she hadn't made the bed that morning. The cool sheets and rumpled comforter looked inviting. Just until her parents arrived, she told herself. She kicked off her shoes and slid beneath the covers and slipped into sleep.

chapter 7

Lizzie awoke late, realizing she'd slept through to morning and remained at Wren Haven. Scrambling to the kitchen, both astonished and panicked, Lizzie took in the rigid back of her grandmother, who leaned with one outstretched arm on the refrigerator. "Mimi?"

Mimi turned. Her eyes appeared pink and glassy, and she clutched a fraying tissue. "Sit down".

Something was not right. Not right at all. She heard no cheery, "Good morning, angel," no crackling of milk hitting cornflakes—in fact, there were no cornflakes on the table at all. Why would Mimi want her to sit down? Even if they jumped into the car this instant, at best she would still be a half hour late to school. Sit down? This made no sense.

Still standing, Lizzie glanced at the wall clock and said, "It's late."

Mimi stepped toward Lizzie but said nothing.

Lizzie's voice rose to a higher pitch. "Mimi, where do you keep the cereal? I need to get going."

Mimi took both of Lizzie's hands in her own, and Lizzie felt the tissue curled in the little finger of Mimi's left hand. "Yesterday, I received a call. You see, my name and number were on the luggage tag."

From cereal to luggage tag? The image of Alice falling down the rabbit hole flickered through Lizzie's mind, eating up another couple of seconds before she felt present enough to ask, "Call? Luggage tag?"

Mimi's lower lip moved, as if she was about to say something, but then didn't. Briefly, she looked down at the floor and took a breath, then looked back up at Lizzie. "There was an accident."

A strange tingling on her scalp caused Lizzie to shudder. She waited, unaware that her jaw was hanging half-open until her drying tongue caused her to swallow.

"The ambulance came, but it was bad." A beat of silence became two, became three. The pressure of Mimi's hands on Lizzie's increased. "They're both gone. Your mom and your dad are gone. The EMTs, the doctors, all tried their best." Mimi sniffled. "But they're both gone."

The rabbit hole image returned, seemingly sending Lizzie down now much faster as she tried to grasp Mimi's words. *Gone? Gone? As in dead?* Lizzie stood still, the scalp tingling turning to a chill that cascaded over her shoulders. It shouldn't be possible. But Mimi put her arms around her and wrapped Lizzie against her soft, broad bosom and Lizzie felt, rather than heard, sob upon sob as Mimi's grief flowed onto Lizzie's collar.

The last car ride with her mother flashed through her mind. She saw the fine vertical line near her mom's mouth. She felt her own fingers scrolling rapidly through her playlist, unthinking, reacting to some unnamed wave of discomfort that now surged again in her gut. The kitchen went blinding white, and she heard a high-pitched tone. She felt hot and cold at the same time. But Mimi continued to hold her, the warmth of Mimi's arms enveloping her. Mimi stroked her hair and slowly the kitchen returned to normal.

Lizzie's mind raced. This couldn't be true. She would just decide it wasn't true, will it not to be true, then everything would be all right.

All right, like when she was little and had a skinned knee and her father had held her and told her it would all be all right.

All right, like when she was eight and had accidentally broken the neighbor's window with her softball and her mother told her she needed to apologize to the neighbor but she'd been afraid to, but she did apologize, and it was all right.

All right, like when she had needed a good grade in algebra and had willed herself through the textbook and willed herself to study instead of hanging out with Shelly and willed herself to get an A- and it was definitely all right.

She willed herself to find a core of steel so she could avoid feeling anything. That's it, Lizzie thought. I will not be one of those soft, sobbing creatures. I will be something else. Something not human. Something that can stand up straight. Something that can think objectively. I'll will that to be true.

Under the kitchen light that had turned to a glare, the horror of what Mimi told her gradually seeped into her pores. She felt Mimi still holding her and stroking her hair. And Mimi never once told her it would be all right.

Mimi released Lizzie, then lurched toward the kitchen sink. She braced herself with both arms on the countertop, pitching forward at a forty-five-degree angle. Lizzie wondered whether Mimi was going to vomit. Instead, she heard a low moan that started from somewhere deep inside Mimi and rose to a wail. Clearly, Mimi had no core of steel to keep her upright.

Mimi's cry reverberated like nothing Lizzie had ever heard. As if a force from somewhere behind her had given her a shove, she flung herself at Mimi's back and clamped her arms around her grandmother as far as they would reach. It was the vibration that

Lizzie would remember for the rest of her life; the vibration that resonated through Mimi's torso and into her own chest. All she could do was rock; rock and hold Mimi, the two of them rocking to a depleted silence. When they finally faced each other again, minutes had passed. Minutes of sighs and no words.

"There are things to do." Mimi sniffled into the tissue. "You won't want to go to school today. I'll be leaving in a few minutes. Virginia will look in on you. We'll go to the funeral home tonight at seven. You'll stay here with me until we can get things sorted out."

For once, a clever retort, a smirk, or even a smug thought seemed irrelevant. Lizzie felt entirely present. Present in Mimi's apartment with Mimi. Her mind was not at school, or in her bedroom with her earbuds in, or hanging out with Shelly.

Mimi shambled into her coat and pulled on a knit hat without looking in the mirror. A tug on either side left the hat slightly askew, but it didn't matter. She kissed Lizzie on the cheek, gave her a tight hug, muttered, "All right, then," gave Lizzie another quick kiss, and left.

Lizzie stood looking at the closed door, finally turning, almost in slow motion, to look around the apartment. Amazing how quickly it had become so familiar. What to do next? That's right, funeral home . . . things to do . . . no school today. This must be what one does.

Yesterday's mail lay shoved at all angles onto the tiny entry hall table. Lizzie began to stack it neatly, then thought a step further and separated the obvious junk mail for tossing. This is the last thing Mimi needs to see, she thought. Better yet, the real mail should go onto Mimi's desk. She sorted, then brought the mail into the room with Mimi's desk where the pull-out sofa-bed remained as disheveled as she'd left it. The bed. I'll make the bed, she told herself.

Before long, Lizzie had the vacuum out, methodically stroking every inch of the wall-to-wall carpet at first, then faster until she covered it at a frenzied pace. She ran the dishwasher, impatient for it to finish its work so she could put away the dishes. A near-violent flipping and fluffing of the sofa cushions produced the welcome physicality of stretching her muscles, but in plumping up the silk toss pillows a seam ripped in one as her plumping became more like punching. Even her thoughts seemed to come at her like punches: Cheap things! Where'd she buy these cheap pillows? Take them back to the store! She tossed them onto the sofa so the rip didn't show.

Irrationally, she ran back into the kitchen and glowered at the dishwasher cycle monitor, cursing it for not being finished. She tore open the under-sink cabinet door and grabbed a large sponge and three different cleansers, then attacked the bathroom. With the first swipe at the tub rim, she skinned her knuckles on the spigot, but continued scrubbing despite her blood dripping onto the white porcelain. The bathroom was perfectly clean thanks to Marietta, Mimi's weekly housekeeper, but she scrubbed until the sponge wore thin and split in two places.

That damned slow dishwasher, she thought, as she returned to the kitchen. About to kick the machine, she spotted a bottle of Windex on the countertop. Windex! She spritzed and swiped at every mirror, both telephones, and the sliding glass doors out onto the patio, then spray polished every wood surface until she was out of cleaning cloths. *Clean cloths, need clean cloths, wash these,* she thought, almost maniacally. She threw them into the washer, along with everything in Mimi's hamper and her own few garments that she'd worn since she'd been at Wren Haven. She swabbed at her damp hairline. Realizing she still wore the same clothes she'd worn to school and slept in last night, she stripped them off, flinging them into the washer, as well. Without measuring, she dumped in the soap powder, then slammed down the lid and snapped on the machine with a satisfying finality.

She stood naked, listening to the water filling the washing machine, slightly out of breath. Aimless for the moment, she wandered back into the kitchen, wondering why she had gone there. Finally, she heard the click that told her the dishwasher was through.

With a handful of paper towels for any that might not be completely dry, Lizzie began unloading the dishes, placing each glass, dish, and utensil into its place with painstaking neatness. That done, she turned her thoughts to herself. Nothing remained to do but shower.

She let the shower pelt her for the longest time, the pins and needles of the stream of water seeming to drive the shock of Mimi's news from the surface of her skin to deep inside her soul. Just standing there with her eyes closed, Lizzie tried to regain control of her thoughts, make some sense of this bizarre morning. What should I be doing now? Should I cry? People cry, don't they? That's right, she remembered, I gave up being human a few hours ago. *Fine.* Shower. Wash the hair. Lather. Rinse. Repeat.

chapter 8

Mimi sat with Reverend Drummond in his office with his assistant, Donna. "I appreciate your seeing me on such short notice." She paused, scanning the minister's desktop, then looked up. "I'm sorry I haven't been here much for the last few years. I moved to Wren Haven, and they have convenient Sunday services there."

"No need to apologize. We've been happy that Jane and her family have continued being part of our congregation. Now tell me about these unfortunate circumstances and what you'd like for arrangements, and we'll do all we can to help."

Mimi took a deep breath. "It happened yesterday morning. Out of the blue I got this telephone call and—the shock of it—but of course I went right away, and the police and the morgue people were all exceedingly kind."

The minister nodded and let her go on.

"It was quite a procedure to go through. Filling out forms,

identifying the bod . . ." Mimi erupted in uncontrollable tears and hiccups. Donna put her arm around her and handed her some tissues. Mimi took a calming breath and continued. "So, the forms, personal effects, it seemed to take forever, but everyone was kind, very sensitive. Could not have been nicer, really. Do you know that a lot of women are now joining the police force?" Mimi glanced between her audience of two. "Sorry, here I am rambling when there is so much to do."

Reverend Drummond took his cue. "And you're using Grayson's?"

"Yes. They've been so responsive. It surprised me when they told me they could retrieve the bod . . . go to the morgue yesterday afternoon and be ready as soon as this evening."

"It doesn't take too long on their end."

"I've just come from there. They needed to know about . . ." Mimi choked. Donna pushed the entire box of tissues toward her.

"Thank you. They needed to know about clothes. And information for the obituaries."

Reverend Drummond just nodded.

Mimi took another tissue. "So, I took care of all that." Sniffle. Another tissue. "I told them cremation would be fine. It's not like we have a family plot."

"Yes, that would be all right. And a funeral? Later this week?"

"Actually, I was thinking sooner rather than later. I hope this doesn't sound callous, but if Grayson's will be ready today, I was hoping you could prepare something for this evening."

"Oh? That quickly? Won't family need some notice?"

"That's just the thing. There isn't much family. You'll remember I lost my husband some years ago."

"Yes, I remember."

"I think my son-in-law has—no, had—a brother, somewhere distant. Or was he a cousin? I don't know, but I remember he didn't even show up to the wedding when Bruce married Jane." Mimi gazed at some indeterminate place over the minister's shoulder, lost in memories. "Do you remember? You married them."

"Yes, it was a lovely wedding. She made a beautiful bride."

"Anyway, I only met the brother, cousin? Whatever he is, we only met once. What was his name? Simon? Stanley? I wouldn't have a clue how to track him down. I'm not even sure he has the same last name. I got the feeling there may have been a family rift at some point." Mimi took a breath and blew her nose. "Yes, there are friends, but they're all nearby. It just seems dreadful and cruel to spend days sitting in a funeral parlor staring at my daughter, at the bod . . ." she sniffed and cleared her throat, "one day after the next. Why put Lizzie through that? Why put myself through that?"

"I see. And I can't say you're wrong."

"So, is there something appropriate you could do this evening? At Grayson's?"

"Of course. The Lord is everywhere. And if you and Lizzie will be at Grayson's, He will be there too. What else can we help with?"

"There are some calls to be made, but I'm not sure . . . My son-in-law worked for the Takstron Corporation."

Donna spoke for the first time. "My husband works there. He'll know who to contact. Let me take care of that. And I know Jane worked for the county. That's easy enough. I can make that call as well. We have a blast email/text list for the congregation, as well as a telephone tree. That will cover a lot of ground. Anyone else?"

"Jane had a best friend, Joyce Adams. Her husband's name is Alex."

The minister tapped a few keys on his keyboard. "Blakely Drive? Sound right?" He turned his screen to Donna, who jotted down the phone number.

Mimi nodded. "Yes, that would be right."

"Okay," Donna said. "I'm sure she'll be happy to cover the friends and neighbors."

Mimi breathed a grateful sigh of relief; grateful to Reverend Drummond for making it easy on her, grateful for Donna's taking charge of the notifications, grateful for Grayson's being able to accommodate them so soon, and grateful for the police and morgue personnel whose names she hadn't even made note of. So much kindness. For the first time since yesterday morning, things seemed somewhat under control. Now she just had to go through the motions. Get through it. Get Lizzie through it.

chapter 9

It must have been three o'clock when Lizzie heard the gentle knock and then the front door opening. Should it have been locked? It didn't matter. Virginia arrived and put her hand on Lizzie's shoulder. Lizzie, seated on the sofa, stared straight ahead. She hoped she said hello but couldn't be sure.

"Lizzie, have you eaten?"

But Lizzie didn't know. She sat with her coat draped over her arm, waiting for seven o'clock.

"I'll put on some water for tea. It'll do you a world of good." Virginia no longer flitted around with the bird-brain act from the prior day and her voice sounded soft and comforting. Loving. "Come sit at the table."

With something of a delayed response, Lizzie stood, holding her coat at her waist. She continued looking straight ahead, not speaking. Virginia gently pried the coat loose and laid it over the back of a dining room chair. Lizzie tugged at the black too-short top. She wanted to sit so the too-short skirt would look less short.

Virginia's eyes swept over her outfit. Virginia, as Lizzie had figured out the day before, was no half-wit. Lizzie's self-conscious tugging of the top down to meet the skirt waistband had to be obvious. Helpless and embarrassed at the scrutiny of her visitor, she could only manage a small shrug and tried to explain, "It's the only skirt I brought. It's black." Suddenly, Lizzie knew the meaning of the word lame.

Virginia gave a sympathetic frown and a small nod, indicating she totally understood. "Of course. Never mind the tea. We'll go see Angie."

And so, on a day when nothing was normal, it seemed the most natural thing in the world for Lizzie to find herself escorted by Virginia, who she hardly knew, to meet someone else she didn't know, for an unknown purpose.

Both stayed quiet as they wound their way through the corridors, Virginia only once breaking the silence by asking, "You don't speak any French, do you?"

Lizzie blinked. "Year and a half in school, but, ah, no, not much."

They stopped at a white door in a dimly lit alcove. Lizzie fairly jumped as Virginia began pounding the door with an open hand and considerable force and shouting at the top of her lungs, "Angie! Angie, I know you're in there!" She kept it up for several minutes, and though Lizzie did not understand any of this surreal experience, she realized some of Virginia's words were not in English and the earlier question about speaking French clicked.

There was a muffled but vehement response from the interior. Undeterred, Virginia continued shouting back and forth with the unseen respondent until the door eventually opened a few inches. At that point, the spewing forth of continually forceful words became more distinct, and Lizzie saw a spray of black bobbing curls and perfectly manicured red nails jabbing through the opening and pointing at a sign next to the door. The sign read:

The Surprise Shoppe
Mme. Angelina Lacroix, Directrice
Mondays and Thursdays only
2:00–5:00 p.m.
All proceeds to the Fellowship Fund

Mme. Lacroix, Lizzie would learn at another point in time, was the acknowledged—grudgingly acknowledged by some—fashion arbiter of Wren Haven, presiding over The Surprise Shoppe, a thrift shop of sorts, which she managed with unyielding policies, like the open hours. Today, however, once Mme. Lacroix listened to Virginia, the shouting subsided to hushed murmurings and much *tsk, tsking* and Lizzie distinctly heard the word morts. A moment later, the door swung open. Had she been able to notice anything beyond her own shock, Lizzie would have observed the most elegant woman she had ever met. The collar of a vibrantly colored silk charmeuse blouse rose at her throat, and the woman wore a tailored black skirt. An observant person might have asked why such a fashion plate existed behind closed doors at Wren Haven. As it was, Madame merely opened her arms, embraced Lizzie for a silent moment, and said simply, "Come."

The surroundings of The Surprise Shoppe might as well have been from another planet. There were racks of clothes, mostly women's apparel. Madame Lacroix flew from one rack to another, tossing various articles to Virginia, then she led them both back to a makeshift dressing room.

The two women pulled a series of garments over Lizzie's head, around her waist and across her shoulders, fitting and murmuring, a pair of half-glasses now perched on Madame's nose. Lizzie made sense of the experience by reasoning, *Good thing I figured out I am not human because obviously I am a plastic doll.*

Madame and Virginia exchanged fragments of comments in some secret code, even though mostly spoken in English.

"Too big."

"Too frumpy."

"Mon Dieu, non."

The two flew back and forth between the racks and the dressing room.

"Much better."

"A belt?"

"Maybe not."

Then, with a sharp snap of her delicate head, Mme. Lacroix approved. She turned Lizzie around to face the mirror. In a plain black shift with a black, lacy, long-fringed shawl over her shoulders, Lizzie observed her solemn and demure reflection. She glanced at her mall-rat togs in the corner and turned her back on them. Lizzie had uttered perhaps no more than a dozen words all day long, but from depths she couldn't understand, she drew the words forward, *"Merci,* madame."

chapter 10

LIZZIE STEELED HERSELF AS SHE ENTERED THE FUNERAL parlor. At ten minutes before the hour, she and Mimi stood alone at the threshold. Lizzie found that even a non-human needed to breathe, but it seemed difficult. She tried to inhale, but the air felt impossibly heavy, and the room bordered on claustrophobic. The cloying sweetness of the several flower arrangements in so confined a space began to produce a headache. Lizzie remained standing in the doorway of the viewing room. Mimi started going around to the various floral gifts, reading the cards. That must be what one does, Lizzie reasoned.

Lizzie had seen a body before. When she had been nine years old, the leader of her Girl Scout troop had died. Lizzie remembered entering the funeral parlor with some trepidation. Holding her father's hand as if she were three years old, she had literally dragged her feet. On that evening, Lizzie recognized only one other young girl, whose name she could not remember; the remainder of the attendees were all adults. Lizzie had not known the deceased particularly well, yet she found herself tearing up as they signed their names in the remembrance book. But that scene, that event, took place long ago, back when she was human. Today would be different since she was no longer one of those soppy creatures.

Once again, Lizzie visualized a hard rod running upward from her midsection until it drove through her heart and her neck and held her head upright. It allowed her to think, *It's better this way. No heart, no tears.* She could face the side-by-side caskets. Step. Step. Step. Two steps more.

Lizzie gazed at her mother. She didn't have her glasses on. Better that way. Less real. That fine line at the corner of her mouth? Gone. She lay there in the blue silk dress so recently bought. It must have been in the luggage in the car. Mimi must have unpacked it for the undertakers. Mimi must have known about the new dress. Of course, she did. A memory of the parting conversation in Mimi's living room flickered through Lizzie's mind. This was the dress her mother had tried on and danced in like a prom queen, asking Lizzie, "Do you like it?" And Lizzie, too cool for silk dresses, had grunted a "yeah," then gone back to her earbuds and texting. Her mother had wanted a friend, and Lizzie had wanted none of it. The surge of guilt, the searing coals in her belly, returned without warning. Lizzie consciously redirected her thoughts: *No, no tears! Feel the steel and brace. Turn away. Just turn away.*

Her father lay in the other casket. A good man. Their family life? Definitely an imperfect, but absurdly normal, life. He traveled much too frequently, three- to four-day stretches at a time. Lizzie never minded; she understood his job demanded it. Did being home less than 100% of the time make him less than 100% of a father? Now gone again. Gone for good. She repeated the line—or was it the lie?—that would get her through the night: If I didn't miss him before, it's not likely I'll miss him now. Not having a heart might have its advantages.

Voices in the background penetrated Lizzie's rumination. "I'm so sorry. So sudden." Lizzie stood with her back to the entryway for another minute, trying to breathe deeply, before turning to face the arriving visitors. First two, then a family of four, then a steady stream, filling the funeral parlor within minutes. She remained standing at the front of the room. Mimi came to stand next to her. Lizzie tried to focus on the faces. Neighbors. The ones who lived next door. The ones who lived at the end of the street. Others she couldn't place.

"Your mother and I worked together."

"I've known your father since high school. We were on the track team together."

The faces and the words began to blend together.

"I was one of your father's customers for many years."

"Your mother worked for me. We all considered her an important member of our team."

"You must be Lizzie. I would know you anywhere. Your father carried your picture in his wallet and would always show me the latest one. He was so proud of his beautiful Lizzie with the golden hair." Suddenly, a whole other form of guilt surged in her gut, making her ashamed of how she willed herself to discard her heart in favor of a steel rod. She needed to think clearly. But not now. No time for that, no time for guilt now. Besides, feelings are for humans.

And then there were the people she knew. Ladies from the church society. Two guys from her father's bowling team. Shelly and her sister, Rachel, and their parents. For once, school gossip didn't matter. In a way, even Shelly didn't matter.

Then there were Mimi's friends from Wren Haven, some of whom Lizzie could now name. In the hour of kind hand extensions and kisses on the cheek, Lizzie felt grateful for her steel core. She kept her back to the caskets and could even manage a dignified smile of acknowledgment for the condolences everyone offered.

Coming into the entry foyer, Herb arrived with a few others. Mimi stepped out into the foyer to speak to Herb, leaving Lizzie alone with the newest arrivals. She shook hands and exchanged polite words, a cheek kiss here and there.

Reverend Drummond stepped up to her and took her hands in his. "Lizzie, I am so terribly sorry. This is such a shock for all of us."

Lizzie nodded. "Thank you. And thank you for being here." But something in his presence felt grating. The presumptuousness of the way he took her hands caused Lizzie's shoulder muscles to tighten.

"Is there anything special you'd like me to do this evening?"

She had the sensation that he expected her to decode a message from outer space. "Do?"

"Yes. For the service."

Lizzie looked at him blankly.

"Lizzie, the remains will be cremated tomorrow, so I'm officiating at the service here this evening. Is there anything in particular you'd like? Certain verses? Special prayers?"

Lizzie found it difficult to grasp anything beyond the immediacy of his hands. Finally, she managed an audible "no."

"All right then. Mimi has chosen a couple of hymns and has things well in hand, anyway. I'm right here if you need me. I'll be here until the end." He gave her hands a little squeeze that felt condescending. It might as well have been a pat on the head.

Cremation. Verses. These were the things Mimi had gone off to do. The minister turned away so the next person could approach Lizzie.

"Verses?" Lizzie heard herself say with a strain in her voice. "Hymns?" she said, her voice now louder, higher pitched. Rev. Drummond looked back over his shoulder, then stepped back toward Lizzie.

"Lizzie," he said, reaching for her hands once again. Lizzie snatched them back, safe under the fringed shawl.

"They read the verses; they sang the hymns every week. In your church." Lizzie glared at the minister. Her voice raised another notch and her right hand flung out from under her shawl toward the caskets. "And this is what happens?"

"Lizzie," he started again, his voice gentle, his eyes sympathetic. "It isn't given to us to know . . ."

Lizzie looked away, defiant, tucking her arms tightly to her ribs.

"I'm sorry," he said again, gently, sympathetically. "Why don't you come visit me in a day or two and . . ."

"What for?" Lizzie spat.

He put his hand on her shoulder and looked as if he might be going to speak again, but Lizzie jerked her shoulder from under his touch. His hand hung limply in the air. The minister took a small breath as if to formulate another remark, then apparently thought better of it, taking a half-step back. He turned away. As he did, Lizzie felt herself scowling, and she again drew her right hand out from under the shawl, this time with her middle finger extended.

Midway in the arc toward the minister's receding back, Lizzie felt the clamp of another hand over hers, collapsing the middle finger onto her fist. It was a large, warm hand, and her knuckles, raw from the frenzied cleaning, stung under it. She snapped her head around to find Mac's open, gentle face, in an expression that didn't need words at all, comforting or otherwise. The steel inside, that strong rod of steel that held her head upright, was gone. Angry at its absence, Lizzie dissolved in large convulsive sobs against Mac's lapel. He held her tight enough that she did not fall as her knees buckled. Embarrassment at the absence of her steel core compounded her fury. Thankfully, Mac's broad chest mostly shielded her from the view of the gathered mourners.

chapter 11

IT FELT LIKE TINY, MENACING CREATURES WERE burrowing into Lizzie's forehead, clawing into her scalp and into her brain as she lay in the dark on Mimi's pull-out sofa bed. *If only . . . if only I'd said that the dress was fabulous, said, "You look beautiful, Mom." If only I'd reached out and said, "Have a good time."*

Lizzie flipped the pillow, searching for a dry spot. In a vicious cycle she saw herself lounging on the floor with her earbuds in while her mother danced, then heard her mother's sigh on that last car ride, the earbuds, the dancing, the sigh, the earbuds . . . It wouldn't have taken much. It wouldn't have taken more than a couple of seconds to reach out . . . *But I didn't even say . . . I didn't even give her something so small, something that wouldn't have taken much.*

She clutched the pillow to her face to stifle her jagged moans as well as she could.

chapter 12

Both Lizzie and Mimi slept as late as they could on Wednesday. Neither pretended to be cheerful; each seemed determined not to weep openly. Lizzie sat down at the breakfast table, hoping her eyes did not look too red. Mimi kept her back to Lizzie while taking an inordinately long time at the stove.

The telephone began to ring at ten o'clock with calls from those who were just finding out. By eleven, the first of many knocks on the door started from the Wren Haven residents who had been unable to travel to the funeral parlor.

"Mimi, I'm so sorry I couldn't make it. With my arthritis, it's difficult for me to get out," one apologized.

"If there's anything I can do, let me know," offered the next. Mimi and Lizzie both nodded politely at the meaninglessness of all the comments. They both had the platitudes down rote and were settling into a sort of suspended animation.

By Wednesday evening, the concerned intrusions of others tapered off. Lizzie considered asking Mimi about the cremated remains, but truthfully did not want to face whatever the next step must be. Instead, she trusted in Reverend Drummond's remark that Mimi had things well in hand and just left it at that. *It doesn't matter anyway*, Lizzie told herself.

Thursday came, and it seemed reading cards and returning calls counted as the new normal, and the most abnormal thing in the world would have been something called school. For a full day, Mimi and Lizzie sat at the table, signing thank-you notes. As doing so became robotic, Lizzie's mind wandered. Thank-you notes seemed about as good a use of time as anything else.

Mimi stretched, then gave Lizzie's forearm a brisk rub. "Feel like some tea? Why don't you put some on? I'll join you." Mimi even tried a cunning smile. "I've got a secret. Edith gave me some of her homemade cookies. They're in the freezer."

"Okay," Lizzie said, turning toward the kitchen, glad to have some other activity to busy her for a few minutes. *Cookies*, she thought cynically. *Monday, Virginia kept trying to distract me with cookies.* Monday was a lifetime ago. Literally, two lifetimes ago. She gave the plastic bag a sharp shake to spill some cookies onto a plate but her fingers fumbled as she tried to put the extras back in the bag. Her eyes welled up and her shoulders quivered. She struggled not to give voice to this new rush of tears, grateful the steam kettle's whistle masked the sound of her blowing her nose with the tissues that she now kept in every pocket. She made more of a clatter than necessary with teacups and spoons and was glad to quell the quaver in her voice enough to finally call out, "Milk and sugar?"

chapter 13

BY TACIT AGREEMENT, MIMI AND LIZZIE DEVOTED Friday, then Saturday and Sunday, to feeling numb. Ironically, Lizzie now felt grateful for the relative anonymity that Wren Haven afforded. It was a good place to pull the covers over her head, figuratively and sometimes literally. What little she and Mimi ate, they ate in the apartment, making quick trips to the Wren Haven convenience store for cold cuts rather than face the pitying faces in the dining room. A dusty can of chicken noodle soup from the back of Mimi's cupboard was a welcome addition. They made popcorn in the microwave and ate it in front of the television. Lizzie picked at the bowl and wondered why she was doing even that because the popcorn was so tasteless.

The one thing they did have an interest in was the local news. They watched for any report on the area where the road had been flooded and sent the car hydroplaning into a tree, but there was nothing; that was yesterday's news, and the only mention was that everything in that region was back to normal after the storm. *Normal* seemed a particularly cruel word. Lizzie threw a few puffs of popcorn at the screen, then grabbed the remote and changed to a home improvement channel.

They began a routine of walking the Wren Haven grounds in the morning and early evening. In the fairer months, a walking club did stretching exercises before setting off through the foliage every morning at eight, but it was February and cold and the paths were muddy from the thunderstorm that had torn through earlier in the week and shredded the fabric of Lizzie's family in the process. So, they staked out a route along the concrete walkways of the dozen or so Wren Haven buildings. The air refreshed them after the stuffiness of the too warm apartment, and Lizzie suspected she was doing a good deed by getting Mimi to move around more than she otherwise might have. Outside, everything seemed gray: the concrete, the bricks of the Wren Haven buildings, even the sky. Yet the drabness was somehow appropriate; gray to match their gray melancholy; half-light to match the half-life they had been left with. Lizzie and Mimi had the grayness and the stillness to themselves. Snow flurries drifted down during one evening stroll. Huge flakes melted against skin, the chill a foil to the warmth beneath a winter coat. No one else ventured out at this hour; the other residents were all snug in their Wren Haven nests.

Mostly they walked in silence. The occasional car passed on its way to the parking lot. Days acquired a sameness, as did the evenings. On Sunday evening, Lizzie bent in the just-past-twilight lamplight to scoop up some of the half-frozen half-inch of snow that had followed the thunderstorm that took her parents' lives. As they broke their stride, one of the lit apartments allowed them to see a slender woman moving around inside.

"Getting comfortable in front of her television," Lizzie remarked.

Mimi answered, saying, "That's Lenore Chambers. She lost a daughter, too. Last year. Breast cancer."

Too. That word, "too." Lizzie didn't mind the crystalized snow numbing her fingers. One thing she was not numb to was that word. For the first time it hit her that she was not the only one grieving. Mimi had lost a family, too.

They both needed peace. Wren Haven was nothing if not peaceful.

Mimi asked, "Do you have gloves? Are you cold?"

"I have gloves." As she pulled an unlined pair of worn leather gloves out of her pocket and put them on, she noticed her knuckles were healing, scabs forming now. "But I have a warmer pair. They're at home. I'll have to remember to put them in the pockets of my coat first thing when I go back."

Mimi raised an eyebrow at the last phrase, the reference to going back home, but merely said, "I have a warmer pair you can have. You'll want them for school tomorrow."

chapter 14

On Monday morning, when Mimi entered Lizzie's makeshift bedroom, Lizzie, already awake and dressed except for running a brush through her hair, said, "I'm almost done." Without a word of discussion, both readied to drive Lizzie to school.

Lizzie already had the apartment door open and one foot in the hallway when Mimi said, "Here, take these gloves."

Nearly cringing at the ugly old-lady gloves—an odd color of yellow with some red flowers embroidered on the back—but not wanting to start an argument and, frankly, having no reason to want to offend Mimi, Lizzie made a show of looking at them appreciatively.

"They were a gift from Greta," Mimi said. "They really know how to make them where she comes from. They're warm. You'll see."

Lizzie shoved them in her coat pocket.

* * *

The commotion of the school hallway and the familiar slide into her homeroom seat seemed a welcome jolt back to the world until Lizzie realized she could hear an indistinct murmur. She couldn't help but see glances coming in her direction. A few of her real friends, those with parents who had known hers, had shown up at the funeral parlor. The other kids didn't know what to do, so they did nothing but talk behind her back.

Making her way to her first class was tougher than she thought it would be. I don't feel normal, she thought. I feel like a piece of seaweed, flaccid, caught in an undertow with no control, nothing to hold on to, being dragged and buffeted.

She was shocked out of the fog of her thought when someone came barreling down the corridor behind her and banged into her shoulder, hard. It wasn't hard enough to knock her down, but it was hard enough to send her books flying.

"Hey!" she yelled reflexively, quickly scanning for whomever it was that apparently mistook her for some sort of punching bag. Still careening down the hall, jabbing some other guy, the obnoxious culprit was evidently Tommy Matthews from homeroom.

"Asshole!" she yelled, a mere cover for surfacing tears and shaking hands. She reached toward two of her books that were in danger of being trampled. She caught the side of someone's shoe across her knuckles, the ones that had, until now, been healing. If she'd been close to tears, the shock of physical pain had driven them back. Instead, she saw stars. She staggered back against the closest lockers, knuckles jammed into the warm salve of her mouth. One book had been kicked a good four feet further away. She watched the book skitter another six feet down the hallway until someone in the crowd picked it up. Jeffrey Snyder. He was bringing it back to her. She quickly reached for the other book before that one, too, got away from her.

Jeffrey handed her the book. Glad that she hadn't dissolved into tears, Lizzie took the book and stacked it on top of the other one lodged on her hip. Jeffrey, the smartest kid in the class, was tall and slender, with curly red hair and wire-rimmed glasses. Hesitating for a moment, he finally said, "Lizzie, I was sorry to hear about . . . about your parents." Then he just stood still, looking at her. He wasn't looking over his shoulder or dashing off with an excuse about being late for the next class. If he felt any discomfort at all in acknowledging her parents' deaths, he didn't show it.

"Thank you," she said. "And thank you for rescuing my book."

She had never seen Jeffrey smile. He was always so serious. Facing her, he seemed about to say something more. Still braced against the locker, Lizzie shifted the weight of her books from one hip to the other.

"My grandmother passed away last year," he said finally. "I know that can't compare to your loss. Sorry, losses . . . but, still, it hit pretty hard."

Lizzie nodded. "Thanks."

The commotion of the corridor swirled around them and they both moved off to their respective classes. Lizzie watched Jeffrey disappear down the hallway ahead of her, thinking that just as the grayness of Wren Haven surroundings had befitted her walks with Mimi, today Jeffrey's seriousness fit her mood perfectly. *I don't want to hear about Shelly's latest crush or be subjected to the cafeteria banter*, she thought. *I just want to sit on a bench somewhere and talk more to Jeffrey. Or maybe just sit next to Jeffrey. Somewhere quiet.*

The day wore on, but the routine motions of school kindled more irritation than comfort. Aside from those who had made it to the funeral home, only three classmates approached her to express sympathy. Try as she might to concentrate, by the last two periods— English and history—her wandering thoughts made it impossible. The words of those who'd offered condolences swirled around in her brain. Aside from Jeffrey, there had been Sarah, who had been in her Girl Scout troop, and Vickie, whom she'd come up through school with since kindergarten. None of these three were in the inner circle of coolness, or even on the periphery. She didn't learn any English or history that day—or math or biology, for that matter—but she left school with an unarticulated feeling that despite the bizarreness of the day she'd learned something worthwhile.

By afternoon pickup time, Lizzie's haze of returning to school had worn off enough for her to feel a tad more alert, yet an attempt at normal conversation betrayed her. To Mimi's, "How was school?" Lizzie's "Oh, good," sounded as forced as it really was. Mimi just nodded and the two of them rode home in silence.

chapter 15

MIMI STIFLED A YAWN AS SHE PUT ON HER BLINKER and waited for the light to change. *Getting up so early to drive to the high school is something I really didn't sign up for. I don't get up this early for water aerobics.*

Lizzie interrupted her thoughts when, two blocks from school, she said, "Just let me out here."

"Nonsense, I'll drive you to the front door, dear."

"No. Just here." In one swift motion Lizzie swung the door open, hopped out, and slammed the door closed again.

Mimi shrugged. *What's gotten into her?* She drove off.

The same scene played out Thursday. On Friday, Mimi drove off less quickly, first scanning the immediate terrain. From the various side streets leading up to the front of the school, lots of kids made their way on foot toward the school. But there were no real residential areas close by. "Got it," she murmured. No adult family members drove their kids to school, or at least not so anyone could tell. Apparently, students who did not take the bus or have their own car and at all costs wanted to avoid the humiliating position of being seen with parents driving them to school, had the parents drop them off several blocks away so they could saunter up to the entrance. Lizzie's request to be picked up a half-hour later at the nearby park also made sense now.

On Saturday morning, Mimi stretched out breakfast, making a great fuss over pancakes with crisp bacon and carefully sliced fruit. She even served the orange juice as a separate course. Quiet time. No pressures. Time for a conversation.

"You know," Mimi began, "I enjoy having you here with me."

Lizzie did not look up, but Mimi caught an unmistakable stiffening of her shoulders. "For the time being," she added quickly. *Okay. Tread carefully.* "It may take a little while to get things sorted out."

Lizzie nodded. "Sure."

"So, while you're visiting," —*good, her shoulders just relaxed*— "maybe you wouldn't mind if we coordinated schedules." Lizzie didn't reply. She just gave a wary look from under her bangs, but Mimi had her attention. "I've kind of got a routine," Mimi said, with an offhand flip in her voice.

Lizzie's lips pursed and her cynicism surfaced as she retorted with a little huff, "Yeah? Like what?"

"Well, there's my water aerobics class. It's at eight o'clock in the morning." Mimi didn't tell her that the water aerobics class happened only on Tuesdays, or that she didn't enjoy it all that much. "So, I was thinking. I talked to Rosa, and she'd be happy to drop you at school in the mornings. She gets off at seven, so it should work out just right."

Rosa was part of the security staff at Wren Haven, and she did indeed get off at seven in the morning. Rosa, young and the type of woman who, even into her elder years, would be considered hot, was nothing like Mimi. Mimi had the impression that Rosa might have a child but had never heard about a husband. She guessed Rosa would be happy to have a few extra dollars for dropping Lizzie at school. Rosa also had a sporty little red car that Mimi suspected ranked a notch or two up on the coolness spectrum.

"That's okay with me," Lizzie said as she snapped a stick of bacon.

"And then there's my line dancing class," Mimi went on with a little side-to-side motion of her head.

Lizzie nearly choked on a mouthful of pancake. "You do line dancing?"

"Well, I'm thinking of joining. The only thing is that it's in the afternoon . . ."

"Well, of course, go line dancing. Don't worry about me."

"But there's the thing about getting you back from school at that hour. So, I checked it out, and Wren Haven has a bus that goes from over near the Jefferson neighborhood about that time. Do you think you could make your way over to Jefferson? They pick up some of the evening staff and bring them here to Wren Haven. You could ride on that bus."

Some referred to Jefferson as "the other side of town." Wren Haven drew a segment of its staff from the town's lower-income district. Many who lived there did not own cars and without the bus would be unable to work at Wren Haven. Some were not much older than Lizzie.

"Sure, I could do that."

Mimi worked to keep her face expressionless but enjoyed a moment of inward triumph. *Is that a glimmer of delight I see? Yes, I think so.*

chapter 16

Lizzie lay in bed, fending off nighttime demons by trying to think back to the time before her unreal life began, the time she thought of as Before Wren Haven. There were two acceptable modes of transportation to school. Most kids went on the school bus. It was just something you did from the time you were in first grade, so there was no real stigma to it. But the super cool kids—that status aspired to by virtually every high school student—arrived by car, preferably driven by oneself or, if not, then driven by another student. Even before the Corridor C incident, Lizzie had felt partially justified in ascribing coolness status to herself by virtue of being Shelly's best friend. Shelly had an older sister, Rachel, and Rach had a car. Rach would ferry Shelly and Lizzie to school and home because that meant she got to drive the extra distance to Lizzie's. Lizzie had suspected that her mother did not particularly like this arrangement, because Rachel made no attempt to hide her smokes from anyone.

At the time, in her own brand of passive-aggressive rebellion, Lizzie had let her mother wonder about what went on in Rachel's car. But now, lying in Mimi's pull-out sofa-bed, Lizzie asked herself why that had mattered. Why had she wanted to torment her mother? No answer. No answer at all. Her mother, truthfully, did not bother Lizzie all that much compared to some of her friends' parents who placed strict constraints on them. Guilt settled on her chest as she lay in bed. She hoped the gremlins of regret would leave her alone tonight.

She now rode to school with Rosa, and it was fine under the circumstances. Rosa always pulled the red sports car, which she claimed to have won in a card game, up to the front of the school with a neat, low-slung swoosh—coolness personified. Lizzie sensed that some of the guys were checking out this action and, in the process, checking her out as well. Too bad she couldn't enjoy it. Maybe someday she would. Maybe next month or next year or next lifetime. But for now, despite Rosa's good humor, she only felt the hollowness in her gut that was so acute that she was sure it was visible to everyone, almost like a doughnut hole. Lizzie, the weird kid with the hole where her stomach should be. Maybe the hole had been burned there by the coals that had blazed in her belly during that last car ride, the ride to Mimi's, when Lizzie's shame at being unable to act like an adult when her mother was sharing adult thoughts with her, treating her as a friend, rather than a kid, had felt like burning coals in the pit of her stomach.

Lizzie attempted to jettison the coals, the burning, by turning on her side and throwing her pillow against the mirrored closet door. *Enough of these horrible, repetitive thoughts! Reliving that ride is keeping me awake and I need to sleep if I'm going to get up on time. Think of something better. Something happier. Think of Rosa.*

It was impossible not to like Rosa. She was chatty and cheerful and always had some new piece of Wren Haven gossip to share. Rosa also had an extensive family, one or another of whom was always up to some antics.

"Mi prima, Luisa, she sign up for beauty school last month."

"Prima?" Lizzie queried.

"Prima, prima! Eh . . . she is the daughter of the sister of my mother."

Lizzie followed the family tree for a moment then filled in, saying, "Oh, cousin."

"Si. Mi cousin Luisa, she sign up for beauty school. You know, you can make good tips as beautician. An' you no have to pay tax."

"Really? No tax? No income tax?"

"No. Cash. No tax."

Something about that sounded off to Lizzie, but she let it slide and listened to Rosa's latest tale.

"Anyway, Luisa get color mix up, and lady who want blonde hair get red hair. Luisa don't know what to do. Lady have eyes close when Luisa realize what happen. Luisa afraid she get throw out of beauty school. So Luisa give her great haircut and tell her how beautiful she look, like nothing wrong. Then, Luisa quick get two amigas—"

"Amigas?"

"Si. Amigas. Eh, friends. She get two friends, also beauty student like her, and they quick come and tell lady how beautiful she look. And lady look in mirror, pretty shock, but Luisa and her friends they tell her how great hair look and she don't believe them but, you know, like, she really want to believe them. So, she leave beauty salon and Luisa hold breath all the time until door close behind her. An' now, you know what? Luisa think she is genius beautician! She say she is going to pick out new hair color for all her client! I cannot believe her!"

Rosa had a full, joyful laugh and a way of looking at the world that little by little helped tug Lizzie, however reluctantly, out of her grief. Lizzie resolved to sign up for Spanish next year.

chapter 17

Wren Haven's afternoon bus riders found Lizzie a curiosity, eyeing her warily at first. After a while, however, this world-weary crowd seemed to assess her as harmless, and they exchanged easy and meaningless banter. Lizzie began to get to know many of the other riders by name.

"Hey, Lizzie, how'd school go today?"

"Not too bad, Silas. How's your knee doing?"

"Gettin' by. Gettin' by." And Lizzie and Silas would amble onto the bus with the rest of them.

Silas had told Lizzie a bit of his back story on one of these rides. He was an older gentleman—and Lizzie did consider him a gentleman—who had worked at Wren Haven since its opening day about twenty years ago. He had had various assignments around the property but now worked tending Wren Haven's extensive plantings. He had shown Lizzie his employee ID card, proud of the fact that he was employee number fourteen and at this point was Wren Haven's longest serving employee, the first thirteen having moved on for various reasons.

His knee was another story. There had been an accident when Wren Haven was still partially under construction. His boss at that time had assigned Silas to clear some of the building debris. A stack of lumber had collapsed on top of him. "I was mostly alright," he'd told Lizzie in a resigned tone, "but the knee was not. I had an operation to fix it up pretty good." He'd gone on to reassure her he could walk "mostly fine." He'd continued, saying, "But for a long time, I thought maybe my working days were over."

Silas did not walk "mostly fine", from what Lizzie could see, but she hadn't wanted to interrupt him.

"My grandson used to drive me to work, but 'bout that same time he took off for college. I'd have been in a peck o' trouble if I couldn't get back to work." Silas looked out the window, probably recalling his earlier Wren Haven days.

He turned back to Lizzie with a grin. "Back then, Wren Haven had a real nice executive director—that's the big boss who runs the whole operation." Lizzie nodded for Silas to go on. "His name was Mr. Sansone. Did I say he was a real nice guy?"

"Yes, you did," Lizzie replied, now leaning forward a bit to hear the rest of the story.

"So, Mr. Sansone had a great idea. He decides to have one of the Wren Haven buses—do you know Wren Haven has a whole fleet of these buses?"

"Yes, I know they have a lot of these buses." *C'mon Silas. What happened?*

"Well, Mr. Sansone decided to have a bus travel on a route all the way over to my neighborhood. So, he was pretty smart. Just look at all the people who ride this bus now." Silas raised his chin to scan the rest of the bus. Then he looked at Lizzie a tad mischievously and grinned a grin that showed all his teeth and all the wrinkles of all his years. With a lowered voice, he added, "But I think he do it just fo' me."

There was a variety of fellow bus riders. Some were high school students and worked just the dinner hour; others comprised an important segment of the small army that kept Wren Haven running day and night.

Mornings with Rosa, afternoon bus rides back to Wren Haven—all provided companionship with people Lizzie would otherwise never have met. This pattern formed a different experience than Lizzie might ever have imagined, and certainly not one that felt unpleasant. But after four weeks, Mimi's references to "getting things sorted out" became less frequent and Lizzie found herself resisting owning up to the truth: she was living at Wren Haven. She was a teenager—Miss Coolness, in fact—living at an old folks' home. That was not normal.

Lizzie had a recurring late-night vision. She knew it was stupid and told herself it was stupid, but in the dark hours on her pull-out sofa-bed she thought about Shelly, and Shelly's taunt the day before leaving for Mimi's that fateful weekend. That taunt ate at her. Like in one of those wavy movie dream sequences, she could see Shelly's face and hear her say, "You think you'll fit in, Liz? We'll have to get you some of those little granny glasses and . . ." Lizzie pulled the pillow over her head to block the image. One night Lizzie dreamed Shelly was no longer her best friend. Someone else was her best friend, but she couldn't see who it was.

Lizzie's half-normal life during school hours was not normal at all once she boarded the Wren Haven bus. No more rides home with Shelly and Rachel. No more normal teenage bedroom to come home to. No more parents. An undertow of resentment tugged at her. Worst of all, she could see no way out of her present circumstances. She was trapped.

The boiling point came one evening a little after eight-thirty. Wandering out to the kitchen, Lizzie passed Mimi, who dozed on the couch with the television tuned to a game show, which was not an uncommon occurrence. The day's mail lay on the hallway console, some opened and some not. One envelope caught Lizzie's eye because it bore the crest of her school. The letter itself was nothing, some announcement about school holidays. What was significant was that it was addressed to Mimi at Wren Haven. That could only mean that Mimi had contacted the school and officially named herself as Lizzie's guardian and changed Lizzie's address to Wren Haven. Shelly's teasing had become reality. There would be no "sorting things out." She was never leaving.

Steaming, Lizzie stormed out of the apartment, tearing through Wren Haven's corridors and up the stairs, taking them two at a time.

Lies! Mimi said I'd only be staying here until things got sorted out, then I'd be going home. Worse, she never actually said I'd be going home, she just let me think it! Sure, I'll be staying here until things get sorted out, and then after they're sorted out too! What a joke! And I fell for it! My own grandmother deceiving me! Haven't I had enough to contend with without being prevented from getting on with my life? I could live by myself. Absolutely I could. What does she think—that I'm just going to retire here? It isn't normal! I want out of here!

Lizzie ran blindly to nowhere in particular except away from Mimi's apartment. She breathed deeply to stave off tears. She passed the library and the music room, both dark. Wren Haven's nightlife had tapered off. Only the pool hall was still lit with the last players. She glimpsed Mac and Herb, barely registering them. The bridge players had broken up and Andy, one of the maintenance workers she rode the bus with, was vacuuming the card room.

Fifty yards past the pool hall, she reached the Great Hall, the venue for parties large and small. A faint aura of warmth still emanated from the enormous fireplace there, but the nighttime lighting scheme cast only a dim light. In the corner was the bar that supplied happy hour on Wednesdays and Saturdays. She brought both her fists down hard on the polished mahogany, then leaned her elbows on the bar and clutched her head, her now-healed knuckles turning white. The mirror behind the bar reflected a distressed creature. Like a bull, she was breathing heatedly through her nostrils, her face an extraordinary shade of red. She saw something else, as well: a couple of rows of various liquor bottles. She had an impulse to grab them and start throwing them at the fireplace, at the mirror, at the floor, but mostly at the absent Mimi. She picked up the first one in the row and then had another idea.

Sometime later, Lizzie felt a hand on her shoulder and heard Mac saying, "What have we here?" Lizzie was half-curled on the floor, a gin bottle askew on the rug, less full than it had been an hour before.

"My goodness, Lizzie, can you stand?"

With a groan that was more of a whimper, Lizzie rose to her feet for only a moment before Mac grabbed her under her arms and supported her as she stumbled alongside him to the nearest bathroom, which happened to be the men's room. With Mac's left palm on her midsection and his right protecting her forehead, Lizzie vomited repeatedly into the toilet.

A half hour later, cleaned up and a good bit steadier, Lizzie sat at the table area near the deserted cafeteria. The usual overhead lighting was off, but there was enough perimeter light to see their way around. Mac pressed against the stainless-steel doors leading into the kitchen. He reappeared a couple of minutes later with some ginger ale and crackers and the two of them sat in the evening half-light of the seating area.

"Now, what's this all about?" Mac asked.

Embarrassed, Lizzie did a terrible job of expressing her sadness and anger and frustration, but she spilled it out without whining too much. At least she wasn't bursting into tears. She supposed that showed some shred of dignity.

"Well, Lizzie, you're not going to solve anything acting this way, you know. In fact, just the opposite."

"Meaning, exactly what, Mac?"

"Well, Mimi—and everyone else—is going to think you need to

be watched."

Watched? Charlie is someone who needs watching. Anyone who needs a little dog to get him back and forth to the dining room needs watching. But me? I'm fifteen! Clumsily tearing at the cellophane of another cracker packet, she just said, "Really?"

"Sure. Like you're not mature enough to be left alone."

They remained in silence for a few minutes. Lizzie shoved another cracker in her mouth, which did absolutely nothing to alleviate her embarrassment at the truth of what Mac said or her embarrassment about the condition in which Mac had found her. Worse, she had no clever quip to toss out to recover any semblance of coolness, any sense that she was not the immature jerk that she now realized she appeared to be.

"I guess you're no worse for wear," Mac summed up. "C'mon. I'll walk you back."

"Thanks, Mac," Lizzie said as they reached Mimi's door. "See you tomorrow."

Lizzie opened the door as quietly as she could. Thankfully, Mimi was still snoozing on the couch. Lizzie sheepishly made her unsteady way to her bed and tumbled in. And, for a change, Lizzie knew that not only would she see Mac the next day but she would be glad to see him.

chapter 18

THE DAYS GREW WARMER. WARM ENOUGH THAT THE jacket one threw on in the morning proved to be inordinately hot by noon.

"Have a good day," Mimi called as Lizzie banged her way out of the apartment to meet Rosa. She took Lizzie's cereal bowl and put it in the dishwasher and clicked it on. Then she walked into the hall and started shuffling through yesterday's mail, ditching the junk mail, and taking the few legitimate bills into the sofa-bed room—what had been her den until a couple of months ago, the room her desk was in. *Don't trip*, she thought automatically as she took an edge of blanket off the floor and tossed it back onto the pulled-out bed. The bed. Left unmade again. But what did she expect? After all, Lizzie was only fifteen.

She pushed Lizzie's assortment of books and cosmetics to the side of the desk's surface, pulled out her checkbook, and wrote several checks. She placed stamps on the envelopes, pushed the chair back under the desk, and shuffled out into the dining-living area. Lizzie's notepad and papers covered half of the dining room table; a couple of pens and highlighters looked as if they might roll off the edge at the slightest vibration. At least Lizzie took her schoolwork seriously.

Mimi absentmindedly dropped the stamped envelopes onto the coffee table. Jane would have been paying her own bills about now. They would need to be sorted out at some point. Sometime soon. She pictured herself entering Jane's home just as she had done so many times before and feeling Jane's tight hug that hadn't changed since she was three. She pictured herself having the same thought she always did upon entering, that Jane had done such a marvelous job with what she had to work with. There would be no hug, no hot coffee waiting. She couldn't face going there yet. She'd only gotten through Daniel's death because Jane had been at her side doing so much for her. Now she'd have to do the same for Lizzie. Soon, though not yet, not today. There would be an entire house to take care of, not to mention the bank accounts, the furnishings, the car. She quickly wiped a couple of tears from her cheeks and allowed herself to plop down on the couch, exhausted, mentally replaying last evening's exchange when she'd simply asked Lizzie whether she'd finished her homework, since she seemed to be engaged in a texting marathon with her earbuds in. Thank goodness Lizzie's answer had been "yes", although with an unmistakable and unwarranted sharpness. What should she have said instead? Maybe, "I'll not have you treating me as an inconvenience in your life? Be grateful you're not in some awful foster home? Be thankful you weren't in the car with them? I wish you were . . ." No, she never would say any of this.

Why was she so tired? It was still early in the morning and she already felt a weariness that made her want to pull a blanket over her head. The sun streamed through the sliding glass doors that led out to the patio. She allowed herself to be mesmerized by the glint of sun off the metal patio furniture. Tired? No, to be honest, it was less fatigue than malaise. Why? She had a home that many seniors would be envious of. And Lizzie? She loved no one more and was now closer than ever to her. She should be happy, right? She reached for the pillow next to her and clutched it to her chest, running her fingers along the silk fabric—and found a rip. Mimi burst into tears. It was all too much.

chapter 19

After yet another night of tossing, when she should have been asleep hours ago, Lizzie enumerated the sources of her anger, sticking in her like a multi-pronged fork. Mainly, she was angry at having no control over where she lived or who she ate dinner with. She hated Wren Haven. She hated that everything was so pretty and so neat. She hated that the old folks' dining room was more elegant than the one in her house.

Although both of her parents were college graduates, Lizzie's family fell into that stratum of the middle class that was not affluent and quite possibly never would be. When anyone outside the family asked, they would just answer that her father was "in sales" and her mother "worked for the county." This always seemed sufficient to elicit a head nod and a knowing, "Ahh."

Coolness demanded some mark of superiority, like not caring about such things as money or social standing. Hence, though

Lizzie pretended to be indifferent, she knew a bit more than she perhaps should have. Like at the neighbors' barbeque last summer. Her father, beer in hand, had sat shoulder to shoulder with Bill Peterman, a long-time friend. "It's a tough business," she overheard her father say. "There's word another division is on the block. Don't think it's mine this time around, but it wouldn't surprise me." That was last summer. It was the first time she had put two and two together. Her father had had a few job changes, though her parents never made a big deal of it. He had recognizable corporate names on his resume but at this point risked having a few too many. There had been a stretch of time when she was in eighth grade when he seemed to be home a lot. That was unusual for him because he normally traveled extensively. That night she connected the dots.

And then there was her mother's job. She did indeed work for the county, scheduling road repair crews. She'd been to her mother's office—no, her mother's cubicle in a government office building—many times since grade school, usually during one of those odd holidays. It was the night of the barbeque that Lizzie had put that piece of the puzzle together as well, realizing that Jane worked at a job that would never be part of the executive ranks but that at some level contributed substantially to the family's financial stability. Coupled with the vignette of her father and Bill Peterman, she had felt an unfamiliar discomfort.

Now, lying in Mimi's pull-out sofa-bed, Lizzie once again connected the dots and better understood her mother's ebullience that weekend. Not only was the weekend in a fancy hotel going to make up for the canceled vacation and the rainy week in the woods, but it was also going to be the career step-up that had been eluding her father for the last decade and a half. And her mother had been happy about the turn in circumstances. It was probably a chance to get the credit cards paid off and maybe put in some better shrubbery. She had bought a new dress, new shoes.

I could have let them share their happiness with me. Now? No chance to do so. No chance to reach out and say, "Have a good time." No more chance to be a daughter. The guilt settled heavily in her chest. She tried turning her face to the pillow to muffle escaping sobs, but when the pillow became too damp to be comfortable for sleeping, she flung it across the room and wiped her tears with the heel of her hand.

chapter 20

THE TWINGE IN HER KNEE AFTER GYM CLASS ONE DAY brought Lizzie's cynicism to the fore yet again: *What? Am I aging prematurely by hanging out at Wren Haven?* Not a good look for Miss Coolness. She gave an inaudible sigh at the thought of Wren Haven, where her makeshift bedroom was half the size of the one she grew up in, just one complaint in the catalog of irritations Lizzie had been mentally itemizing day by day.

And what about Shelly? She hardly saw her anymore except for about ten minutes after classes ended each day. Shelly was the one person who would understand how Lizzie chafed at always having to be on her best behavior, lest Mac be proven right.

Before long, the chafing rubbed her emotions raw again. She had been too curt with Mimi once too often and soon genuine resentment returned.

One evening she slammed her textbook loudly enough to get Mimi's attention.

"Don't you have more homework to do?"

"It doesn't matter. I'm not going to pass this class, anyway."

"Why? You've always been a good student."

"There's a term paper due for this class and all my research is at home. Without it, I'm going to flunk."

To Lizzie's exasperation, Mimi just continued filling in another word of the crossword puzzle she was working on. Then, without looking up, she replied in a nearly languid voice with, "Well, that's easy enough. We can go to your parents' house and pick up whatever you need. We'll go Saturday. Maybe you'd like to get some different clothes while you're there."

Lizzie hadn't missed the implied message. "Pick up whatever you need" meant pick her things up and bring them back to Wren Haven, the prison. Mimi had just spoken volumes and what Lizzie had intended as an expression of anger, Mimi had managed to exacerbate. But anger didn't matter, not really. It would be the incentive she needed to find a solution to her situation. Something different to think about tonight.

chapter 21

As they entered the familiar foyer, Lizzie flicked the light switch, to no effect. What was with the light?

Mimi grabbed up the mail overflowing the mail slot basket and began sifting through it. She shook her head and muttered, "Electric, telephone, internet. All these bills that haven't been paid. Gracious."

Halfway down the corridor to her bedroom, Lizzie stopped short. She'd never thought about electric bills.

Lizzie surveyed what had been her bedroom. What was so great about anything here? The frames of the wall-hung photos didn't match, and she'd never liked the one of her middle-school graduation. Her parents had bought the furniture when she was eleven and by now it was old and worn. But this was home, not an old folks' home. A normal home. Or it used to be. It used to have a normal family living here. It used to have electricity.

She could hear Mimi in the kitchen, the refrigerator door open.

coolness to the wind

Of course, anything that had been in the refrigerator would be spoiled. She could hear Mimi cleaning it out.

Fifteen minutes later, Mimi appeared on the doorstep of Lizzie's bedroom. Her eyes scanned left to right above a quizzical open mouth as she took in Lizzie lounging on her bed instead of filling a suitcase.

Mimi took one step into the room and then picked up a large stuffed rabbit that Lizzie's father had brought home from his travels one Christmas. Maybe Easter.

"Wouldn't you like to bring the rabbit with you?" Mimi cooed. "He's so soft and pretty." Mimi stroked his foot-long ears, then cuddled it close enough to rub the fur against her cheek.

Lizzie barely kept her temper as she sprang from the bed and grabbed the stuffed animal from Mimi's arms and flung it against the wall. "Baby thing. Should have been thrown away a long time ago." The rabbit bounced off the wall and onto the bed.

"Lizzie!" Mimi was clearly astonished.

Lizzie spun to face Mimi. "I'm staying. I'll be fine here by myself."

"Lizzie, you can't—"

"Yes, I can. You can't force me to leave!" Her voice rose. "What are you going to do, drag me to the car?"

Before she'd uttered the last syllable, Mimi slapped her across the face. Hard. So hard that it caused her to stagger back. It was the last thing she had expected. Debating, cajoling, crying, anything but slapping. The shock of it caught her up short, momentarily depriving her of breath.

"I know you're angry about the hand you feel you've been dealt," Mimi slung at her, raising her voice, "but you'll not take it out on me." She finished with a sharp jerk of her head, "Now get whatever you want. I'll wait for you in the car."

The slam of the front door sent another tremor through Lizzie, almost like another slap. Lizzie exploded in tears, grateful she didn't have to worry about anyone else hearing or seeing her humiliation.

She wished she was crying for her parents but, to be honest, she was crying for herself. The planned defiant speech had come out more like a petulant child's whine, underscoring her helplessness. Still refusing to pack anything, she grabbed the rabbit and hurled it at the mirror above her dresser. A sharp shattering of glass would have been satisfying. Instead, she heard only a dull thump as the rabbit bounced to the floor.

Lizzie dropped to the edge of the bed. She stared at the wall, then up toward the ceiling. The peeling paint in one corner sparked a memory of her parents arguing over whether the house needed repainting, about which, for some reason, she felt absolutely nothing.

Lizzie flopped back onto the mattress and rubbed her eyes. She had had visions of riding her bicycle to the supermarket to buy groceries and once again riding to school with Shelly and Rachel. In her late-night scheming, it had seemed that was all she needed to do. She could do that. But what about those bills? As if to emphasize her failed attempt at striking out on her own, the afternoon sun slipped behind a cloud. Lizzie gave an involuntary rub of her arms, then automatically started toward the thermostat. Once again, she stopped in her tracks. Right, she thought, no electricity, no heat. Great.

Arms crossed, she stood at the threshold of her bedroom and pondered this for a minute, then sprinted over to her dresser, yanking out the top drawer. She reached to the rear of the drawer where she'd been stashing her singles and fives and tens since she was old enough to appreciate that money could buy things. She counted it out. A disappointing hundred and forty-five dollars. Would that pay the bills? How much were electric bills? She separated the wad into two and tucked the bills into her pockets.

She stood there dumbly, hands still in her pockets. What could she do? Stay here in the dark? In a freezing cold house? Oh, and the bike. She winced at remembering its wracked-up front wheel. So much for that idea. Her father had been going to get around to fixing it, just like he was going to get around to fixing the loose tile in the kitchen and the drafty bathroom window. Without the bike, she couldn't even get food. It would be a lot harder than it had seemed every night for the last week when she had been visualizing her freedom. Defeat. Mimi wins. She wanted to rip the ears off the idiot rabbit lying on the floor. Instead, she gave it a kick and the poor rabbit flew under the bed, out of sight.

For the second time in as many months, Lizzie packed a bag, the largest one still in the hall closet, this time seething with genuine resentment, not just annoyance at an inconvenient weekend.

She wasn't ready to leave yet. More to buy time so Mimi wouldn't see she had been crying than out of any sentiment, she walked around the house. She jiggled the bathroom window trying to seat it better in its frame, to no effect.

She stood at the door to her parents' bedroom. The bedspread was an off-color match to the window drapes, but close enough, as she remembered her mother saying last summer when they were hitting the sales. Funny, the bedspread was slightly askew, the door to the clothes closet ajar. Last minute packing, she thought. Packing by people who used to be alive.

She took a step into the bedroom. Tentatively, she opened the lid to the jewelry box on the top of the dresser but couldn't bring herself to touch anything. Despite the cool temperature of the house, the air felt thick enough to choke her. Scanning the contents of the jewelry box, she felt her breathing quicken to a hyperventilating state. Suddenly she wanted nothing more than to flee this room, this house. She snapped the lid of the jewelry box closed.

Lizzie stumbled as she tried to maneuver the large suitcase down the front steps. The messenger bag slung over her left shoulder to haul her laptop computer and half-finished research papers threatened to slide off in the process. She tried her best to keep her head bowed down enough that Mimi would not get any satisfaction from seeing any tear residue that might have escaped her palm swipes.

Lizzie tossed her suitcase into the back seat, then slumped into the front passenger seat. She expected Mimi to peel out of the driveway in a huff, but she just sat there, looking at her.

"Wouldn't you like to bring your TV?"

Now that was an idea. Lizzie did have a TV. Some off-brand TV her father had picked out for a birthday present. It even came with a karaoke attachment that she had never used, so far off her wish list that it never would have crossed her mind to ask for one. But he had seemed so pleased with his choice that when she opened it up, she made a fuss and hugged and kissed him and knew she had made his day. For once a parental memory made her feel good, glad she had made his day. Even so, Lizzie inhaled a lungful of oxygen to stave off tears as he came to mind. He had been a good father.

Ignoring the suffocating sensation of a minute ago, Lizzie re-entered the house. The TV would work fine. And she'd have her own computer. When Mimi was watching her game shows, or whatever she had on before she fell asleep, Lizzie could seclude herself with something watchable.

"So, anything good on TV tonight?" Mimi tried as they finally pulled out of the neighborhood.

What could she do? Just be mad at Mimi for the rest of her life? In no scenario did that work. Mimi had asked a civilized question. She could at least give her a civil answer. Lizzie carefully modulated her response to be respectful but not enthusiastic or loving. "You ever watch the show with the gay guys?"

"Gay guys? Nooo. What kind of TV show with gay guys?"

Had she shocked her by talking about gay men? Couldn't worry about that now. "Nothing bad. They teach some straight guy about cooking and about decorating."

"Decorating! You know the room you've been sleeping in? I've never bothered with any real decorating in there. Do you think we could pick up some ideas to make it prettier?"

At least she hadn't said "your room." Lizzie supposed that was a concession. "It's on tonight," was all she said. And with that a truce of sorts was declared.

chapter 22

"Damn!" With her elbow on her knee, Lizzie followed her verbal exasperation by smacking her palm to her forehead.

The expletive elicited a disapproving look from Silas, who sat next to her on the Wren Haven bus. Lizzie rarely swore, but this, this! This fell into the category of the outrageous, the unimaginable, perhaps even contemptible. Her cell phone dangled in her other hand. All she wanted to do was reach Shelly, finish the conversation they'd been in the middle of when Rachel pulled up, and now the phone wouldn't work. Lizzie closed her eyes and allowed herself a moan of frustration. The scene at home a few days ago popped to mind. Of course. The phone worked. The cell service had been cancelled for non-payment. She had an irrational vision of jumping off the bus and running screaming down the middle of the street.

Silas stared at Lizzie, still appearing disapproving.

"Sorry, Silas. It's just that my cell phone died and now I can't get hold of a friend I wanted to talk to." Lizzie shook her head, then said to herself, "This is not normal."

"You use your cell phone a lot?"

"Of course. Everyone does. Who can get by without a cell—"? She didn't finish her statement because of the way Silas looked at her. "What?"

"I don't have a cell phone."

"You left it at home?"

"No, I don't have a cell phone. Don't own one. Period. Never have."

"Never? How do you live without a cell phone?"

"No, never. What do I need a cell phone for? I get on the bus, I go to work at Wren Haven. I come home on the bus, I eat, I sleep, I get back on the bus. What do I need a cell phone for?"

She rubbed her forehead. Maybe she'd just have to remember she wasn't human. Only humans need cell phones, right? Or maybe this bus was part of the Wren Haven parallel universe where cell phones didn't exist.

Silas stared at the phone in Lizzie's hand and then up at Lizzie. "My grandson has a cell phone. I don't know why he needs it. There's a perfectly good regular phone in the kitchen." He shrugged. "What's so important it can't wait 'til he gets back in the kitchen?"

What was so important? Well, finishing the conversation with Shelly for one thing. Were there other people who didn't own cell phones? Lizzie did not know any. Or hadn't until Silas spoke. Did Mimi have a cell? She could swear Mimi did, but come to think of it, she couldn't remember seeing her use it even once in the last couple of months.

Funny, but focusing on cell phones jogged her to remember something else. She hadn't thought anything of it then, but yesterday—no, the day before—when she'd texted Shelly, she hadn't received an answer. *Strange.* And hadn't that happened one day last week, as well? Maybe Silas was speaking pure wisdom—for more reasons than he knew.

chapter 23

"Thanks for getting me out, Herb," Mimi said. She took a relaxing deep breath and looked around at the décor. "I needed to get away from the apartment and away from Wren Haven for a bit. This is perfect." They were in a modest but pleasant restaurant not far from Wren Haven, a glass of wine at each place setting. No din of the Wren Haven dining room, no Snowball begging for belly rubs, no Lizzie. The only background sounds came from a soft instrumental over some decent speakers and the servers bustling to other tables in the half-filled room. Cute round vases on each table held fresh yellow and pink flowers.

"Rough time?"

"You wouldn't believe the scene last week. I had to take Lizzie back home to gather some school materials, some notes, and her computer and so forth. She needed more clothes than she arrived with, for sure. She must be sick of wearing those by now. After a half hour I saw she hadn't packed anything, and she launched into a tirade about how she wanted to stay in the house. Alone!" With a sigh, Mimi slowly closed her eyes and then looked heavenward. "Why me?"

Herb squeezed her hand and then let go as the server brought their salads.

"These are supposed to be my golden years! Those last years with Daniel were not easy between the doctors and the treatments and the bills. Well, you know what I mean. You went through something similar with Doris."

Herb nodded and gave Mimi a small, calm smile.

"And then going through the anguish of selling the house—I felt like a traitor, selling the life we had had together. That was so hard. So hard." She gave a small shake of her head and glanced at the server hurrying to the next table. "When I moved to Wren Haven, I thought that this was my new life; built-in social activities, new friends." She patted Herb's hand. "And a sunny apartment of my own choice, just right for one."

Mimi sighed. "If I had known I was destined to have a grown roommate," emphasizing the last word with a side-to-side head motion and rolling eyes, "I would have chosen a larger model. One with more space. A lot more space."

They both ate slowly, relaxing physically and mentally. It was a relief, really, not to feel like having to keep up a conversation with a half-dozen other people.

"Sorry I'm not a more cheerful dinner companion, Herb."

Herb smiled. "That's alright. We all have these trials in life. Not the same trials but ups and downs just the same."

"I suppose so. It's just that this one was so unexpected." Mimi put her fork down. "It's like my lifecycle has been upended. And it's going to last for years." Mimi didn't even try to hide her exasperation. "Herb, every other day I'm thinking that I can't go through these teenage years again."

Herb dabbed with his napkin and then said, "Ahh. Jane?"

Mimi blinked. Without realizing it, she was recalling the stretch of her life decades ago when it was Jane, not Lizzie, who she was desperately trying to manage.

"What was she like at that age?"

"Just as bad, I suppose. But those were different times."

"Different?"

"Sure. I didn't have to worry about what she was getting up to on her computer and I knew her friends and her friends' families—knew all the parents enough to pick up the phone and call if I needed to—and I wasn't having to contend with a child who had been wrenched from her home and family and everything familiar to her."

Herb chuckled. "And what were you like at her age?"

At this Mimi giggled, nearly choking on the lettuce she'd just put into her mouth. "Probably worse. One night I was so angry with my father that I stayed out all night. They had the police out looking for me."

Herb drew his lips inward with the corners slightly turned up, the look that told Mimi he couldn't resist a little teasing. "Oh, so Lizzie's perfectly normal." They both chuckled.

Herb began buttering a roll. "You know, Miriam, a philosopher, or maybe a very religious person . . ."

Mimi regarded Herb warily.

". . . the type of person who dedicates a lifetime to thinking deeply about such things, might have a different perspective." Butter knife in hand, he slowly looked up at Mimi.

Mimi's shoulders sagged. Really, Herb? Tonight I would rather just be able to blow off some steam, not have a philosophical discussion. She sat in silence for a few seconds, then sighed. "How so?"

"Well, someone from a more contemplative walk of life might draw your attention to the fact that having a teenager foisted upon you is not the only shock you've had lately."

Mimi crossed her arms and considered Herb over the top of her glasses.

"They might point out that you've also just lost your only daughter, your only child, in fact."

At that Mimi looked down at her empty salad plate, nodded, then took a deep breath, returning her gaze to Herb.

"So . . ." Herb drew the word out with a little wave of his hand, evidently waiting for Mimi to finish the thought.

"So maybe this child has come into my life to fill a void." Her whole upper body moved in a small rocking motion. She couldn't deny it. This explanation made more sense than any other.

The server's clearing of the salad plates jogged her back to the present and put her in a happier mood. "Like I said, Herb. This is just what I needed. You are just what I needed. Tonight is perfect. Thank you." Mimi smiled and reached for Herb's hand.

chapter 24

THE INFAMOUS TERM PAPER WAS THE SECRET THORN Lizzie thought she had to stick in Mimi's side, and she cultivated it the way one irritates a hangnail, disliking the pain but continuing to do so because it creates a perverse stimulus.

Late one afternoon, in one of her more obnoxious moods, Lizzie decided to goad Mimi by blatantly turning on the living room television—having absolutely nothing worth watching on at that hour made it so much the better—during what was usually homework time. She chose to emanate a particular strain of sullenness designed to raise Mimi's hackles—volume a little too loud, remote clicking too quick and too forceful.

Mimi sat in her favorite living room chair, filling in a crossword puzzle, not responding.

Internally, Lizzie gave an exasperated huff.

A good ten minutes later, in her annoyingly languid style, Mimi simply asked, "Done with your geometry homework?"

"Yeah."

"Biology?"

"Doesn't matter."

"Doesn't matter?"

"Nah. I'm flunking biology, anyway."

Mimi continued filling in her crossword puzzle, not even lifting her eyelids. "And why's that?"

Ha. I'll get her with this one. "I can't finish my term paper, and without that I can't pass, so I'm going to flunk anyway, so it doesn't matter if I do the homework." *There. How's she going to argue with that?*

Finally, Mimi laid her crossword puzzle down, placing the pencil in her lap. She looked up at Lizzie. "I thought we went and picked up all your notes and your computer for that paper."

"Not enough. I need to go get some research help at the library but because I have to take the afternoon bus back here, I can't stay late at school to get the librarian's help." Lizzie resisted the urge to glance at Mimi to see whether she had managed to provoke her and instead just tried to see Mimi's reflection in the glass of the patio door.

"Well, why don't you go down to the computer center?"

Computer center? This most unexpected recommendation snapped Lizzie out of her cynical slouch on the sofa. She squinted at Mimi's reflection. *The voice is casual but, is that . . . is that a smirk I see?*

Mimi continued in that dry, even tone, "Sure. Wren Haven's computer center is very up with the times. There's even an instructor. It's over near the pharmacy. You know where that is."

Sure enough, as Lizzie discovered the next day, there was a large and well-equipped computer room. Peering in the glass-fronted door, she saw three rows of computer stations, apparently set up for classes. All empty. However, a good-looking young man sat at the front of the classroom, engrossed in whatever was on his laptop screen.

"Mrs. Van Nostrand," he said, not looking up as Lizzie entered. "You're right on time."

"Excuse me?"

At her response, he eyed his visitor. "Mrs. Van Nostrand? My four o'clock?" He gave his head a little shake. "You're not Mrs. Van Nostrand, I take it?"

"No. I'm Lizzie Olsen. I just came in to . . . to . . ."

"Well, help yourself," he said with an offhanded gesture toward the computer stations.

"Are you the computer instructor?"

"James Heathwood. Pleased to meet you, Lizzie Olsen," he said with a smile, standing and extending his hand. "I am the computer instructor and here to impart wisdom twice a week, but sometimes my students don't show up. I never know why. Maybe they forget, maybe they find something better to do. But I show up, and it's a good job for me. When they don't show up, I can get some studying in."

James looked the part of the professional instructor, like someone who enjoyed his job and took it seriously. He presented a professional appearance in a crisp white dress shirt, tie, and a corduroy sport jacket. This was someone who wanted to treat his students respectfully. He wore glasses. He looked cheerful. From his brief introduction, it was evident that he had an amiable manner, the kind of personality that would make taking instruction from him easy and pleasant.

It turned out James was a graduate student in psychology at the nearby university, transplanted from London. Computer instruction at Wren Haven was a part-time gig that kept him afloat financially. He was able to give Lizzie a few research tips and seemed happy enough to chat. Lizzie, for her part, made a friend that afternoon.

Over the next couple of weeks, Lizzie gave the paper earnest effort, but it was turning out to be more work than she had initially thought it would be. About midway through her draft, she asked James to critique it, which he did. Then he gave her an unexpected suggestion: "Come back on Thursday. We'll have George look at it."

Lizzie had no idea who George was, but she dutifully returned on Thursday. She found James and George huddled over her paper. George, a slim man with thick glasses, looked vaguely familiar, but Lizzie couldn't place him. He wore the sort of uniform of the retired gentlemen of Wren Haven: khakis—never jeans—and a cotton shirt that he could throw a jacket over for dinner in the dining hall. Without preamble, he addressed her. "Lizzie, you're writing a paper about epidemics. Do some real research. Start with the repeated measles outbreaks in Boston in the late 17th century, early 18th century. That'll get you going in the right direction. You get stuck, you come see me, but I've got to go now." George took a few quick steps toward the door.

A bit taken aback, Lizzie glanced anxiously at James and then called to George, "Wait! Why Boston? What do measles have to do with COVID-19?"

George stopped short and turned to her. "All epidemics have some things in common. All need to be studied as to how they transmit and how quickly they spread."

Lizzie frantically scrawled notes on a spiral-bound pad.

"You've got to know—"

Lizzie glanced up from her scribbling, wanting to scream, "Hold on! Give me a break!"

"Aw, hell," he said. "You might as well use the real thing. Come on."

George was already halfway out the door. James gave her an ear-to-ear smile and made a shooing motion. Lizzie scooped up her notebook and miscellaneous belongings and chased after George, catching up to him halfway down the hall. James had better be right. This guy could be an axe murderer for all she knew, and she didn't know who he was or where he was leading her.

George walked briskly, leaning slightly forward as if afraid of being late for something. Lizzie scurried after him, taking an extra-long stride now and then to keep up with him all the way to the third floor of the adjoining building. He opened the front door of an apartment and looked back at her. "Well? Are you coming?"

Déjà vu hit Lizzie. It was the damp afternoon when Virginia had collected her after school. She'd felt uneasy then but no harm had come to her. But Virginia wasn't a man and she wasn't beckoning Lizzie into a strange apartment. Put your big girl pants on, Lizzie. If you thought you could have taken tennis champ Virginia, then slender George would be no contest, either. She followed him in. George led her into a room that occupied the same position as her room in Mimi's apartment. However, it had a totally different feel and look, all brass and mahogany and leather, the absolute stereotype of a man's study. "Sit anywhere."

Lizzie seated herself in a maroon leather wing chair.

George crouched down and pulled a cardboard box out of a closet and began rifling its contents. Lizzie sat looking at George's back as he plowed through what looked to be some voluminous documents. She knew she'd never met him before, but he looked familiar. She'd probably seen him around. Maybe in the dining hall.

"George!" Lizzie heard a shrill voice from another room. "Are you pulling out all that dusty old stuff again?" Though singles occupied most of the Wren Haven households, couples resided there as well. What was George's last name? She cast an eye over the walls. Degrees, several of them, like what you'd see in a doctor's office, covered half a wall. One George Duff had excelled himself at the University of Virginia and Cornell University, among others.

"Oh, be quiet, Janna."

"I just vacuumed in there," the woman replied, her voice no sweeter as she stomped to the doorway, "and I don't intend to . . . oh, we have company," she said as she noticed Lizzie on George's leather chair.

Lizzie stood and extended her hand. "Lizzie Olsen. I live with my grandmother, Mimi Kidder, in the next building."

The woman returned the shake. "Janna Duff. I live with this grouch here."

George rolled his eyes at this introduction. "Janna, you just go back to whatever you were doing. Lizzie and I have important work to do."

Lizzie held her breath, hoping she was not stirring up some marital discord.

"Important work! All that musty old stuff? Ought to have gotten rid of it a long time ago. Shouldn't even have brought it when we moved here." Janna marched off.

Poor George. Then it struck Lizzie why she recognized him. Wren Haven's entry foyer, the one she came in when she hopped off the bus after school, designed as a gathering place where people could get their mail, have a cup of coffee, and generally hang out, had several library-style sofas and chairs. George made a habit of commandeering the furthermost sofa and surrounding himself with piles of newspapers. She had once wondered how many hours it would take a person to wade through such a stack and why anyone would even want to spend so much time reading all those newspapers. At the time, she had just racked it up to what some retired people must spend their day doing and never gave it another thought. But now that she heard Janna blowing from one room to another, she knew better. Poor George.

"Okay, cutie pie. This is what we want," George said with a grin as he turned around and stood up with some difficulty.

Lizzie enjoyed a private chuckle at the contrast between her new nickname and her own trepidation of perhaps being sent off with an axe murderer just ten minutes ago.

George was waving a sheaf of papers like the blueprint to a lost treasure and, yes, an undeniable grin spread across his face. He tossed the packet onto a coffee table between them and pulled up a chair with casters. She heard a knee creak as he sat down and noticed him give it a quick rub. Nevertheless, George immediately launched into his lecture. This was a man totally focused. He was no longer brusque. He was calm, direct, and his voice had lost the edge it had in replying to Janna.

"This is the earliest data we have on AIDS," he said. "At the time, we were charting where the cases were springing up. You can see . . ."

There were tables of statistics. Pages of tables. Maps. Graphs. By the time George started in about correlations among cohorts, Lizzie felt herself sinking in way over her head, but she continued taking copious notes, hoping to make sense of them later. She glanced at the letterhead of George's material, reading it upside down: Centers for Disease Control and Prevention, Atlanta, GA. This was the real thing. Something clicked. Those plaques on the wall suddenly made sense—Doctor of Medicine, Distinguished Service, Honors, a photo of him speaking at a podium. George had been a research scientist. She paid attention as closely as she could, given the firehose of information coming at her.

"What's a cohort?" she asked.

"Now we're getting somewhere!" George exclaimed with another grin. And Lizzie wondered how she could have ever imagined him as an axe murderer.

Little did she know it at the time, but Lizzie would get an A on that paper. What she did know was that George was a goldmine of information.

Lizzie made a point of dropping by the computer center during James's workdays, and if his Wren Haven students didn't show up, they chatted about anything and everything. If James had a student, she often just sat at a free station and started her homework, a change of scenery from Mimi's pleasant but sometimes confining apartment. Occasionally, James would set up the "Will Return Shortly" sign near his computer and they would go to Wren Haven's tiny ice cream parlor, but usually they would just sit in the empty computer center and complain to each other about academic demands. Lizzie took great pride in explaining American football to James. She suspected that James found her and the stories of her friends to be excellent case studies for his adolescent psychology class, but she didn't mind. It felt good to have a friend—a friend who was neither a peer nor a senior citizen.

chapter 25

O NE DAY, SOMETHING REMARKABLE HAPPENED. LIZZIE forgot to be angry. It was the first Saturday in May. She lazed in bed, staring at the leaves outside her window, now full, green, and healthy.

Ten minutes later, over a bowl of cornflakes, she tried to discern what was different, what was missing from her "old" life, her "before" life. Mulling over what she would have been doing had she been at home with her parents, she decided it was chores. Saturday had always been the day for cleaning her room, running errands, and always some inane project one of her parents would decide they needed her to do. Not fun. Not the way to spend a Saturday. There were no projects here at Wren Haven. No garage to organize, no flowerbeds to weed. Marietta came and cleaned once a week, and Mimi's apartment was always spotless. Dry cleaning and shoe repairs got picked up and delivered right to the front door. And because they always took dinner in the dining hall, grocery shopping was minimal, and Mimi usually did it while Lizzie was at school. Yes, life at Wren Haven certainly was different and, now able to be a bit more objective, Lizzie decided that parts of the lifestyle were not so bad. So, this was her daydream as she sat in her nightgown eating cornflakes, staring through the sliding glass door at what was going to be a perfect, beautiful day.

"Penny for your thoughts," Mimi said over the top of the *Wren Haven News*.

"Oh, I was just thinking about my bicycle. It was a great bike, but I had it in a bike rack at the supermarket and someone rammed into it and then it was wonky to ride, so that was the end of it." She left out the part about her father's promise to fix it. Lizzie pictured him with a screwdriver and a wrench. He would have spent all day trying but, truthfully, he just wasn't the mechanical type. At moments like this, she felt a deep pang of loss.

"Is that right? Well, that's not so hard to take care of. Go get dressed."

Pulling on her jeans, Lizzie could hear Mimi on the phone.

"Henry? You still have those bicycles?"

There was a pause before Mimi continued, "Well, you come by here. I've got a buddy for you."

Twenty minutes later, Henry rode up on a bright blue bicycle, towing a matching one alongside. It matched except for the fact that the seat of the towed bike had been adjusted for legs considerably shorter than Henry's. Lizzie noticed a few water droplets sparkling on the fender and suspected that Henry had given the bikes a quick cleaning before coming over.

Henry seemed to be on the younger side of the Wren Haven population. His hair was barely silvering at the temples and the contours of his tee shirt suggested a well-developed musculature.

It's true, Lizzie thought, as she gave the pedals the first few pumps, you never forget how to ride a bicycle. She rode shoulder to shoulder with Henry until they entered one of the driveways leading out of the Wren Haven campus, then she fell behind him, letting him lead. Henry showed her paths out behind the Wren Haven property she never would have guessed were there. He took her to a strip mall not far away. There was a pizza place where they had pretty good slices for lunch. It crossed Lizzie's mind that if it hadn't been too far for Shelly, it would be a great place to meet up.

She and Henry rode for hours. The spring air invigorated her skin and her leg muscles felt reawakened. Henry was a fine conversationalist and an excellent bicycling companion.

Arriving back at Mimi's, Lizzie was not exactly looking forward to an unexciting evening of dinner in the well-appointed dining hall and then finishing her term paper. However, Mimi had something different in store.

"Herb and I are going to a movie in the auditorium tonight. You can join us if you'd like."

Lizzie tried to size up this unexpected invitation without being too obvious before she answered. "I'd hate to tag along on your date."

"Nonsense. You're always welcome. Herb likes you."

Lizzie only made a small grimace as she dropped down at the kitchen table and began to flip through Mimi's *People* magazine. How could she read this inane stuff? Movie stars. Who cared?

"Besides, Herb's got a tagalong, too. You'd be doing us a favor to round out the party."

Lizzie laid her hands flat against the magazine, impassive.

"Herb's grandson is visiting. He's about your age. You might have fun."

Lizzie peered at her grandmother from under her bangs, doing her best to appear agonized. "Aw, Mimi, a setup? A blind date?" She set her elbow on the table, the heel of her hand holding up her head to alleviate the pain and grief of it all.

"You don't have to come. I just thought you'd like to do a favor for Herb. He's been nice to you."

That was true. Herb had driven her to a concert she'd wanted to go to and taken her shopping when Mimi was sick in bed last week.

And he'd given her a proper reading lamp for Mimi's desk so she could use it for homework instead of using the dining room table. A movie was a small thing to ask. And whatever movie was showing had to be more entertaining than the term paper that was almost done and could wait until tomorrow.

"Okay," Lizzie said neutrally. "What time?"

chapter 26

Mimi noticed Lizzie was wearing black pants and a black stretch top. The top had sparkles around the neckline and looked brand new. Lizzie had also put on a little makeup. *Miss Coolness is back,* Mimi thought with a lightness absent of any anger. She resisted the urge to tell Lizzie she looked nice, figuring that such a compliment from a senior citizen, a grandmother no less, might take the shine off. Instead, she just asked, "Ready?"

They met Herb and Rod outside the auditorium. Introductions duly made, they each grabbed a bag of the popcorn being handed out and went in and found four seats together.

As the auditorium filled, Mimi could hear Lizzie and Rod conversing in first-date normalcy.

"Nice theater," Rod remarked.

"Yeah, I like the way I can stretch out," Lizzie said, extending her legs. "All the aisles and corridors are pretty spacious because some residents have walkers or canes and need the space to maneuver." She threw a few puffs of popcorn into her mouth. "You here for the weekend?"

Rod swallowed a mouthful, then with a one-shouldered shrug answered, "Mmhmm. Going home tomorrow. My parents went away for the weekend, and they thought it would be a good chance for me to bond with my grandfather." With a glance in Lizzie's direction, he added, "Since I'll be going off to college. And it's not too long of a drive here."

* * *

"Wonderful show," Mimi assessed as they left after the end. "Lizzie, it's such a lovely evening. Why don't you show Rod around the campus? He probably hasn't seen any of the other buildings or our fitness center."

The two younger ones didn't need any further encouragement to take off by themselves. As they turned out of sight at the end of the corridor, Mimi surprised herself with an affectionate thought. Three months ago, who would have thought she'd be setting her granddaughter up on a date? And for the first time since that horrible accident, Mimi realized she'd forgotten to be angry. Angry at the pain of loss, angry at being saddled with a teenager to raise again, angry at God for taking her daughter and her daughter's husband for no good reason.

Herb also seemed to focus on the two young people as they disappeared around the bend. "He's a nice kid," he said, "but his parents have him in this all-boys prep school. Well, not all boys, but it was once, and the boys still way outnumber the girls." Herb took Mimi's hand as they walked toward Mimi's apartment. The crowd had thinned out with everyone going their own way. "So, how's he going to meet some sweet young thing?" Herb nuzzled close to her ear, and they both smiled. Mimi was glad she'd forgotten to be angry.

chapter 27

A COUPLE OF DAYS LATER, LIZZIE CAME IN FROM SCHOOL to find Mimi at the desk in the sofa-bed room. She was huddled over a slew of papers with a hand calculator.

"Hi, sweetie," Mimi greeted her without looking up. "Have a good day?"

"Fine." Lizzie looked over Mimi's shoulder. "What're you doing?"

"Oh, the usual. Just balancing my checkbook. Reconciling with the bank statement."

"It looks like a lot of work." Lizzie plopped down on the sofa-bed, glad that for once she'd made it up before leaving for school.

Mimi shrugged. "Yeah. It is."

"Don't you have a computer program for that?" Lizzie then glanced at the antiquated computer on the left side of the desk. She guessed not.

"Your grandfather always took care of this sort of thing and set himself up with his own method," Mimi waved at the computer, "but when I went to his spreadsheet, I couldn't see that it was any more efficient than the old-fashioned way." She picked up the calculator and gently tapped it on the desk for emphasis. "To tell you the truth, though, I know I'm the only one still doing it this way and, frankly, my eyes are not what they used to be. And it's so tedious. It seems to take so long." She raised her glasses and rubbed her right eye. She sounded tired.

Lizzie listened and nodded. "My mother has . . ." she began, then cleared her throat and started again. "I know my parents used a software package to track their bank accounts." She hadn't done this before, but she could give it a shot. "Would you like me to try installing the same thing for you? Like anything, you'd have to learn to use it." She looked again at Mimi's out-of-date computer, a big, clunky thing. She knew Mimi used it for the occasional email, but not much more than that. It was probably awfully slow, too.

"We could put it on my laptop if you'd like. It's pretty fast. You might find the entire process goes more quickly." Lizzie took a step closer to the desk and looked over Mimi's shoulder. "Do you do this every month?"

"Yes."

"I hate to see you doing so much work."

"Do you think it's possible to get me more modernized? There are a hundred things I'd rather be doing than this," she said, picking up a handful of paper and tossing it back down on the desk.

"I could give it a try. And I'm sure James could give me a hand if necessary. I think he's in this afternoon."

Lizzie shuffled all the papers together and put them in the messenger bag with her laptop and threw in the calculator for good measure. She was about to leave the apartment and then stopped short. "Mimi, I'm sure there will be a cost for the software."

"Oh, of course, dear." Mimi reached for her handbag on the kitchen table and pulled out her credit card. "Here, use this."

When Lizzie got to the computer center, she found James

engaged with another resident. They were sitting side by side in the front row.

"Mrs. Van Nostrand, you're doing just great."

"I just knew this internet surfing would be the best thing!" the petite, older woman said.

Seeing Lizzie come in, James concluded his tutoring. "Remember, anything you want to refer to in the future, just bookmark it. See you next week."

Mrs. Van Nostrand left with a satisfied smile and a slight swagger. Well earned, Lizzie thought. She must be about Greta's age.

James leaned back and clasped his hands behind his head. "Miss Olsen, how are you today?"

"I'm okay, but I have a real project that I might need your help on." She explained the bank reconciliation quest.

"Why don't you just sit down and see how far you get and yell if you get stumped?"

"Perfect. Are you here for long?"

"Another hour and a half. It shouldn't take anywhere near that long."

Lizzie spent a diligent fifteen minutes and got the program installed before James checked on her.

"Okay. Let's see how you're doing," he called from his side of the instructor's table. "Have you created a password yet?"

Lizzie nodded her head. "Just did. I used Mimi's address, Wrenhaven plus Mimi's unit number. Letters and numbers."

"Lizzie, that's too obvious. Someone could easily guess that."

Lizzie backspaced, then stared at the screen for a moment. "Okay. How about HavWrenen plus the unit number?"

"Much better. Easy enough to remember, but not so obvious that anyone else would be likely to guess. And you've got at least one upper and one lowercase letter?"

"Yup."

"Fine. And for good measure, add a special character, like a percentage sign or punctuation mark."

Lizzie typed again. "Okay. I'm good."

That turned out to be the straightforward part when she saw the next fields to fill in. Oh, no. Now what? I don't want to screw this up now that I told Mimi I could get this up and running. Just swallow my pride and ask for help. I'm sure I'm not the first person to feel inept. He is the instructor, after all. "James, it's asking for account numbers, and I look at this statement and I'm not really sure . . ."

James slid next to Lizzie and took his first look at the assorted papers Lizzie had spread out on the desk. "I see Mimi uses the RealBank branch right across the hall."

"Who wouldn't? It's so convenient and they have an ATM and everything."

He took the several spread-out papers and tamped them together in a neat stack. "I see what you mean. There are numbers and codes all over this statement. If you're not used to reading them, they can be confusing." He took a minute to familiarize himself with the statements and then began his explanation. "Right here you've got a special number identifying the account owner as a Wren Haven resident."

"Got it."

James continued pointing to various numbers on the printed document and explaining them. Then he pointed to the screen and said, "This field is asking for the primary account number. I can see that's throwing you, because it's not labeled the same way on the statement, but it's right here." He pointed to the upper right part of the statement and she typed the account number into the form. He guided Lizzie through a few more fields and walked her through the process of downloading the account data.

He gave Lizzie a tutorial on entering new data, then finished by saying, "Now, let's make sure that the balance on your most recent statement matches the balance for the same date in the computer program. We just hop over to actions, click reconcile, and voila!

Down here, a zero difference means you're reconciled with the bank statement."

"Thank you, James," Lizzie said, gathering up the papers and laptop, eager to report back to Mimi. Maybe now she'd let her get rid of that older computer and free up some space on that desk. The two of them could just use her laptop. She would have to pay more attention in business class. This was all stuff she could only vaguely remember and now she actually needed to understand it.

"Mission accomplished," Lizzie announced as she came through the door with a slight bounce in her step and a little wave of the credit card before gently slapping it in Mimi's palm.

"Fantastic! And fast!"

Lizzie slid the laptop onto the desk surface, gave a sharp nod, and said, "No problem." Honestly, it felt good to do something for Mimi; to feel capable, to feel less like a dependent child. "Mimi, I'd be happy to do this for you. You know, when your statement comes in the mail. And the program is already on my laptop."

"Oh, Lizzie, would you? You wouldn't mind?"

"Of course not. I'd be happy to." She allowed herself another moment of satisfaction, then opened her geometry book with a genuine intent to study.

chapter 28

It was a Thursday afternoon and Lizzie and Shelly were walking toward the Jefferson neighborhood after school. They had reached the steps of the library, their usual after school hangout, where they could see anyone else who was going home this way—which wasn't too many kids—or just hang out by themselves. Shelly threw her books on the steps and did some stretching lunges. Lizzie sat with her books on her lap, looking down the street. She didn't see anyone walking or driving by that she knew. In a few minutes, Rachel would pull up to collect Shelly and then Lizzie would continue on to the Jefferson bus stop. Until then, they could analyze the hidden meaning of some school gossip, complain about their teachers, or just waste time.

Today, Lizzie was feeling slightly guilty about being deceptive. Not deceptive, really, just that she had this secret she was carrying around, and you don't keep secrets from your best friend—not your best friend since you were six years old. Why was she keeping this from Shelly? She didn't know, exactly, but it didn't make her feel good.

"Had something good happen to me on Saturday," Lizzie started.

"Saturday? What, at the old folks' home?"

"Yeah." Lizzie was staring out across the street. "There was a movie," she started again, but Shelly interrupted her.

"Did anyone see the end, or were they all asleep?"

Lizzie ignored Shelly's quip. "At first I didn't want to go . . ."

"Yeah, I wouldn't want to go either and have to sit through all that snoring."

Lizzie hadn't expected this. She and Shelly had always given each other a hard time in jest, but now she was trying to share something important, and Shelly was tuning her out. In fact, Shelly seemed to be on a roll with some self-invented brand of humor that was not humorous in the least.

"It sounds like you're turning into one of them. I'll have to call you Grandma Lizzie, get you some of those little granny glasses. Pretty soon you'll be shuffling around." Shelly hunched over, took some tiny steps, and scuffed the soles of her shoes on the pavement.

Rod was nice. They'd had an enjoyable time after the movie. Lizzie had walked him all around the campus, showing him the small town that was Wren Haven: the pharmacy, fitness center, computer center, and bank. Then they'd shot a couple of games of pool. And he'd called her every night since then. He was going to drive—what was it? An hour? Three-quarters?—to see her again this Saturday. They were going to go out to a real movie theater and get real popcorn and . . . and Lizzie wanted to share this with her absolute BFF but here was Shelly, acting like a jerk, shuffling up and down the sidewalk in front of the library.

Lizzie looked down at the books on her lap. Peeking out from between the pages of her biology book was a large A, prominent on the upper right corner of her term paper on epidemics. George Duff and his brisk stride came to mind while she watched Shelly, now laughing at her own pantomime. There was something wrong here.

Lizzie didn't laugh. "They don't shuffle!"

Exactly then, Rachel pulled up. "See you tomorrow, Liz," Shelly called as she grabbed her books and made for Rachel's car.

"They walk better than you do," Lizzie half-shouted as Shelly bounded into Rach's car, knowing full well Shelly was already out of earshot. *She's such a jerk that she doesn't even know what a jerk she's being.* Lizzie hoisted her books onto her hip and headed for Jefferson with a quicker than usual, firm step.

Lizzie entered the Wren Haven lobby with all the rest of the regular riders from the Jefferson bus. At the far end she saw George Duff, peering over the top of his newspaper and trying to act like he wasn't watching for her. This had been going on ever since he gave Lizzie her first tutorial in epidemiological transmissions. Most days she'd breeze over with a "Hey, George, how's it going?" and he'd act surprised to see her. Sometimes Lizzie would have a genuine question to get her to the next stage of her term paper and he'd talk her through it. Other days she'd just sit with him before heading off to Mimi's; sometimes she'd ask about whether he was going to one Wren Haven event or another. George preferred to play the resident grouch, jabbing his finger at some newspaper article and complaining about the terrible state of world affairs. She was careful never to ask about Janna, surmising that George's territory in the lobby behind his stack of newspapers was his refuge from her.

"Hey, George," Lizzie greeted him as she plopped down on the chair across from him, trying to look and sound nonchalant.

"Hi, Lizzie. How are you, cutie pie?"

"Pretty good," she responded noncommittally.

"How'd school go today?"

"Pretty good."

"So? Everything's pretty good?"

"Pretty good." After that scene with Shelly, things were far from pretty good. She'd been silent all the way back to Wren Haven, and she had probably been a bit rude to Tamika, whom she'd recently gotten into the habit of sitting next to on the way to Wren Haven. But right now, sitting here with George, she was glad to have something else on her mind.

George was pretending to be engrossed in his paper, tilting his head back to get a better angle through his bifocals.

"Got my term paper back."

"Oh, how did you do?" he asked in a mode somewhere between mild and matter of fact. Lizzie did notice, however, that with his apparent interest in tilting his head to get a better focus on his newspaper, his eye was trying to covertly glance toward the books on her lap.

"Uh, pretty good." With a smile that she was doing a terrible job of trying to suppress, she pulled the paper with its A out from between the pages of her book and gave it a quick wave in his direction.

George gave her the biggest smile she'd ever seen from him. Even better, he played along, nonchalantly. "Oh, I guess that's pretty good."

"Thanks, George. I couldn't have done it without you."

"Bah," he returned, resuming his crusty act and giving her a wave of his hand. "Get out of here."

Lizzie jumped up and took two steps toward the hallway that led to Mimi's apartment, then looked back at George or, rather, the back of George's head with its thinning hair, tilted back to scan the next news story. Then, impulsively, she threw coolness to the wind and went back to the rear of the sofa where George was sitting, squeezed the top of his left arm and gave him an awkward hug from behind, saying, "Thanks again, George," and then ran off toward Mimi's before George could respond.

She now felt super good about the grade on her paper and about having thanked George. However, all these super good feelings were not enough to compensate for the super bad feelings regarding Shelly. Why hadn't she told Shelly about Rod until today? Why had Shelly blown off her conversation in favor of her juvenile shuffling act? And, perhaps most important, why was she now asking herself all these questions about the person who had been her absolutely, unequivocally, very best, lifelong friend?

After dropping her books at Mimi's, she dashed to the computer center. James was in. He didn't have any students today, but he was busily typing something into the computer at the instructor's station. He heard her come in. He glanced up but did not stop typing.

"Hi, Lizzie. Have a seat."

She sat at a computer screen in the front row. James kept typing. He went on for another two minutes.

"James—" she started.

He cut her off with, "Shhh." He typed some more. "One minute, Lizzie."

Lizzie felt terrible. *First, Shelly treats me like dirt and now James can't be bothered.* She leafed through some Wren Haven materials stacked at the end of the table—notices of upcoming events, a copy of the Wren Haven Residents Directory and a map of the hiking trail. Then she folded her arms on the desk and put her head down.

Another minute and a half later, she heard James say, "Done!" She looked up. He was standing now and stretching as if he'd been sitting for hours. It turned out he had been.

"Luckily, I had two cancelations this afternoon," he said. "I was able to get this last paper out of the way."

"You mean it doesn't stop?"

"Doesn't what stop?"

"Term papers. In college."

James laughed. "Especially not in college! There are lots more! In fact, next year I start my thesis and that'll be a year of writing something like a book." He snapped his laptop closed and beamed at her. "What's up?"

"Eh, nothing."

James, the budding psychologist, folded his arms on the desk, not prompting Lizzie in the least, creating the kind of silence that felt like an uncomfortable vacuum.

"Got an A on my biology paper," Lizzie said, trying a more chipper tone.

"Uh-huh."

Lizzie was now attempting to affect boredom with her chin cupped in her palm, tracing an unseen design on the desktop.

"Want to go for a walk?" he suggested.

"Sure," she said, glad to insert some motion into the conversation.

"So, how was school today?" he asked.

"Okay. I got an A on—"

"So you said."

"Oh, right."

"Anything else new?"

"Not really." Trying to put her thoughts into words sounded ridiculous, even to herself. *What am I going to say? My best friend made a joke and now I feel lousy?*

"Want to go to the ice cream parlor?"

"Nah."

"Let's go out."

"Okay."

They exited the lower-level corridor through large glass doors leading out to one of the courtyards of the Wren Haven complex. Two residents, a man and a woman, were trying to enter from the other side and James saved them the trouble of fumbling for their key by holding the door for them to enter.

James got the conversation going by asking, "Do you know them?"

"Not well. I think their name is Conyers, or Congers, something like that. They're bridge players. Bridge is big here at Wren Haven. You should come by the card room any night after dinner. It's Wren Haven's hot nightlife spot."

James gave a neutral "uh huh" and Lizzie lapsed into silence again.

"Glorious weather," James said, looking up into the late afternoon cerulean sky. There were fine wisps of white clouds catching golden glints of the late afternoon sun at their edges. "I must say, I don't miss the London weather."

This remark caught Lizzie's attention. "No? It's not like here?"

"No, it's not like here, Lizzie. There is ever so much more rain, for starters."

They wandered over to the small playground. Whoever designed Wren Haven deserved credit for incorporating almost anything a senior citizen could want, including this playground for visiting grandchildren or, in some cases, great-grandchildren. Like the computer center, it was sometimes used and appreciated by the residents, but not in great demand. Lizzie sat on one swing, not swinging, just lazing back and forth a bit and looking down at the toes of her sneakers and the designs they made in the sand.

James sat on the edge of the sandbox opposite her. "In fact, standard back-to-school shopping includes acquiring pencils, notebooks, an umbrella, and wellies—those are boots, Lizzie." He paused, now appearing to contemplate the sand as well. "In fact, my father is building an ark in his backyard."

Lizzie was silent, still engrossed in the sand at her feet.

James continued, "I figure I can sell tickets for the next great flood."

At this, Lizzie gazed in his direction, her head resting on the chain of the swing, with a mild smile to match her now contemplative mood, knowing he was putting her on.

"What do you miss about home, James?"

"Oh, family, of course." He waited a moment, then asked, as kindly as he could, "Missing your mum and dad? Missing your family?"

Most days Lizzie was past crying for her parents. Though the pain was still there, it was no longer quite so raw; like the skinned knuckles that had scabbed over and diminished to scars. "Mimi is my family now," was her only reply.

Lizzie stopped playing with the little mound of sand she'd made with the toe of her sneaker. "Any friends? Miss any friends?"

James took a moment to consult the horizon before answering, "Yeah. I miss my teammates from my football—sorry, soccer—club. A lot of good times there; a lot of terrific mates."

"Ever have a best friend? Someone you could absolutely trust? Someone who knew all your secrets? All your fears?"

James thought for a few seconds. "There's my older brother, of course. He's married—a lovely girl, by the way, my sister-in-law—and they have one baby and another on the way. So, we've very different lives now, but I suppose we'll always be close."

"Different lives," Lizzie repeated, almost under her breath, as she swung gently, gazing out toward where the sun would be setting. The sky was already taking on a more golden cast. She returned her gaze to James. "Anyone else?"

"Well, yeah. There was Jeremy."

"Was?"

"Yeah." An almost-smile now came to James's face. "We were best friends for so long; always over each other's houses, getting into one scrape or another together. We were inseparable."

"What happened?"

"That's the funny thing," James said, looking Lizzie square in the face now. "Nothing 'happened.' It's just that . . . gosh, I've never given it much thought but, looking back, I suppose I was always the better student. I can't say there was any jealousy between us, because, well, he was always the better athlete, to be fair. But somehow, as my course load at school became heavier, he'd be giving me a rough time about spending so much time with my books instead of being out on the field. I suppose there were one too many instances like that and eventually he stopped bothering me about it. Funny thing, though, I didn't feel left out. More like relieved. I guess you could say we'd outgrown one another. I must have been about your age."

"Outgrown," Lizzie murmured. "Outgrown." The warm, diminishing rays of the evening sunset warmed the metal chain of the swing and she rocked with her head against the chain for a good minute longer.

James rolled a few grains of sand between his fingers and seemed deep into his own thoughts. Then he angled his head up at Lizzie and asked, "Have you ever thought about becoming a psychologist?"

chapter 29

WHERE WAS IT? LIZZIE TOOK A HANDFUL OF hangers and tossed them onto the sofa-bed. *Ah, here.* Surprisingly, not too wrinkled.

"Find what you were looking for?" Mimi asked, leaning against the doorjamb.

Lizzie gave a little start. "Oh, Mimi, you scared me. I didn't know you were home." She paused, holding the black dress up and examining it for flaws. "I'd had this all the way in the back of the closet." She stood with the closet door open, holding the black dress from so many months ago, the one Madame Lacroix had found for her when . . . well, for that time in February.

"Uh huh," Mimi said, almost under her breath. Mimi came closer and began to inspect the fabric with Lizzie. "Looks okay, honey. No spots that I see. No pulls." Mimi fingered the fabric. "Why on earth are you dragging this out today?"

Lizzie didn't respond. She held the dress up against herself to see her reflection in the full-length mirror. Finally, she said softly, "Rod's senior prom."

She didn't even finish the sentence before Mimi clapped her hands and gave a little squeal of joy.

"I haven't said yes," Lizzie said in a cautious tone.

"Of course, you'll go," Mimi interrupted. "And you must have a new dress. This was very nice for the last time you wore it, but now . . ." Her voice picked up to a more cheerful tone before continuing, "It's May, and pink would be so much nicer, or maybe a pale yellow?"

Lizzie interrupted her with, "Mimi, black is better. Black is in."

Mimi looked down at the dress, then back at Lizzie. "Of course, dear, of course. Why don't you slip it on and we'll take a better look?"

As Lizzie changed, Mimi perched on the edge of the sofa-bed with a decidedly quizzical look on her face and scratched her head. "Do they wear short dresses now? Prom used to be the occasion for evening gowns." She paused and Lizzie noted a look of genuine concern on Mimi's brow. "It's important that you have the right thing. I'd want you to fit in with everyone else."

"Either. Mostly long but short can be cool. And, like I said, black is the thing right now."

The two looked into the mirror together and almost telepathically decided it was still a shapeless shift. The last time it hadn't mattered and had matched the despondency of the circumstances. But now it did matter, and this dress was nowhere near acceptable.

Lizzie slumped down on the arm of the sofa, still staring at herself in the full-length mirror that somehow emphasized the stringy hair hanging over her shoulders. Mimi left the room and returned several minutes later with the small stool she used to elevate her feet when watching TV, a cushion full of pins, and a spectacular pair of black patent-leather spike-heeled shoes. "Here, why don't you try these? Hop on up," she said as she dropped the stool at Lizzie's feet.

Lizzie had the shoes on in an instant. She almost squealed.

"Mimi, where did you get these shoes? They're gorgeous!"

Mimi tapped the nail of her index finger against her teeth before asking, "Do they fit?"

Lizzie nearly sprang onto the stool. "Perfectly! Wherever did you get them?" Maybe it was the contrast with the disappointment of old the dress, but the materializing of the shoes sent a spark of excitement up from Lizzie's now well-shod toes straight to her lips, which she could feel stretching upward as far as they could go.

Mimi did not respond. Instead, she knelt on the floor and began to pin up the hem of the dress.

"Oh, that's much better," Mimi said, fingering the hem, running her fingertips over the shortened length. Mimi inserted a few more pins, continuing to work without a word.

Lizzie glanced down at Mimi, who seemed small from the height of her vantage point on top of the stool. Her excitement over the shoes dampened at Mimi's silence. *Was there a problem?* "Mimi? Is something wrong?"

Mimi took a deep breath, then said, "The shoes were in your mother's suitcase." Mimi sighed a little, looking down at the carpet. "They looked brand new," she said as she resumed pinning. "They were still in the shoebox."

"Oh." Lizzie felt as if a baseball had been thrown at her gut; thrown and torn open the wound that had been the singed hole in her stomach last February. "I'll need to break them in."

Mimi nodded and fussed with a few of the pins.

Fifteen minutes later, Mimi and Lizzie stared at each other in the mirror. Spectacular shoes; not a spectacular dress.

Mimi sat back on her heels, hands in her lap. "I think we've got a good excuse to go shopping for something new. Too late today, but one day next week after you get home from school we can go—"

"Mimi, the prom is Tuesday and, anyway, I haven't told Rod I would definitely go with him. I only just met him, really."

Mimi shot up from the stool to face Lizzie, hands on her hips. "The prom is Tuesday and you haven't given that poor boy an answer yet? Get on the phone this minute! And don't worry about the dress. We'll figure something out."

"You're right, I suppose. If you think it's reasonable to—"

With a fully extended arm and the kind of expression that suggested there would be no argument, Mimi pointed toward the hallway phone. "Go!"

Returning to her bedroom a tad sheepishly but with a small smile, Lizzie found Mimi in a decidedly take-charge frame of mind, her earlier exasperation having morphed into a more upbeat idea. "Wear the shoes. We'll get this taken care of. Bring your jeans and tee shirt. Let's go."

Lizzie gathered up her discarded clothes from where she'd tossed them on the sofa-bed and scampered after Mimi, who was now halfway to the door.

She followed Mimi to the craft room on the second floor. Two women in the corner held soldering irons as they worked on a large piece of stained glass. They did not look up from their work. Another cluster of four women fit pieces of blue fabric onto a large quilt. Lizzie followed Mimi over to a sewing machine where a solitary woman sat stitching small pieces of bright yellow fabric. A thought popped into Lizzie's head: *I'll bet that's a summer dress for a granddaughter.*

"Rosalie, I thought we'd find you here," Mimi said in greeting.

Rosalie looked up but did not answer, giving the impression that she did not appreciate being interrupted. Lizzie stood there in the dress with pins in it and the spike heels she'd never worn before, feeling like an unwelcome mannequin.

"Got a little problem here," Mimi said, taking Lizzie's elbow and steering her in Rosalie's direction. "Senior prom. Tuesday."

Rosalie sat back in her chair and let her glasses-on-a-chain drop to her chest. She looked Lizzie up and down, then put her glasses back on and reached to feel the fabric. "Lovely silk. Can't get this anymore. Wish I could." The glasses dropped to her chest again, and she turned her attention to Mimi. "You've definitely got a problem." She took Lizzie's other elbow and turned her around to see the back. "Definite problem." She sat back in her chair again, then reached for a straw tote bag beneath the sewing machine. She pulled out a cell phone and hit the speed dial. "Saul," she said in a brusque tone, "need you over here. Bring the books and the tape." Rosalie went back to stitching on the sewing machine.

Mimi gave Lizzie a couple of firm pats on her forearm. "It'll be okay," she whispered. "Rosalie and Saul will take care of you."

About two minutes later, a gentleman in an open-collared shirt entered the craft room, carrying a half-dozen large catalogue-like books under his arms. He walked quickly, purposefully, almost like George.

The women in the quilting group murmured among themselves. Circumspect, Lizzie took in more of her surroundings. *Straight pins, soldering irons, and someone named Saul, all in one room. Tell me this isn't a parallel universe.*

Rosalie gestured to Lizzie and said to Saul in the same brusque tone, "Senior prom."

Lizzie felt herself being scrutinized, nobody speaking to her, just pushing her in every direction for inspection. If this is what it's like to be a fashion model, she thought, it's not anywhere as glamorous as it's cracked up to be. Maybe she shouldn't have told Mimi about Rod's invitation. She could have just made some excuse about trying on the dress, cleaning out the closet or something, and when she saw it looked awful, just not gone. It's not like she'd known him all that long, like going with him was an obligation. But maybe they could transform this sack into something wearable. Better than feeling guilty if she let Mimi put a new one on her credit card, and she knew Mimi would do that to make her happy. Those dresses were expensive, the good ones, anyway—anything she'd want to wear. There wasn't much left of that hundred and forty-five she'd stuffed in her pockets a few weeks ago. If she'd known a prom dress was on the horizon, she could have saved it and maybe found something online.

An even bigger surprise interrupted her regrets and anxieties. Saul started grabbing the fabric of the dress at strategic points. "Beautiful silk," he said to his wife.

Rosalie gave him a little shrug without smiling. "Gorgeous." She began flipping through the huge books that Saul had brought.

"Arms up," Saul said perfunctorily. Lizzie raised her arms outward. Saul began taking measurements all over her body, some in embarrassing places. Nobody paid attention, except Mimi. Mimi looked on and gave Lizzie one of her tight-lipped smiles and a reassuring squeeze of her eyes.

Saul finished and came to look over Rosalie's shoulder at the page she had opened. Her index finger carelessly traced something on the page. "Maybe this new designer?" Rosalie suggested. "His neckline would be good for her."

From Lizzie's vantage point, it didn't look like photographs on the page. There were images that looked more like sketches. Rosalie moistened her finger and flipped to the next page.

"Try . . . you know, the one who always works in silk," Saul said, reaching for another catalogue, or magazine, or whatever these books were. Then he seemed to change his mind. "No, too old, I saw something . . ." He reached for another book.

"Okay, we'll take it from here," Rosalie said. "Come back Monday." She went back to the stitching she had been working on when they arrived. Mimi motioned with her chin toward a nearby ladies' room where Lizzie could change out of the dress in order to leave it with Rosalie.

Taking the stairs back to Mimi's apartment, Lizzie, now in her jeans and tee shirt, turned to Mimi. She didn't have to pretend to be flabbergasted. "Mimi, we left the dress with those people! Who are they?"

"Rosalie and Saul Glassman? Didn't you meet them at dinner one night?"

By now I would have thought I'd met everyone here, buzzed through Lizzie's mind. "No, I don't think so."

"Rosalie and Saul owned one of the largest high-end garment workshops in Manhattan and several overseas. Still own them, in fact. I think their children more or less run the businesses for them now. You can go to the boutiques on Madison Avenue or Rodeo Drive and see all the latest designs. Everything gets made somewhere, and a lot of the clothing comes out of Rosalie and Saul's workshops. Did you see the names on those sketches? Did you see the dates on those books that Saul brought?"

"No." No, Mimi, Saul's tape measuring distracted me.

"Next season's styles," Mimi said conspiratorially.

Lizzie's jaw dropped open. This time it wasn't in sarcasm, and it wasn't an act.

"All right," Mimi said, the take-charge tone returning to her voice, "dress, shoes, the next thing is hair. Why don't we walk over to Mr. Donnie right now and make an appointment for, what is it, Tuesday? We'll make it for three hours before Rod comes to pick you up."

Mimi was clearly having fun making plans for Lizzie, but at the mention of her hair in the same sentence as Mr. Donnie, Lizzie experienced the kind of shock reserved for the most shocking of horror movies. *How to get out of this one?* Lizzie had seen Donnie's Wren Haven clientele. He did a great job for those with thinning hair, sort of puffing it up, but invariably they left his chair with what Lizzie could only think of as hairspray tortoise shells. His expertise was stuck in some other decade and Lizzie needed to be squarely in the present, or perhaps the future, along with her dress.

"That's okay, Mimi. My hair is fine like it is."

Mimi ignored her. They were heading toward Mr. Don's, Wren Haven's on-premises beauty salon.

"Mimi, I like it this way," Lizzie tried again, hearing something like desperation creep into her voice as they got closer to Mr. Don's House of Beauty. "You know, long. I've been letting it grow long. I like it this way."

Mimi broke her pace, turned toward Lizzie, and reached for a hank of hair. She gave the ends a good look and shook her head. "Your ends are all split; you've at least got to get a trim. While he's at it, I'm sure he'll have an idea for something more suitable for the prom than the same style you get out of the shower with."

Lizzie cringed as they approached the salon. Then she exhaled in relief. The sign bearing a clock with moveable hands that hung on the door indicated that Mr. Donnie closed at 5:00 pm on Saturdays. It was now ten past. Below the clock, a handwritten scrawl said, Closed Sunday.

Mimi stared dumbly at the sign. Lizzie was inwardly ecstatic until Mimi said, "No problem. I'll come down on Monday when you're at school and make an appointment for Tuesday."

"Provided he has an opening," Lizzie said. "It's possible he's booked solid."

"Don't worry about that," Mimi replied with a dismissive wave and a lift of her chin. "Virginia always gets her hair done on Tuesday afternoons. If need be, I'm sure she'll give you her slot." That settled, at least in Mimi's mind, she said, "Ready for dinner?"

Lizzie didn't feel like eating.

chapter 30

WHY NOW? WHY DID THE GREMLINS OF guilt have to find her tonight?

It had been an okay day, as days at Wren Haven went. First an early morning ride with Henry, always a feel-good time. Then, after lunch, after willing herself to get serious, she had another term paper out of the way. Later, the hopeful visit with Rosalie and Saul—fingers crossed, she believed they could do something with the dress. But it was the shoes. The beautiful, black, spike-heeled shoes. Her mother's shoes.

Last year, Lizzie and her mother had discovered they were now the same shoe size and would occasionally swap shoes. Jane would borrow the old moccasins to amble out to the mailbox on a Saturday morning and Lizzie would grab the pair of her mother's brown pumps on the days she wore her favorite brown jeans.

But that was not what she was thinking about now. She was trying to recollect, and it was hazy through whatever gossip Shelly must have been relaying over her cell as she lounged on the floor, but bits were coming back. The navy-blue dress. The twirling around in front of the mirror. The shoes. Something about not being broken in. A little rub at the heel. Better bring another pair, just in case. How impossible it was to enjoy yourself when wearing uncomfortable shoes.

So, all the guilt surged again—a surge like an ocean wave engulfing her. The guilt over ignoring the blue dress and her mother's joy over the new dress and now the black shoes that she was going to benefit from. *I could have not ignored the dancing. I could have at least given her as much attention as I would have given Shelly. I could have shared her excitement. She wanted me to share her excitement, to be a friend, but it was more important for me to be cool; too cool for a blue dress. Too cool for dancing in front of a mirror. Too cool to say, "Have a good time." And now, no do-overs. No going back and no going forward in that scene.*

Tomorrow Lizzie would be angry at having to carry this guilt. Tonight, she needed to turn the pillow to where it was not yet wet as she lay in the dark on the pull-out sofa-bed.

chapter 31

"Rosa, what am I going to do?" Lizzie whined on Monday morning.

"But maybe Mr. Donnie give you nice haircut, Lizzie. Maybe you worry too much."

"Rosa, I've seen maybe seventy-five clients leave Mr. Don's, and I've never once seen a haircut I'd like to have."

"But maybe all those ladies they tell Mr. Donnie how they like him cut their hair and he just do what they tell him. You know, like they say, 'give the customer what the customer want.'"

"I suppose," Lizzie said, hearing the doubt in her voice as she looked out the window at nothing in particular. "It just seems like a colossal risk, knowing what his work usually looks like and hoping that I'll be the one in a hundred who comes out with a decent cut."

"Si, I understan', Lizzie." Rosa grew equally thoughtful. "If I you, I be worry, too."

They drove in silence for another minute, then Rosa snapped

her fingers and shot Lizzie one of her megawatt smiles. "I know! Luisa can do your hair!"

"Luisa? The one who gets the color mixed up? Are you crazy?" If Lizzie was apprehensive at the prospect of putting her hair in Mr. Don's hands, it absolutely horrified her to imagine letting Luisa anywhere near her hair.

"Oh, that," Rosa said with a short toss of her wrist. "She much better now. I sometime go to see her at work and her customer all come out look fabulous. Like movie stars."

"Rosa, has Luisa graduated from beauty school yet?"

"Next month. We have big party for her."

Lizzie weighed her options, taking refuge in the passing scenery. Mr. Don's tortoise shell hair or the color maniac. Maybe.

"How much do you think she'd charge me?"

Rosa waved her hand. "Nothing. She do as favor for me. An' believe me, she owe me plenty favor." Rosa was clearly pleased with her solution. So pleased, in fact, that Lizzie intuited that she might offend Rosa if she turned her down. Great, she thought. Now she had two people she could possibly offend over her hair. Four people to offend if she counted Virginia and Mr. Don. The urge to scream on the Jefferson bus over her dead cell phone was nothing compared to how she now wanted to scream, "Leave me alone! Leave my hair alone!" Worse, like a dream sequence in a movie, or a nightmare, Lizzie saw herself in the shapeless black shift, sporting a hairspray tortoise shell by Mr. Don. She saw Rod way ahead of her, disappearing into a crowd because Lizzie could not keep up with him as she ever so slowly shuffled toward the dance floor.

Lizzie shook herself back to the present. Rosa handed her a cell phone. "Call Mimi. Tell her not bother to make appointment with Mr. Don. Tell her Rosa take care of an' you afraid to hurt my feelings if you say no."

True enough, thought Lizzie, and dialed.

chapter 32

Returning home after school on Monday, Lizzie waited for Mimi to return from her book club so they could go to the craft room to reclaim her dress. Rod had already called her twice, once to remind Lizzie the prom was tomorrow night, and again ten minutes later to remind her he'd pick her up at six.

"Lizzie, you here?" Mimi called, entering the apartment. "Let's go pick up your dress. I just passed Gladys, and she said Rosalie was in the craft room pressing it earlier. Bring the shoes."

How does Gladys know about my dress? Right, she thought. Wren Haven is essentially a small town and news travels like wildfire. I'm newsworthy? A fifteen-year-old getting dressed up for a senior prom—of course I am.

As they opened the glass doors to the craft room, they saw the black dress on a padded hanger hanging on a high hook attached to an ironing board. Rosalie was once again at the sewing machine, working on the child-size dress.

Mimi took the hanger off the hook and handed it to Lizzie. "Go slip it on in the restroom and let us see." As Lizzie pulled the craft room door open to exit, she half-turned and saw Mimi put her hand on Rosalie's shoulder and say, "Thank you, friend." Rosalie just nodded.

No one was more surprised than Lizzie at the transformation. Her heels click, click, clicked on the tile floor of the craft room. As she entered, even the stained-glass workers looked up to check her out. "Nice work, Rosalie," one of them called out.

Rosalie let her glasses fall on their chain to assess her handiwork and Lizzie's reaction.

Lizzie felt positively giddy. Gone was the shapeless shift with the modest round neckline. Instead, Lizzie wore a perfectly fitted sheath that fell to fingertip length. The dress now lightly skimmed her slim figure. All the prior remarks about the beautiful fabric made sense. In fact, in this light she could see it was not a bland black at all. It had a subtle, iridescent design woven throughout. The sleeves were gone altogether, and hot pink piping outlined a sweetheart neckline—not that Lizzie had much cleavage to show off, but if she had, this is where it would be. Best of all, there was a slit rising three-quarters up Lizzie's left thigh, with a provocative little pink bow at the top.

Lizzie giggled at Mimi's astonished expression. Mimi was actually holding her breath!

Rosalie leaned toward Mimi and said, "Don't worry. Black pantyhose. Get her some black pantyhose and she'll be fine." Mimi exhaled with a relieved laugh, splaying her hand on her chest.

Lizzie's "Thank you, Rosalie," felt inadequate compared to the miracle Rosalie had performed, but she hoped it was obvious that Rosalie's several hours of alterations could not have been more appreciated.

chapter 33

Lizzie wasn't concentrating much at school on Tuesday, not that it mattered. The term was winding down anyway. She'd still have to pass her final exams, but . . . whatever. Rosa was picking her up from school this afternoon so she wouldn't have to wait for the Jefferson bus. While her mind was on Luisa and the impending haircut, Shelly caught her in the hallway.

"Hey Liz, where you been? Haven't seen you in the last few days. What's up?"

Lizzie decided to give her a break. After all, she'd been her best friend since they were six. "Got some new shoes. Spikes."

"Yeah?" Shelly gave her an acknowledgment with a lower lip jut-out and a side head-tilt. But, Lizzie noticed, she didn't ask why or where she'd gotten the shoes.

Lizzie took a half-step away from Shelly. Shelly smelled. Shelly smelled like the smoke from Rachel's car. How had she ever tolerated that smell? She'd always hated it. "I'm thinking about going out for swim team next year. I figure I can train in the Wren Haven pool over the summer."

Obviously uninterested in Lizzie's swimming aspirations, Shelly was wound up with some excitement of her own. "My mom and dad said we're taking a beach house for the summer. I hope they got one where there are plenty of guys. See you after school. Regular place."

"Uh, no, Shel. I've got something else to do. I'm getting picked up right after school."

"A hot time at the old folks' home?"

"Yeah, Shel, that's it. See you 'round." For a moment James flashed into Lizzie's consciousness before she made her way to the last class of the day.

chapter 34

THE SCENE LIZZIE ENCOUNTERED UPON ENTERING Mimi's apartment confirmed that Wren Haven was the parallel universe she'd always suspected.

Sitting with Mimi at the dining room table was a woman with tufts of hair sticking out at all angles from her head. Moreover, most of the hair was black, but the ends of the tufts were different colors, several colors! Some red, some gold, a bit of purple here and there. The woman's eyes were heavily lined in black beneath lids with as many colors as the hair. Bright red lipstick finished off the look. But the sight of this woman was not nearly as shocking as the fact that she and Mimi were sitting and chatting amiably, like old pals. They each held glasses of half-consumed iced tea. They were sharing a laugh about who knows what. *The aliens have landed, and they've landed at Wren Haven. They've captured my grandmother and left this look-alike in her place.*

"Oh, Lizzie, here you are," Mimi greeted her. "Here's Luisa, who's come to do your hair!" Of course. Luisa. Somehow, Lizzie had expected a version of Prima Rosa; sexy, vibrant Rosa with the luxurious long black hair.

"Hello, Luisa," Lizzie said with what she hoped resembled a cordial welcome. Luisa stood. She wore something like harem pants, but these gathered at the knees like knickers. Her tank top revealed a good deal more than usual Wren Haven attire.

Luisa immediately reached to feel Lizzie's hair, running her fingers through it with intent.

Lizzie battled between an inward cringe and addressing the lull in the conversation with a veneer of politeness. "Thanks for coming. I appreciate your coming all the way over here."

"I give you color first, then you take shower, shampoo out."

At the word *color* a quiver of apprehension went right to the roots of every one of Lizzie's hairs. She remembered the tale of the color mishap, observed the colors—all of them— on Luisa's head, and considered that Luisa was here as a favor to Rosa. She didn't quite know how to respond.

Lizzie resolved to never again take Mimi for granted when she heard her break in with "Do you think color is necessary? Lizzie has such lovely blonde hair." Mimi took a strand of her hair on the other side of her head and held it up. "See how it catches the light?"

Luisa circled to Lizzie's back. "Mmm," she murmured; the scientist, deep into her examination, again grabbing a handful of hair. "Is maybe not necessary, but for special occasion could be more special." She twisted herself around to look Lizzie in the face. "You no want color?"

Mimi started to clear the glasses from the table. Lizzie saw her opening and took a step away from where they had been standing, drawing Luisa with her. She leaned toward Luisa and in a just-between-us-girls under-voice said, "That's very nice of you to offer, Luisa, but I think my grandmother . . . well, you know about grandmothers . . . they like to keep their little girls natural looking."

She had no idea what Luisa's experience with grandmothers might be, but this felt like the best shot at avoiding Luisa's coloring ideas. She just hoped that over their little tea party Mimi hadn't described the black dress. That would totally give lie to her argument. Lizzie held her breath.

"Si. Grandmothers. Abuelas. You go take shower, shampoo hair, then I cut."

"Take your time, Lizzie," Mimi called. "Luisa and I will just have another glass of iced tea."

She didn't know what Mimi put into the iced tea that made the two of them find so much in common, but whatever it was, it worked. She pulled the shower curtain closed.

* * *

"So, what style haircut you like?" Luisa stood over her with a pair of scissors in her hand. They might as well have been a guillotine. "Could do a lot of different styles with this much hair." Luisa combed and parted, combed and separated ominously.

I've got to speak up! Lizzie thought in a panic. What could she say? Don't scalp me? Don't make me look like a circus clown? Come back when you've passed your licensing exam?

Mimi didn't seem to be paying attention to the drama unfolding in the middle of her kitchen. She leaned against the doorjamb, nonchalantly thumbing through one of those damned *People* magazines. *Mimi, help! What do I say?* Lizzie pleaded silently. Maybe this was where Reverend Drummond's prayers should come in. Luisa's scissors made threatening snippy-snip sounds that sounded like she was sharpening a knife.

"Oh, look at all the nice styles these celebrities have," Mimi said mildly. She flipped a few pages and held one open for Lizzie and Luisa to look at. Lizzie's finger flew to the center of the right-hand page.

Luisa stopped her snippy-snips and looked over Lizzie's shoulder. "Oh, si, everybody like her haircut. Very glamorous. No problem."

If Lizzie hadn't closed her eyes with a sigh of relief, she would have seen Mimi winking at her.

chapter 35

Herb finished taking the photos of Rod and Lizzie, and Mimi slipped her hand into his. She'd forgotten how fun life could be. Look at them! Who would think that a slinky black cocktail dress could contain such sweetness? The bit of makeup was superfluous; the bloom of youth was no hyperbole. Not only was Herb visiting Mimi to see Lizzie and Rod off, but somehow, at around a quarter of six, Mimi's apartment became a popular place. Virginia dropped by to ask Lizzie about a computer question ("Tonight? The prom? Oh, certainly this can wait, and how splendid you look!"). Greta knocked, hoping to borrow a cup of sugar. (Really, Greta, couldn't you have thought of any less transparent excuse?) and Alice came to ask Mimi if she'd heard a funny noise that was somehow forgotten the moment she glimpsed Lizzie and Rod from the doorway.

As Lizzie subjected herself to inspection by all the "accidental" drop-ins, Mimi slipped into her bedroom and opened her jewelry box. She drew out the strand of pearls just as she had envisioned doing before drifting off to sleep every night since the hem-pinning episode. They were to have been Jane's—not now! No tears tonight! She took a quick swipe at the corner of each eye. Spreading the pearls across both palms as if in presentation, she took a step toward the bedroom door. Through the doorframe she could see Lizzie and Rod still receiving admiring comments. She rolled the large center pearl between her fingers, looked down at the large orbs, and then up across the living room at Lizzie in the black dress. Miriam, you know better than this, she silently scolded herself. The pearls were from her era, not Lizzie's. She'd managed to pull the dress out of the hat, so to speak, and Lizzie was obviously delighted to be wearing next season's cut. She didn't want to spoil the moment. Clasping them around Lizzie's neck wouldn't bring Jane back. She took a step back and with another small sigh carefully draped the pearls back into the jewelry box. She was about to close the lid when her knuckles grazed the sharp edge of a large, diamond-shaped ring, onyx in a distinctively decorative gold frame. Perfect.

Without ceremony Mimi slipped the ring onto Lizzie's finger while Lizzie continued accepting the effervescent compliments, smiling and blushing. Rod looked on and appeared pleased that his date was worthy of so much attention.

At Mimi's touch, Lizzie glanced quickly at the ring. A fleeting look crossed Lizzie's face—recognition?—before Rod tugged on her hand to leave.

chapter 36

Prom night had been a total success. Rod had been a good sport through the dozen photographs Herb had wanted to take. Lizzie had tried, and mostly succeeded, to not think about the last time so many people had come by to see her and Mimi.

Mimi also had to be given credit. Not only did she get Lizzie out the door looking great and feeling great, but somehow between line dancing and book club and water aerobics had managed to educate herself about what was called the "after party" and had not once asked Rod what time he'd have Lizzie home.

So, it had indeed been a big deal, and Lizzie was now officially half of a couple with Rod. But now it was Wednesday and she was back in school, and here was Shelly coming down the hall.

"Hey, Liz, great news. My parents said you could come to our beach house for a week. You've got to come. I don't know what I'll do if it turns out there are no guys and I'm stuck there with just

Rachel."

"Gee, thanks, Shel."

Just then, Amy Connors came by and tapped Shelly in a silly game of tag, then flew down the hall. "Hey!" Shelly yelled and raced after Amy.

Lizzie stood in the hallway watching Shelly run down the hall, nearly skidding at one point, before veering off to her next class. Shelly hadn't noticed her great haircut, had never once asked why she had a new pair of spikes, and now she was running around playing tag like a kid. Lizzie passed a mirror and saw the circles under her eyes. She might just be too busy to go to Shelly's beach house this summer.

With that as the afternoon's realization, Lizzie looked forward to a civilized dinner in the Wren Haven dining room.

chapter 37

Rarely did the Wren Haven dinner conversation reflect as much ire as it did this evening. Tonight, everyone seemed to have an idea or an opinion on a planned revolt against the new scooter rules. They weren't the type of scooters meant for kids, but motorized one-person vehicles, a definite step up from a wheelchair, usually with a basket on the front like one might have on a bicycle. The scooters had become so popular among Wren Haven residents that actual traffic jams were occurring at the elevators and at the dining hall entrance. The valet parking for the scooters that had been instituted right after New Year's had been well accepted, but the new rules pertaining to scooters were beyond reason. The rules included speed limits, driving only on the right side of the hallway (after all, what if there was someone on foot going slowly using the right-hand handrail?) and the coup de grâce, a requirement to obtain a Wren Haven driving license! The latter was especially offensive since the test would be administered by Ricky, a member of the security staff likely over twenty-one but who, with his too large cap and too large collar, looked about fourteen. Ideas for a protest ranged from deliberately exceeding the speed limit to keep the security staff in a sweat for a couple of days, to installing obnoxious hee-haw-sounding horns and driving past the administration offices en masse.

Lizzie sat listening politely to the grousing, fighting off the drowsiness from the prior late prom night, silently thankful Mimi did not need a scooter to get around. Then something else struck her. Mimi didn't need one now, but five, ten years from now? Who knew? Suddenly gratitude swelled for Wren Haven's line dancing and water aerobics classes and, for the first time, Lizzie became consciously appreciative Mimi was health-aware enough to take part in them.

chapter 38

The first Saturday in June dawned unseasonably warm. It was the kind of early summer weather that made one mild and drowsy, even upon waking, even if one had managed to get a full night's sleep, the kind of sleep possible when the gremlins of guilt had decided to go elsewhere for the night.

Lizzie had been fishing in her closet for something lighter weight to wear when some old photographs fluttered down from the shelf above. She didn't know the people in most of them, but one caught her eye. There was Jane, a much younger Jane, probably about age nineteen. This must have been the summer trip to Europe she'd heard about and ignored, mentally filing it under ancient history.

Jane wore a tank top and cutoffs and bore a backpack and—and a large onyx ring. Diamond-shaped. In a distinctive gold frame. Lizzie brought the photo over to the dresser and grabbed the ring from the top drawer where she had tossed it after the prom. They were unmistakably the same. Lizzie plopped onto the edge of the unmade pull-out bed, stunned.

Mimi could have gone to her parents' home any day while she was at school and been back here with Lizzie none the wiser. That's how she happened to have the ring. And what about the damned ashes? Where were those? Did she just throw them to the wind without even asking?

The rage that had lain dormant began to smolder. What began as a tiny spark quickly ignited up Lizzie's spine. Her hands became fists, nearly wrinkling the photo. Lizzie charged into the kitchen where Mimi was finishing a cup of coffee and reading *The Wren Haven News*.

"How could you?" Lizzie shouted, slamming both the ring and the photograph onto the kitchen table. "What did you do? Raid my mother's jewelry box? What else did you steal out of our house?" With emphasis on the "else" Lizzie paced around the small kitchen like a caged lion, feeling heat rising from under her collar all the way up to her temples.

Mimi sat impassively.

Lizzie continued her rant. "I do not believe this. My own grandmother! Looting her own daughter's possessions!" Feeling at a loss for anything further to accuse Mimi of, she leaned against the stove, arms folded, head bent. Mimi's ensuing silence felt like an even bigger insult.

"Are you done?" Mimi finally ventured.

This did nothing but set Lizzie off again at no less a decibel volume, accompanied by three quick strides around the small kitchen. "Done? Done? Yes, I'm done. Done with you, done with this place, done with pretending that I've got anything like a normal life!"

Mimi said nothing. She turned the page of her newspaper, which did nothing but further infuriate Lizzie.

Finally, with a scrape of chair legs, Lizzie yanked the side chair away from the table and dropped onto it, glaring at Mimi. "Well?"

she demanded. Another uncomfortable silence.

Mimi calmly took another sip of her coffee before replying, "Well," and calmly folding her newspaper and laying it on the table.

"Well, what?"

"Well, there are some things that needed to be sorted out, and—"

"We're back to that? Things that needed to be sorted out?"

"Yes, these are the things that needed doing so you can move on. So I can move on. So we can both move on. Do you realize it's been nearly four months?"

"Boy, do I realize it. It feels like four years!"

"Mm-hmm."

"And anything that is in that house should belong to me."

"Yes, dear, you are correct. It does. And everything is safe. And waiting in storage."

Lizzie came down a decibel or two. "What do you mean?"

"Darling, the house needed to be sold."

"Sold? You sold my house?" This was beyond belief! She'd sold the house? The house that she'd continued to have late-night fantasies about returning to some day? Words failed her.

"Yes. That's why everything is in storage. At some point, when you feel ready, we can go through things and decide what to do with everything. But I thought it was too easy for jewelry to get lost in the moving, so I gathered up the best pieces and have them here. This ring," she said, picking it up from the table, sort of weighing it in her palm, "is one of them. They are all yours and you are welcome to them. I just hadn't wanted to open the wound too soon."

Mimi looked at Lizzie, hesitated for a moment or two, and then cocked her head to the right. "Frankly, I don't know what you're ready to handle and what you're not. One day you're a mature young lady and the next day you're throwing a temper tantrum." Mimi gave a wide sweep of her hand and a slow dip of her chin, indicating that Lizzie's current deportment fell into the tantrum category. "For example, you haven't expressed the slightest interest in your parents' ashes. Many people would surmise that you're repressing or going through some other sort of processing stage."

Humiliation washed over Lizzie, landing hard in her stomach, as she recalled Mac's warning: People are going to think you need watching. Where could she go with this? The house had already been sold. Nothing was stolen; everything waited for her. She kept silent. Now it was an embarrassed silence. Frankly, a guilty silence. She had embarrassed herself and insulted Mimi when, in fact, Mimi had done nothing but safeguard Lizzie's property and Lizzie's feelings. Couldn't she ever get anything right? She wanted to pull a cover over her head and hide from herself, from Mimi, and from the rest of the world.

"And," Mimi continued, a tad more upbeat, "there is some excellent news. It turns out the real estate market in that neighborhood is fairly strong right now. You'll be able to go to any college you want." Mimi gave her one of her loving, grandmotherly smiles.

"College?" Lizzie asked, feeling awkward and stupid at this change of topic.

"Sure," Mimi went on, her familiar drawl sneaking in. "It's just two years away; a matter of months, really."

"Months?" Was this possible? Possible that she wasn't trapped at Wren Haven for the rest of her life? Fragments of the conversation bombarded her as she sat there. Moving on. College. You are welcome to them. Ashes.

Lizzie tried to retain a shred of self-righteous indignation as she demanded, "What about the ashes?"

"They're in the storage unit as well. Give it some thought. Summer's coming. Without your schoolwork you'll have more time to decide what you want to do with them."

Now, too ashamed to even look at Mimi, Lizzie cast her eyes at the kitchen tile. "Hmm, yes," Lizzie said, this time wanly, "more time." *Time to get things sorted out.*

chapter 39

For days after the verbal explosion in the kitchen, Mimi mentally replayed the conversation, usually accompanied by self-recrimination over what had gotten the two of them to that point. One way of working off her own frustrations was to pour what energy she had into Wren Haven's physical fitness activities.

One morning after water aerobics class, Mimi lingered, just floating in the pool. Everyone else had gone to the locker room, their distant voices garbled through the water.

Lizzie's accusations were cruel, unwarranted, ungrateful . . . but she was only fifteen. What would she have thought at fifteen? What would Jane . . . Could she do this? Could she think of Jane without crying? If she couldn't, then it was good to be in the pool where the addition of a few tears wouldn't matter. But she thought . . . she thought she could do it. Jane. Her blonde hair. Her father's slender frame. How beautiful she looked in her wedding gown. The cookies she baked at age ten, trying to surprise her, and how she pretended to be reading in the next room in case Jane set the place on fire. Good times. A good life, if too short. She hoped Jane thought it a good life. She hoped she'd been happy. She hoped she'd had as many magical moments with Lizzie as she'd had with her.

Lizzie. Lizzie in her short, black prom dress. Maybe a few more magical moments remained.

chapter 40

Boarding the Wren Haven bus one late June afternoon, Lizzie plopped down next to Tamika. Tamika was a couple of years older than Lizzie. Lizzie was under the impression that Tamika was a senior, but they hardly ever talked about school. Tamika was part of the dinnertime waitstaff at Wren Haven. Most of the time they sat together, sometimes Tamika next to the window, sometimes Lizzie did. It didn't matter. Today Tamika was window-side, staring out. She sat with her backpack on her lap, clutching the requisite Wren Haven necktie in one hand.

"Hey, Tamika, what's up?"

Tamika didn't reply, but Lizzie took little note. She was preoccupied herself, already sifting through some final exam material she had picked up on her way out, one page of which was totally new stuff.

"Tamika, you ever hear of—"

Tamika punched her fist into the seatback in front of her and abruptly shifted a half-turn further toward the window, causing Lizzie to jump, clutching her books to her chest and instinctively edging toward the aisle, away from Tamika. She realized she was holding her breath. Had she said or done something?

Tamika stared out the window, stone still. Strange. They were friends. Not like Lizzie and Shelly, of course, but bus-riding comrades. A half-minute later, Lizzie had a more rational thought: maybe she was not the object of Tamika's unexpected fury. Whether she was or wasn't, Lizzie was still somewhat afraid to relax back into her seat.

Another half-minute on, with no fist apparently coming her way, Lizzie, truly baffled, asked, "What's the matter?"

Whatever anger had welled up in Lizzie in Mimi's kitchen was not the half of Tamika's glowering rage. "That bitch, Pawling. I oughta not show up. Let that bitch hustle them tables herself. Bitch."

Sylvia Pawling managed the dining hall staff like a marine sergeant, but she was one reason Wren Haven's large operation ran like a well-oiled machine. The potential for chaos was everywhere, from bottlenecks of residents arriving on scooters to mass rebellion against the salt-free soup, yet one mealtime followed another with nary a snag. Sylvia Pawling was a big reason. Though lovable was not a word that would spring to mind in describing Sylvia, she was far from abusive. She was just all business, as her job demanded, as far as Lizzie could see. Nobody had ever had any real problem with her as far as she knew. But, then again, Lizzie had never worked for her.

"Did she do something to you?"

"I axed her for a loan, and she wouldn't give it to me. I tol' her she could take payments out of my paycheck, but she say no, somethin' 'bout they not set up for it. Bitch."

"Well, that's true. I know from talking to Albert—he's the Wren Haven accountant—that there are departments and budgets and—"

Tamika kicked the seat in front of her so hard that she again startled Lizzie, causing her to nearly spill her books and papers. This time she was not so sure that Tamika wouldn't turn on her.

Tamika's tirade continued. "All them rich White people up there. They got money. They could give me a loan if they wanted." Tamika's voice was a notch louder than it usually was. Her fingers tightened on the necktie.

Rich White people? Yes, residents' apartments were nice, but far from palatial, and judging from the recurring dinnertime conversation of the escalating cost of living, Lizzie rather doubted that many would describe their circumstances as Tamika apparently perceived them. And what was with the reference to White people? She scanned the benches across the aisle. The few rows ahead. The couple of rows behind. Okay. She got it. Or got it as much as she could. There were more people riding this bus that looked like Tamika and more residents in the Wren Haven dining hall that looked like her. But somehow, she didn't believe that totally explained whatever was going on today. Tamika was awfully bitter about something. What? Whatever it was had something to do with money, a loan of money. Lizzie didn't know what was eating Tamika, but she knew Sylvia Pawling was right—a Wren Haven staff member couldn't just hand out loans. She'd learned that from Albert.

Albert was Wren Haven's go-to guy for charges that appeared on residents' monthly account statements. Albert's office was not the easiest to find, being at the end of a manmade rabbit warren, the one part of Wren Haven not smartly polished. He sat at a modern computer screen but had a dusty, old-fashioned electric adding machine at the side of his desk, a leftover from the prior occupant. The day Mimi had sent her to Albert to inquire about a charge on her monthly invoice he had not looked up as Lizzie entered his office, but merely gave an indistinguishable grunt that could have been a moan to acknowledge a visitor, or an indication that he did not enjoy his work, his office, or an intrusion into his space.

"Albert?"

"Yessss," came the reply with a deep breath as he took the paper

Lizzie extended.

"My name is Lizzie. Mimi Kidder, my grandmother, lives in unit 218. She wants to know what this charge for sixty-five dollars is."

Albert typed a few keystrokes. A few more. He scratched the beginning of a five o'clock shadow sprouting from a grayish complexion, then leaned back and put his thumbs in the belt cinching his generous waistline. "Activity fee. Water aerobics started up again last month."

"Oh, well, that makes sense."

Perhaps it was the brightness of Lizzie's response, or perhaps it was just that Albert was happy for once to not have to fend off a continuing stream of complaints from another cantankerous Wren Haven resident. Like water on a drying plant, Albert seemed to come to life. He was nice. He spent a half hour explaining departments and budgets and debits and credits and suddenly the basic accounting Lizzie had slouched her way through all year made sense. At that moment, Lizzie had resolved to pay more attention during her business class.

Tamika was still steaming to Lizzie's right.

Why had she opened her big mouth? Was that her real motivation? Did she actually think she was going to help Tamika? Or was she just trying to show off how much she knew? Like she was superior because she had an inside track to the Wren Haven empire, Tamika's employer? The smoldering coals in her belly gave her the honest answer.

They rode in silence for the next mile and a half or so, Tamika continuing to stare out the window. Still sensing the hostility churning inside Tamika, Lizzie reached for her gentlest tone and asked, "What do you need the money for?" suspecting she might not want to hear the answer.

She thought she discerned a slight tip of Tamika's head, first left, then right; if she wasn't mistaken, Tamika's fury was giving way to something else; there might have been an extra blink or two of her eyes.

Uh-oh. Tamika seemed embarrassed about something. She'd poked into territory somewhere in the land of humiliation. Look what she'd done. Lizzie's silent prayer was simple: Earth, just open up and swallow me whole.

"Prom dress," Tamika muttered, still looking out the window. Lizzie said nothing. A long minute later, Tamika's voice dropped to a near whisper. "I been saving my paychecks and then got the cash from the bank a couple of days ago. Somebody musta been watching me leave the bank 'cause my wallet got lifted. By the time I got home, my wallet was gone. The wallet and all the money. A month of workin' and a month of paychecks, all gone."

What could she say to that? I'm so sorry? How lame. How useless. Lizzie stared out the window as well.

More to defuse the time bomb sitting next to her than anything else, Lizzie ventured, "What's his name? What's your boyfriend's name?"

"Louis."

"Is he cute?"

Lizzie saw a small smile, an affectionate smile.

"Yeah. He's cute. And real nice." Tamika's smile faded. "He already bought the prom tickets. I don't know what I'm going to tell him." Tamika swallowed. "And I can't ask my grandma. I just can't."

"You live with your grandmother?"

Tamika nodded. "Yes."

"Me too."

They rode a while longer. Trying to compensate for her blunder a few minutes ago, Lizzie mentally toted up her own net worth. She had a bank account with about fifty bucks in it, but she'd never had an ATM card to get at it. And the bank was near home, not near Wren Haven. She remembered the day her mother had taken her to the bank to open the account in her own name. She'd been about seven when her mother had taught her about banks and kept stressing the word savings in that exaggerated tone she used when she really wanted to ingrain something. But she'd never told her what she was saving for. Lizzie wondered now if it was for a prom dress.

So she had fifty-odd bucks in the bank and there was the dwindling remains of the hundred and forty-five she'd taken from her dresser drawer. How much did a prom dress cost? For sure a lot more than both stashes combined, even if she could get her hands on all of it. Ask Mimi? There was something not right about that, either. For starters, there was the fact that Mimi didn't even know Tamika. Damn, this was a rough spot for Tamika to be in, and a tougher one for Lizzie to think a way out of now that she'd opened her big mouth and acted concerned. The silence was worse than the punching and kicking. One more thing to feel guilty about.

After several excruciatingly long minutes, Lizzie could feel the inspiration light bulb go on: call Madame Lacroix! Her fingers searched for her cell phone, finding the usual pocket empty. Right. Canceled for non-payment. How could she have forgotten? The bus kept bouncing along, the same as every day. And anyway, the Surprise Shoppe's selection of formal wear might miss the mark in a big way. She'd better not set up expectations she couldn't deliver on, and she'd better not ask Madame for a favor that she would try her best to fulfill but that could end in ingratitude and maybe cause hard feelings.

The bus kept bouncing along. Bounce, bounce. *Think, think.* There was one viable solution. It might work. If it didn't, there would be little downside—a downside she was willing to risk. But how would Tamika react? This was not an unreasonable consideration given the afternoon's display of violence. There were expressions for what Lizzie had in mind, and they weren't pleasant: adding insult to injury; no good deed goes unpunished. There was another expression that she wished had come to mind earlier: mind your own business.

So, with apprehension, Lizzie rummaged around in Mimi's hall closet later that afternoon. "Mimi, where are your shopping bags?"

Mimi looked up from the book she was reading. "Top shelf. I tuck the nicer ones behind the box on the floor."

Mimi probably wondered why she was tearing apart her neatly organized closet. By now, Lizzie had the entire collection of shopping bags spread out on the floor. There were two nice plastic-coated ones used for gifts. One had a Christmas motif. She put it aside. The other had lilacs all over it. She wondered what had come in it. It was pretty. Maybe too pretty. She didn't want anything too showy, so the lilac bag went back into the closet with the Christmas bag and Lizzie settled on a plain black shopping bag with an understated label and sturdy cord handles. Simple enough to not be pretentious, and—great!—there was tissue paper inside.

Lizzie looked over her shoulder to where Mimi had resumed her reading in the living room. Good. She hadn't caused too much of a commotion.

chapter 41

"Mimi, I'll meet you in the dining hall," Lizzie called around dinnertime, then sprinted out the door.

Lizzie scanned the dining hall and saw Tamika taking orders from a table near the windows. Waiting until Tamika moved away toward an area where no one else sat within earshot, Lizzie discreetly tucked the shopping bag containing the black dress under Tamika's arm. "See if this works," she blurted, and scooted off before Tamika could respond.

Mimi, Virginia, and Mac were just entering the dining room. Lizzie sprinted over to meet them. The hostess seated them further away from the entrance and Lizzie sat with her back to where she suspected Tamika might be working.

It would be some days before Lizzie saw Tamika again. Some kids had exams, some didn't, and it threw the usual schedule off. But on a Thursday afternoon as Lizzie approached the Jefferson bus stop, she noticed the younger riders gathered together, talking. Most of these were the kids who, like Tamika, made up a large segment of the evening wait staff. Most held similar pieces of letterhead paper; some held envelopes in their other hand. They were giggling and pointing to each other's letters. Lizzie could detect an occasional joyous whoop among the murmur. Still a hundred feet away, Lizzie saw the Wren Haven bus pull up and everyone file on. She ran ahead and hopped on as well, the last one to board. She slid next to Tamika.

"Hey, Tamika. What'cha got?" Lizzie panted, nodding toward the paper Tamika held. Tamika handed the paper to Lizzie with an unsuccessful attempt to stifle a look of happy satisfaction.

> *Dear Miss Jones,*
>
> *In recognition of your devoted service to the Wren Haven retirement community and the satisfactory completion of secondary education, the Wren Haven Fellowship Fund is pleased to award you $8,000 to support your pursuit of higher education.*

Details followed about filling out forms and transferring funds.

"The seniors who work at Wren Haven got these letters from our guidance counselors today. I'll be able to start college in September."

"Excellent," Lizzie said, handing the letter back to Tamika. "Congratulations."

Tamika was indeed happy now, looking out the window. Not with a big expression of elation, but a daydreamy, everything's okay kind of smile.

Lizzie felt good for Tamika and was happy to indulge in her own daydreaming as the bus bounced along, glad for once to not be thinking ahead to that night's homework.

"Oh! I almost forgot! I thought you'd want to see . . ." Tamika rooted around in her backpack. She pulled out a photograph and passed it to Lizzie. There was Tamika in the black dress, a tall, slender boy in a tux holding her hand.

Lizzie handed the picture back to her and in a tone low enough that no one else could hear, said, "You fill it out better than I did." And they shared a laugh.

chapter 42

Lizzie boarded the Jefferson bus back to Wren Haven for her last ride of the academic year. The school year had been winding down over the prior week and, having no more exams, she allowed herself to relax. Though the end of classes provided a grim reminder that the coming months would be an opportunity for a less restrictive social life for her classmates while hers had been truncated, she had to admit there had been little else to concern her. What she had initially thought of as the unreality of Wren Haven—everything perfectly clean and manicured, everyone perfectly civilized and cordial—had gradually become reality. Her reality. She didn't quite know what to make of the situation. She told herself it didn't matter, that she didn't have to make sense of anything. In a couple of years, she'd be off to college and then live a life of her own choosing. Until then, the abnormality of living in a retirement community could be endured; would be endured.

As part of her escape from such abnormality, Lizzie had borrowed the latest bestseller from the Wren Haven library, a thriller. It was a can't-put-it-down page-turner, so engrossing that Lizzie and Mimi were late to the dining hall that evening. By the time they arrived, a distinct buzz circulated. Everyone was talking about poor Evelyn. Even Greta's cheerful chirping was subdued. Evelyn had lost her scooter license.

Such a silly mishap could have happened to anyone.

The accident happened on the skybridge, the glass-wall-enclosed walkway that connected two of Wren Haven's main buildings. Evelyn had been heading west, on her way to the pharmacy. Charlie and Snowball approached from the opposite direction. Snowball, recognizing Evelyn, who usually had a playful belly rub for him, raced toward her. Fearful that she might hit Snowball, Evelyn veered to the right, toppling one of the artificial palm trees, which in turn crashed into the floor-to-ceiling glass wall. Glass shards fell to the ground below, scaring a flock of ducks wandering across the street beneath. Between the falling glass and the squawking ducks, Amos Tucker, driving through just then, swerved up over the curb and into the hydrangea bushes. Meanwhile, Harriet's German shepherd, hearing the commotion and Snowball's barking from two corridors away, raced down the skybridge with Harriet in tow. The leash between Harriet's hand and the shepherd's neck caught Charlie at the back of the knees and he went over on top of Evelyn, spilling her and the scooter onto the floor.

No one was hurt, but the next day Ricky, unfortunately the most junior member of the security department, had the unpleasant duty of informing Evelyn they couldn't let the incident go unnoticed and needed to revoke her scooter license.

The seriousness of the situation could not be underestimated. Evelyn lived a fair distance from the dining room, and she depended on her scooter to get around. She hadn't shown up to dinner yet, even at this late hour and, rumor had it, she'd asked to have her dinner sent to her. Wren Haven's organization allowed meal delivery, but not as a matter of routine. One usually only had dinner sent if quite ill and truly unable to make it to the dining hall.

What mobility options did Evelyn have? A clunky walker? A cane while holding the handrails in the hallways? Both would make for slow and arduous trips. A wheelchair? Wheelchairs had significant drawbacks. First, one had to actually learn to use those things. Second, they were cumbersome. But the most important aspect was what no one wanted to say out loud. At Wren Haven, using a wheelchair violated the community's standard of coolness. Just as no one at Lizzie's high school wanted to be seen being dropped off, no one at Wren Haven wanted to be seen in a wheelchair. Wheelchairs were for old people. Motorized scooters were for cool seniors.

chapter 43

"School's out," Mimi said as she poured herself another cup of coffee.

Lizzie looked up from her cornflakes with residual drowsiness as Mimi continued a now well-caffeinated line of thought.

"Let's celebrate and go to the mall for manicures. It will feel good to get off the Wren Haven property for a change."

"Wow. Sure." Maybe she could shake off some of the intermittent claustrophobia induced by the all-encompassing daily Wren Haven life.

Sitting side-by-side at the nail salon, they debated the various colors, Lizzie deciding to go for a metallic green. "Don't worry, Mimi, I'm not joining some demonic cult. Besides, how much trouble can I get into at Wren Haven?" They both giggled.

Lizzie tingled at the smooth feel of the warm soaking water as she watched the manicurist assembling her tools. "This is fun." To think, just a few weeks ago, she and Mimi had been at each other's throats. And it wasn't that long ago that she'd declared Mimi her prison warden. And now they were BFFs? Well, life in a parallel universe . . .

They window-shopped for another hour afterward, critiquing the horrible acid yellow that seemed to be the coming season's trendy color, compared fabric qualities and prices at various establishments, and Lizzie periodically admired her new fingertips. They browsed make-up, Lizzie not being able to bypass the lip gloss display. She teased Mimi by holding up a metallic green sample. "Oh, look, a perfect match!"

With a short half-laugh, and a tight shake of her head, Mimi said, "No!"

Near the wide entrance to the mall's most upscale store, Mimi tapped Lizzie's arm. "Wait here. I need to pick up a greeting card across the way."

"Okay, I'll be in the jewelry department."

The diamonds were indeed dazzling. Where did one wear such jewelry? Certainly not to senior prom. Voices at the other end of the counter interrupted Lizzie's observations. They came from two individuals who were obviously employees. A middle-aged man addressed a younger woman. She stood with her hands clasped penitently, head lowered at a forty-five-degree angle. They faced the far display case.

He bobbed his head in front of her face and jabbed at the display case. "Why did you put those bracelets all the way over there?"

The young woman said nothing.

"Why didn't you put them in the center of the display?"

"I thought . . ."

He interrupted her. "You thought? You *thought*?"

The young woman couldn't have been more than a couple of years older than Lizzie. Lizzie tried to assess the situation at a distance, focusing on the younger employee. This might be the woman's first real job. She appeared smartly dressed in a crisp summer dress and moderate wedge sandals. Far better than her own jeans and tee shirt, Lizzie thought, unconsciously running a hand down her thigh. She'd bet that the young woman had gone out and bought the outfit just for this job. Working in the fine jewelry department of the best department store? It was probably the dream job she thought she wanted. But look at the treatment she's receiving. Her mother's words came back to her: "Don't stare." Lizzie pretended to be perusing the sapphires, but continued to eavesdrop, cringing at the man's persistent berating.

"I'm all set," Mimi said cheerfully as she rejoined Lizzie. "Let's get some lunch." The man's heated voice, loud enough to be heard all the way down to the end of the counter, caused Mimi to give him a quick glance before gently cupping Lizzie's elbow to leave.

At the café, they ordered lunch, but Lizzie remained quiet, still feeling the humiliation of the poor junior employee. "That man. He showed zero respect for that employee who had probably shown up for work on time and done her best to arrange the merchandise."

"Mmm?" Mimi looked up from her handbag where she'd replaced the cloth she used to clean her reading glasses.

"That man! What an obnoxious boss! Maybe she's young and maybe she's inexperienced, but is that any reason to embarrass her in front of all the other employees and in front of the customers? It's not like he caught her stealing something. It was only over placing some bracelets a few inches to the right or to the left of where he would have placed it—his idea of arranging some jewelry, and she'll probably go home in tears."

Mimi picked up her menu. "You don't think he could have been trying to guide her? To instruct her in a sales technique?"

"No, I think he used her arrangement of the bracelets to show who's the boss. To show her, and all the other employees within earshot." Her hand trembled slightly as she reached for her glass of water. "I never want to be like that."

Lizzie caught Mimi's look across the table. The jovial countenance of the bantering over lip gloss had evaporated.

Mimi asked, "What do you want to be like? Who do you want to be?"

Lizzie opened her mouth to answer, but she had no words. Who did she want to be? This question stunned Lizzie as much as if the long-ago genie had once again appeared to demand an answer, a genuine answer. She might not know who she wanted to be, but now she sure knew who she didn't want to be. As the server put her tuna sandwich on the table, Lizzie marveled at the abstract notion that she might be able to construct her own future. Neither coolness nor lip gloss figured in any of it.

chapter 44

THE SCHOOL YEAR OUT, LIZZIE HAD PLANNED TO RELISH a late sleep-in, but it was not to be. At 7:00 am she got a call from Mac.

"Why don't you come and play golf with us?"

"Golf? I've never played golf."

"Doesn't matter. We've got enough players. We need a seer."

"A seer? What's a seer?"

"Doesn't matter. Come. You'll find out."

Twenty minutes later, she stood in the lobby where Mac said he'd pick her up. They rode the shuttle bus to the golf course where they met Virginia, Herb, and a petite woman named Winnie. The three waited for Mac and Lizzie in a golf cart; Herb was driving. Mac sat in front with Herb. Lizzie, glad to be slim, squeezed in between the two women in the back.

"Got Lizzie to come along to be our seer," Mac announced unceremoniously.

"Welcome, Lizzie," Winnie said with a smile. "We've got a good day today."

"Great day," Herb echoed.

"Virginia," Lizzie whispered, leaning to her left, "what's a seer?" The only thing Lizzie could make out of the word seer conjured up images of gypsies and fortune tellers at carnivals—nothing remotely related to golfing at Wren Haven, A Continuing Care Retirement Community.

Virginia didn't respond.

"Virginia?" Lizzie whispered again, but Virginia still did not respond. She looked straight ahead and squinted under her eyeshade.

Had she said something to offend Virginia? Why the silent treatment? Lizzie tried once more. "Virginia?" this time tapping her arm.

Virginia turned to Lizzie with her characteristic warmth, patting her back on the forearm. "Nice to have you along, Lizzie." Lizzie then realized Virginia was deaf in her right ear.

They pulled up to the first tee and piled out. Virginia teed up first. The brunch conversation of some months back suddenly came back to her. Lizzie remembered that Virginia held some championship title and had an impressive swing. So, this was it: golf. Must be.

"Get ready," Mac said to Lizzie, putting his sunglasses on to watch Virginia.

"Ready for what? What do I do?"

"You've got to see. You're the seer."

"See what?"

"See where the ball goes. The rest of us don't have such good eyesight anymore. Got to know where the ball goes."

Hearing the thwack of the club, Lizzie hopped forward a step or two for a better view and shaded her eyes against the sun, straining to follow the arch of the ball. The foursome all turned and looked at her. "Well?" they all asked in uneven unison.

Hoping she hadn't mistaken a glint of sunlight for the ball, Lizzie pronounced with some uncertainty, "Off to the right."

"What?" Virginia said.

"You've done it again, Ginny," Winnie said. "It's out of sight!"

"I know it's taken flight," Virginia said. "Where'd it land?"

"Ginny," Herb said, a bit exasperated, "did you forget your hearing aid again?" He tapped his ear for emphasis.

"Oh," Virginia mumbled, then put her hand in her pocket, pulled out her hearing aid, and inserted it. "Thank you. That's much better," she said with a grin.

Lizzie shot a surreptitious glance at Herb. He gave a small shrug. Lizzie returned Herb's shrug with a suppressed chuckle.

They golfed for hours, but it felt healthy to be out in the fresh air and it got to be fun to be the arbiter the foursome looked to. Lizzie got into the spirit and began hamming it up, narrating a play-by-play that got everyone laughing.

"And it's a forward pass by Herb. Wow! Into the end zone!"

"Oh! Too bad for Winnie. A gutter ball!"

"Well done, Mac! It's a pop fly to center field!"

At the last hole, Mac took Lizzie aside and said, "I've had enough riding around. You feel like walking back? We can drop the others off at the shuttle stop."

"Great!" said Lizzie, in the best mood she'd been in probably since the day she'd found herself parachuted into Wren Haven.

Mac drove back to the shuttle bus stop, announcing, "Here you go. Lizzie 'n I'll get the cart back." The others departed with tired waves, Mac and Lizzie watching them walk the short distance to the shuttle bus and file on. As the bus pulled out of sight, Mac made no move to drive off, just sat with his hands on the wheel as if considering something. Finally, he turned to Lizzie and said, "You want to drive?"

"Sure!" What a nice guy. But a pang of the unspoken dampened her enthusiasm. Surely they must both be thinking the same thing—that she wouldn't have a dad to teach her how to drive.

They swapped seats, and Mac coached her through the stopping and going. Predictably, Lizzie lurched forward, nearly got them into a ditch, and finally got the hang of it. By the time they pulled up to the clubhouse, Lizzie felt quite proud of herself. She parked between two other golf carts, inching up for perfect alignment.

"Thanks, Mac," Lizzie said, genuinely happy.

"Don't mention it, kid."

They started their walk back to the main building complex, first circling around to the other side of the golf shed. Off to the side, its canopy askew, sat another golf cart, a smaller, older model.

"Hey, Roy!" Mac shouted. A few seconds later Roy, the employee who kept the golf course running, appeared at the doorway wiping his hands on a rag.

"Hey, Roy," Mac said, "what's with the cart here?"

"Oh, that." Roy shrugged. "Pat Hodges ran it too close to that old apple tree over near the third hole. You know, the one with the low-hanging branch. He racked up the canopy. It's old anyway, so we're just getting rid of it. Still runs, but it's not worth getting fixed. It's just there until the guy comes to take it away. I expected him to come a few days ago, but he never showed up. I think he's forgotten about us." With that, Roy disappeared into the shed again.

Mac and Lizzie looked at each other. They stood a long minute looking over the cart, then looked at each other again. Roy was nowhere in sight. They were completely alone. Except for the birds and the rustling of leaves as the summer breeze picked up, it was absolutely quiet.

"Seems a shame to just junk it if it still runs," Lizzie whispered, although she didn't know why she needed to lower her voice. "Looks like he hit more than just a tree branch."

Mac came around to the front left to join Lizzie. "I see what you're saying." Mac scratched the back of his neck as he surveyed the rather large dent on the front left side. The headlight, although still intact, looked like a giant had pressed his thumb over it, smooshing it into the body. Mac's dry humor came into play with, "Guess he should have had a seer with him." With his thumb and index finger, he tested the screws that connected the canopy to the chassis. "Mm-hmm. Wouldn't take much to set this right or, better yet, just take it off."

It seemed to Lizzie that they could virtually read each other's minds.

"Better let me take it this time," Mac said.

Without another word, Lizzie climbed into the passenger seat. They headed toward the residential area, hitting a rough patch or two and getting jostled a bit. Golf carts rarely traveled this stretch of ground. "What are you going to do with it?" Lizzie asked.

"Don't know. Got any ideas?"

"Seems we should be able to make some good use of it for something."

Mac pulled up to an entrance at the back side of one of the Wren Haven buildings Lizzie had never seen before. She peered out from under the cockeyed canopy to get her bearings among the buildings.

"This is the closest entrance to the wood shop," Mac explained. "Maybe some of the boys will give me a hand." He stopped the cart and sat in silence for a moment, as if second-guessing the wisdom of leading Lizzie down the path of theft, deceit, and general skullduggery. Then he reached into his pocket and pulled out a ring of keys. He selected one and handed it to Lizzie. "Here. See if you can open that door."

"You're going to drive it in?"

"I can't very well work on it out here. All the tools are in there."

Finding it tough to argue with that logic, Lizzie jumped out with the keys, fumbled a bit at the lock, then pulled the door open. The resulting entrance allowed Mac ample margin on either side. It opened onto a corridor much like the many corridors in Wren Haven, but a good deal dimmer. Seeing no one else in the corridor, she swung the door open as wide as possible and waved Mac forward.

He drove in, passed Lizzie, then continued down the corridor a short distance. After seeing the back end of the cart disappear to the left, Lizzie quickly closed the door, making sure it auto-locked then half skipped, half ran after the cart. She hadn't been into these bowels of Wren Haven before. In the pottery studio on her left, two women worked at their wheels while a third placed objects into a kiln for firing. Inside an even larger room on her right stood rows of looms, many of which had colorful yarn threaded through and half-woven pieces that looked as if they were projects in progress. Who knew weaving would be such a popular pastime at a retirement community that so many looms would be required? She chuckled at her own cynical fantasy of turning Wren Haven into a sweatshop.

The squeal of a buzz saw and the scent of freshly sawn wood diverted Lizzie's thoughts as she came up to the wood shop on her left. The space was even larger than the weaving studio. From the little Lizzie knew of wood shops, this one appeared well equipped. Her father had had an electric saw on a workbench in their garage and a few other tools, but nothing like this operation. A half-dozen different tables sported electric saws. Several additional workbenches stood generously spaced apart. Various kinds of wood, all organized and stacked neatly in large racks against the far wall, awaited the ambition and creativity of residents. Mac and three other men now surrounded the cart, looking it over just as Mac and Lizzie had done out on the golf course. One of them wore protective goggles and held a piece of wood that looked like it could be the leg of a chair.

"I don't know, Mac," one of them said, running his hand over the chassis. "This is just a wood shop, and you've got a hunk of metal here."

"Hey, Carl," the second man said to the one holding the chair leg, "what do you think? I think Mac is right. Look at how it's bolted here."

Carl pushed his goggles up on his forehead and put the chair leg down on a nearby workbench. He peered into the cart and ran his fingers along the seam that connected the canopy to the body. He said nothing, but gave a curt nod of his head, then turned to the others and nodded again.

Lizzie handed Mac's keys back to him. "What should I do?" she asked.

"Nothing right now," he said. "Trust me. Carl can handle this. Why don't you go back to Mimi's and then check in on us later this afternoon? It must be getting on to lunchtime, anyway." Lizzie folded her arms and shuffled from one foot to the other before Mac suggested, "Maybe you can think of something useful to do with this jalopy."

At that, she brightened a bit and said, "Okay. See you later." She took a couple of steps toward the door to the inner corridor, then turned back toward Mac. "Good game today!" she shouted over her shoulder and gave him a wave as she half bounced toward the door.

* * *

"Have fun?" Mimi asked as Lizzie sat down at the table.

"Mm-hmm," Lizzie managed through a mouthful of sandwich.

"Don't talk with your mouth full."

Lizzie took a swig of milk. "I'm the seer."

"And a seer is?"

"I'm the one who can see where the ball goes." She looked at Mimi. They both kept a straight face for all of one-and-a-half seconds, then both cracked up.

"But if Virginia doesn't have her hearing aid in, it doesn't matter if I can see where the ball goes because she can't hear when I tell her." They both sputtered and laughed even harder. One thing Lizzie had learned while living at Wren Haven was that older people could often laugh at their infirmities. At least Mimi could. She regularly quipped about all the pills she had to take and how she ought to buy stock in drug companies. And if the foursome today could have her along as a seer, they obviously were not hypersensitive to their declining physical abilities. But how declining could they be if the bunch of them could go out at the crack of dawn and shoot 18 holes? Okay, fifteen before they called it quits.

Laughing like this differed from the conventional manners she'd been brought up with. Don't stare. Look away. Don't make fun. Don't call attention.

She'd learned that lesson at the shopping mall one day. She couldn't have been more than seven or eight. She'd been sitting at one of the waiting benches in the middle of the mall watching a man with crutches and leg braces slowly make his way from one shop to the next, his legs stiff with the braces, his shoulders coordinating the swing of the crutches with his metal-encased legs.

"Don't stare," her mother had hissed as she jerked Lizzie's little arm. "It's not polite."

"I wasn't staring. I was watching. And anyway, he's walking in the other direction. He doesn't know I'm watching," Lizzie had argued. But her mother had just pulled her off in the opposite direction toward the parking lot.

Lizzie refilled her glass with milk. Obviously, today's laughter didn't square with the snippet of civilized behavior she'd been taught. There were other comparisons she could make, too. For example, one wasn't supposed to stare, or take special notice, but somehow it was kind to help a blind person or an elderly person across the street if they were having difficulty. Whatever.

Having this laugh with Mimi felt different. But then, many things felt different here at Wren Haven. Perhaps it really was a parallel universe. How about absconding with abandoned golf carts? Did making off with community property fall into the category of unusual but acceptable behavior? Could it? Under what circumstances? What if there was a good reason? She was pretty sure that her and Mac's feeling like having an escapade didn't fall into the category of good reason. Would putting the cart to good use make it justifiable? The thoughts ricocheting around in her head seemed too immense for a soft summer's day, so she just swallowed the rest of her milk.

chapter 45

Lizzie awoke much later in the afternoon. She'd stretched out on Mimi's patio lounge chair with her novel splayed across her chest. *Don't tell me I'm getting as bad as all these old folks, taking naps all the time,* she thought,. Then she remembered how warm and enveloping the sun had felt and how the words on the page had become less interesting.

As she brought herself to wakefulness, she became aware of an uncomfortable feeling that she'd missed something important, something important that had come to her in a dream that she wanted to grasp back. The cusp of the dream slipped away. She closed her eyes again, desperately trying to return to where she'd left off in the dream. Important. Terribly important. Blind people. Lame people. Trying to cross the street; no, not trying to cross the street, but trying to get from one place to another. Who were these people? Recalling her dream only half worked. She could only see snatches of it. The people in her dream . . . there was the man from the mall so many years ago, the man with the leg braces. There were others. There was . . . "Ha!" she cried out and opened her eyes. She put her hands behind her head with a self-satisfied grin and enjoyed another moment in the sun, now no longer so high in the sky. She stretched again and looked at her watch, the one she had taken to wearing in the absence of her cell phone. 4:35!

"Mimi! If I'm not back when you're ready to leave for dinner, I'll meet you in the dining hall," she called out as she dashed out the door. Now to find her way back to the wood shop.

These corridors all look alike, she thought with irritation. But she was looking for something else as well. At least they were nice and wide.

"Mac!" she called as she burst into the wood shop. A huge fan whizzed near the golf cart, drying the paint that now had the golf cart looking fresh and shiny.

"Oh Lizzie, you're just in the nick of time. What do you think?" Mac asked as he gestured toward what had once been a golf cart. Gone was the green and white canvas canopy. Gone was the dent on the front left. Gone was the green and white Wren Haven logo. The cart was now an innocuous shade of tan. It turned out that the headlight had just become dislocated. Once the fender was straightened out, the headlight had only needed to be righted with a couple of screws.

"Amazing! How'd you guys do all this?"

One of the men busied himself with wiping off the seats and the floor mats with a damp cloth. Another buffed the chrome with a chamois. The paint wasn't precisely the gleaming gloss of a showroom model, but beyond that it looked brand new. "Carl deserves most of the credit," the one with the chamois said. Carl had returned to the saw near the window with his chair leg.

The fellow with the cloth straightened up and said, "Carl used to own an auto body shop. Knows how to do stuff a lot more complicated than this. He used to straighten out race cars. Built a few, too."

Lizzie circled the cart, looking it over, squatting down to examine where the great dent had been. "Great work, Carl," Lizzie yelled over the buzz of the saw that he now had going. Carl just gave her a wave without turning around.

Mac leaned against one of the workbenches, taking in Lizzie's delight. "You want to take her back?"

"Back?"

"Back to the golf shed."

"No!" Lizzie replied, as if returning the cart to the shed was the stupidest thing she'd ever heard. "No, I don't want to take it back!"

"I know it's a different color now, but maybe Roy can use it for running around the course, fixing up the sprinklers, that sort of thing."

Roy didn't seem that interested in this cart a few hours ago, so no, I don't think I want to give this nice little run-about back to him, Lizzie thought, a thought that must have been written on her face.

"You want to give it to the security guards?" Mac tried.

"No! No, the security guards have enough of their own. They have an entire fleet of real cars."

"It's taking up a lot of room in here," the guy with the buffing cloth said. "You got a better idea?"

Lizzie shifted from one foot to the other. "Maybe." She took a step to the right, one to the left, still examining the vehicle. Nobody said anything. The high-pitched squeal of Carl's saw still ran in the background. She looked up and realized she had their attention. "Where does Evelyn Martin live?"

At quarter past five, Lizzie silently pulled up to Evelyn's front door and knocked.

"Hold on," came a thin voice from inside. Lizzie could hear a shuffling sound. It seemed an eternity until Evelyn opened the door.

"Oh Lizzie, what are you doing here?"

Lizzie made a sweeping gesture toward the cart behind her. "I thought you could use a ride to the dining hall."

Evelyn looked from Lizzie to the cart as if it were an apparition, then a smile started at the corners of her mouth and her eyebrows went up. "For me?"

"If you'd like . . ." Lizzie stumbled. "If not, that's okay. It was just a thought."

Evelyn beamed.

"I can get you as far as to where they have valet service. You might want to bring your walking stick."

"You wait right there, little miss. I'll be right with you." Evelyn hobbled away, perhaps a little sprightlier. She returned, having swapped her slippers for regular leather shoes, combed her hair, and applied some lipstick. She also brought the cane she used to hang from the basket of her scooter, closed the door behind her, and touched the cart, as if making sure it was not a mirage. It took her a minute to get settled in the passenger seat, but once Lizzie was behind the wheel Evelyn looked at her as if setting out on an adventure and said, "Tally ho!"

Lizzie giggled. "Tally ho it is!" She pulled forward. As Lizzie had previously observed, the corridors were plenty wide enough. They were designed to be wide enough to accommodate a couple of scooters—or wheelchairs—passing each other, abreast of a couple of pedestrians on either side. The darker truth was, this being a senior citizens' residence, the architects had envisioned that paramedics might someday need to maneuver a gurney. So Lizzie had plenty of latitude when they passed George and Janna Duff in the hallway. Both looked a little surprised, but they waved as Lizzie and Evelyn passed. Lizzie nodded and Evelyn waved back.

"I feel like Miss America!" Evelyn said, and Lizzie felt a little sad that such a small thing as a ride in a golf cart could create such disproportionate happiness.

Only once did they have a close call. As Charlie was leaving his apartment for dinner, Snowball dashed into the hall in front of the cart. Lizzie did a combination swerve and brake. She took it a little slower after that.

More people were in the hallways as they approached the dining hall, everyone heading into dinner. "Hey, look at Evelyn!" she heard someone say. Evelyn gave a decidedly Miss America wave.

The young scooter valet looked as if he were seeing a flying saucer when they pulled up, but just shrugged and said, "Pretty cool."

chapter 46

I FELT A CLAP ON MY SHOULDER AS I MADE MY WAY TO THE dining hall.

"How's it going, Mac?"

I turned to see Gregory and Beth Cox.

"Just fine, Greg, and with you?"

"Eh, chugging along, chugging along."

"Will you and Beth join our table for dinner?"

"Sure," Beth and Greg answered in unison..

We had to elbow our way through the crowd that had gathered at the entrance to the dining hall. Many were gazing down the corridor and I saw a couple of people tapping others on the shoulder.

We bypassed the hostess and I gestured to the table where Mimi, Virginia, and Greta were already seated. There was an empty seat near Mimi that I surmised she was saving for Lizzie.

Once seated, I could see the corridor. Lizzie drove the cart through the small knot of people, and Evelyn waved. Some residents waved back.

The hostess seated Evelyn at the table nearest the entrance.

"That's an awfully nice thing you're doing for Evelyn, sweetie," Mimi said under her breath as Lizzie took a seat between us.

"It's nothing," Lizzie said as she took an onion roll from the breadbasket, but she looked a bit flustered. The two of us shared the secret of the great golf cart caper. Lizzie peered out from under her bangs at me. I gave her what I hoped she understood to be an approving nod.

By the third day since Lizzie had begun transporting Evelyn, more people waited in the corridor for Lizzie and Evelyn to arrive. This time the onlookers clapped as they arrived. Evelyn waved as if she were Miss America.

"Seems you and Evelyn are creating quite a little stir," Mimi said as Lizzie joined her, the Glassmans, and me. Mimi's pride was clear, but I sensed a note of concern, as well.

"I had trouble getting through the crowd," Lizzie said. "The valet didn't look too pleased. Why are people applauding?"

Saul looked toward the dining room entrance. The crowd had dispersed. "Showing appreciation, probably," he offered.

"But Evelyn's the one who got the ride. And they can all get to the dining hall by themselves, so what do they care?"

Rosalie affected an exaggerated frown and shrugged. "Sometimes it's just nice to recognize that someone does something for someone else without expecting anything in return."

I glanced over at Mimi, now silent but leaning forward attentively, and wondered what concerned her.

Two days later, I stood half-way down the corridor with others to observe the arrival of the golf cart. So many people lined the corridor that I genuinely worried Lizzie might hit someone. Someone held a sign reading, "Free Evelyn." Lizzie threw a concerned glance at Evelyn, but Evelyn just smiled and waved.

I chuckled to myself. The celebrity status of not having a license sure tickled Evelyn.

John McElroy had been a railroad conductor in his day. He slapped his old conductor's cap on Lizzie's head as she drove by. It nearly covered her eyebrows, but Lizzie just gave a good-natured grin and pushed it further back on her head.

The following evening the welcoming crowd was larger than ever. Not only was the "Free Evelyn" poster in evidence, but there was another taped to a wall. It read, "Stop the Tyranny of Unjust License Revocation." What had been cheery clapping yesterday became rhythmical. Chants of "Go, Evie! Go, Evie!" filled the hallway. A small group on the right sang, "We Shall Overcome."

Evelyn smiled and waved, but at this point no one could deny the truth: Lizzie had started a protest movement. Lizzie and Evelyn passed me in the corridor and John McElroy's conductor's cap slipped forward, threating Lizzie's field of vision. She yanked it off, flinging it upside down on the seat between Evelyn and herself.

A moment later, a coin whizzed past her cheek, clearly startling her. Then another grazed her shoulder. People threw coins and bills into the cap.

"For the bail bond fund!" someone yelled.

* * *

All of us around the table had just finished ordering dessert.

Lizzie asked, "What's a bail bond fund?"

"A what?" Mimi said, obviously taken aback. "Why?"

"That's what someone in the crowd said. Look." Lizzie raised the conductor's cap and jingled the contents for her tablemates.

Herb leaned forward. "A bail bond fund is a collection of money to get someone out of jail."

Mimi and Lizzie looked at each other. In unison, they said, "The letter."

"What letter?" I asked.

Mimi made a hand-flick of annoyance. "We got a letter from Howard Fulbright, the Executive Director, asking Lizzie to attend a meeting tomorrow at two o'clock."

Lizzie sounded equally annoyed, but perhaps a little scared as well. "It sounds more like 'Report to my office' if you ask me," she said.

Thinking back to the growing crowd welcoming the golf cart each evening, the Wren Haven grapevine apparently had a piece of information yet to reach some of us, something to do with driving Evelyn to dinner and back each night. Lizzie took the folded letter from her pocket and shook it open.

I took the letter, written on suitably impressive Wren Haven letterhead, and read it. I couldn't help myself from spouting, "Aw, this is ridiculous." I threw my napkin down on the table and shot up from my chair. "Lizzie, come with me."

Lizzie followed me across the dining hall as I scanned the room looking for Mike Mullaney. I spied my rotund, balding friend two tables away just as he finished the last bites of what looked to be a scrumptious peach cobbler. Half of his tablemates had already left. I took a vacant chair next to him and motioned for Lizzie to sit next to me.

"Hello, Mac," the balding fellow said jovially. "Who's this you've got with you?"

We shook hands and I said, "This here is Lizzie Olsen, Mimi Kidder's granddaughter."

Lizzie extended her hand, and Mike shook it.

"Ah, yes," Mike said, appraising Lizzie through his bifocals. "Lizzie of the glamorous black dress, I hear tell."

Lizzie blushed. Mike leaned toward her and said, "Herb showed me the photos."

I dove in. "Mike, that a-hole, Fulbright, has summoned Lizzie to his office tomorrow and we're thinking it might have something to do with the fact that Lizzie's been giving Evelyn Martin a ride to the dining hall in the evenings."

"You mean you think it has something to do with so many people turning out to support Lizzie doing something the administration is clearly failing to do and is, in fact, responsible for?

"That's right. You think you could go along with her? You know," he added with a touch of sarcasm, "make sure this poor young thing doesn't get lost on her way to those intimidating offices."

"Why sure," Mike said, putting his fork down. "Lizzie, tell me what this is all about."

"Thanks, Mike." I rose to leave, patted Lizzie's shoulder, and said, "You're in expert hands. I'll see you later." I took off to return to our table.

As I returned to the table, Herb said, "Machete Mike! That's a good move, Mac."

"Who is Machete Mike, and what's he doing with my granddaughter?" Mimi wanted to know.

"Oh, I know Mike," Alice said. "No one wanted to go up against him."

"Mike is retired now," Herb said, "but he was, and would still be, I'll wager, the best defense lawyer in the state."

"Defense lawyer!" Mimi cried. "What . . . ?"

"Don't worry, Mimi," I cut in, patting her forearm, "he's just going to walk over with her tomorrow to make sure Fulbright doesn't scare the bejeezus out of her, which is what I am sure he has in mind."

Mimi looked at Alice. "Alice, you would know. You were a lawyer."

"Am! Still am a member of the American Bar Association and licensed to practice in three states," she retorted with playful pride and a smile.

Anyone who knew her had a high regard for the sensible, articulate Alice. She made eye contact with the rest of us. "Herb's right," she said, her tone serious. "They call him Machete Mike because he slashes the opposition to shreds."

chapter 47

Lizzie met Mike at the appointed elevator. He carried a newspaper under his arm.

She wore a pink sundress for the interrogation they both surmised was in store for her. The dress was pretty but a couple of years old and, in truth, on the verge of being outgrown. "I've never been on this floor before," Lizzie said to Mike as they got off the elevator and faced an imposing set of mahogany doors with a large brass plaque evidently intended to impress, reading Executive Offices.

Mike, however, did not seem impressed. He just sauntered ahead, occasionally slapping his newspaper against his thigh.

"Ah, yes," he mused, "home of the great and powerful Oz."

Fulbright could have been a resident himself. His white hair was decidedly thin on top, and he wore gold-rimmed glasses. He had a physique that gave the impression of a muffin popping out on top of his white shirt collar, and a round face of a pink hue that probably caused his doctor to prescribe blood pressure medication. Clearly, he was acquainted with Mike.

"What are you doing here?" he snapped when Mike followed Lizzie into the office.

Mike brought his hand up to his chest and looked around innocently, as if he couldn't believe he was the object of Fulbright's address, which caused Fulbright's face to glow the slightest bit more pinkish. "So nice to see you again, Howard," Mike said, just a tad beyond solicitously. "Why, I just walked little Lizzie over so that she wouldn't get lost among the corridors of this vast empire." He gave an unnecessary sweep of his free hand, then, uninvited, sat in one of the two chairs opposite Fulbright. Lizzie took the other chair. "She's never been to this floor before, have you, Lizzie?"

Lizzie assumed the sweetest, most wide-eyed expression she could and shook her head.

"Don't mind me," Mike said. "I'll just sit here and read my paper. You two conduct whatever business you need to, and then I'll see this little tyke back home."

In a stage whisper behind his hand to Fulbright, he added, "Told her grandma I wouldn't let the little darlin' out of my sight."

He sat back, crossed an ankle over the other knee and opened his paper expansively.

"Don't give me that," Fulbright spat back. "By now this little conniver knows every nook and cranny of this campus."

He glared at Lizzie, but she kept her composure and said nothing. Mike turned a page of his newspaper and held it like a shield between himself and Fulbright.

Fulbright seemed to take a moment to decide how to proceed given this unexpected turn of events with Machete Mike showing up. He addressed himself to Lizzie.

"Now, about this rabble-rousing. We had a nice, quiet retirement community here before you showed up. What have you got to say for yourself?"

The last sentence was more of a challenge than a question, but

Lizzie did not take the bait.

"All I did was help Evelyn get to dinner and back." She licked her lips and opened her eyes even wider, assuming an amazed expression implying that she could not believe her next statement. "Ricky took her scooter license away."

"Indeed, he did. At my insistence. We have the safety of our residents to consider, and we can't tolerate reckless driving that imperils others."

"Got any witnesses to this purported reckless driving?" Mike inquired from behind his newspaper in the way he might ask a grocer if he had any riper tomatoes.

Fulbright literally bared his teeth as he turned his attention from Lizzie to the back of Mike's newspaper. "Amos Tucker. And I'll have you know he narrowly escaped perishing as a result of the falling glass when he was driving beneath the skybridge."

"Is that right?" Mike drawled again, this time sounding like he'd just read about an unbelievable real estate deal. He peered out from the edge of his newspaper. "Sounds like what Amos would have been able to see from down below was falling glass, not reckless driving."

Mike went back behind his newspaper screen but said, "What a shame you've got such faulty construction here that glass falls out of the walls. Hope Amos doesn't bring a suit against Wren Haven."

Mike lowered the paper to his lap, looking up at the ceiling, nodded and put his index finger to his chin.

"Oh, and against the contractor, of course." He crinkled his brow. "Maybe the city's Department of Buildings too."

After another moment of consulting the ceiling, he said no more, but gave a side bob of his head and casually went back behind the cover of his newspaper.

Fulbright had gone one shade pinker and was glaring at Mike's newsprint screen.

"There is nothing wrong with our construction. It was Evelyn Martin's fault. She lost control of her vehicle, so she has to lose her license. Those are the rules."

He turned to Lizzie, saying, "And I can't have you, missy, contravening the consequences of those rules and starting protest riots."

He let that sit a moment, then leaned back in his chair and folded his hands across his rounded midsection, apparently satisfied that he'd gained the upper hand.

"You know, Lizzie," he said, now examining his fingernails, "we have other rules here at Wren Haven, as well." He paused for dramatic effect, then inclined his head back and literally looked down his nose at her. "Rules about the minimum age for Wren Haven residents."

Mike slowly and carefully folded back one side of his paper, obviously to create the appearance of deliberately speaking to Lizzie, complete with angling his head to evoke sage thoughtfulness.

"Isn't Wren Haven such a wonderful place? Always looking out for our residents, even their health; putting the 'care' in 'continuing care retirement community.' Even anticipating that some residents might need a caregiver to live with them. How fortunate Mimi is to have her loving granddaughter at her side now that she is battling the infirmities of advancing age."

He half-turned his head toward Fulbright. "Of course, a caregiver would not be an official resident, would they, Howard? And, therefore, not be subject to rules applying to residents."

Just as Mike was readying to add, Wouldn't you agree? Fulbright grabbed a pencil on his desk and looked as if he was going to snap it in two.

Mike ignored him and turned to Lizzie. "I guess Mimi's been taking those water aerobics classes to strengthen her heart." He finished with an "Mm-hmm" and repositioned his paper.

Fulbright upped his attack. "Mimi isn't sick. I've seen her hopping around with all those line-dancing people. And besides, we're not talking about sick people, we're talking about unruly behavior being instigated by outsiders, like this one here." He finished by brandishing his pencil like a fencing foil.

"All I did was help Evelyn get to dinner and back." Feeling the slightest bit devilish, she added ever so sweetly with a straight face, "Ricky took her scooter license away."

Fulbright's face had gone from pink to red. "We can't have reckless driving at Wren Haven!"

There was a slight rustle of the newspaper and once again Machete Mike, unseen, asked, "Got any witnesses to this alleged reckless driving?" deliberately drawing out the word alleged.

Again, Fulbright waited, as if collecting his thoughts while glaring at Mike's newspaper.

"Charlie Burke," he said finally. "In fact, Charlie and his dog were also victims of Evelyn Martin's reckless driving. They both could have been seriously hurt."

Once again, Mike peeked out from the side of his paper. "Is that right?" he asked again, sounding amazed. "And Charlie's a reliable witness? I hear tell Charlie's a tad forgetful." Mike disappeared behind his newspaper again.

By now, Fulbright was doing a little rocking motion back and forth over his blotter, as if he were a dog straining at the leash.

Mike, still holding either side of the newspaper, let it buckle onto his lap.

"I wonder, Lizzie," he said in his best by-the-way tone of voice, "on your rides with Evelyn, did she ever discuss the event that deprived her of her sole means of transportation to the dining hall?"

"Oh yes," Lizzie answered, trying to evoke innocence itself. "She said she was trying to avoid Snowball, who was running toward her, and avoid Charlie, who was being pulled by Snowball."

"Is that right?" Mike responded, cocking his head and sounding more amazed than ever. He looked at Fulbright. "Sounds to me, Howard, that if you're looking for a scapegoat for that falling glass, you'd do better to euthanize that vicious hound, Snowball."

Mike disappeared behind his paper again.

With a little imagination, one could almost see steam coming out from beneath Fulbright's tight collar.

"You know perfectly well that Charlie needs that little dog to get him around. No one in his right mind would think that two-pound ball of fuzz was any danger for a human on a motorized vehicle. And another thing . . ." Fulbright stopped mid-sentence as his assistant, Lorraine, came in and put a file on his desk, although he did not look up at her.

Over her shoulder, Lizzie heard Mike say, "Why, Lorraine, how are you?" The newspaper was down again. "So long since I've seen you. Things are well?"

Given the red-faced Fulbright who was not even looking at her or the silver-tongued Mike Mullaney who had chosen this moment to pay court to her, Lorraine seemed delighted to exchange a word or two.

"Fine, Mike. And Mary? And your son?"

"Both fine. My boy's working for the state now. The governor asked him to head up the health department, starting next month. He's already got an entire laundry list of problems to tackle, he tells me. He's going to start with inspections of dining establishments."

Lizzie looked from Mike to Lorraine and back to Mike again. I don't know where he's going with this, but I have the feeling I'm in the presence of a master.

"Oh? Dining establishments?" Lorraine echoed.

Lizzie couldn't help thinking, This is probably the most interesting conversation she's had all week.

Mike now emphasized with an upward hand-sweep, "Oh, yeah. You wouldn't believe how lax some places are. Inadequate refrigeration, more tables in their space than they're licensed for, allowing people to bring their pets in . . ." with just the slightest emphasis on the word pets, so slight that had one not been following the conversation it could have been missed it altogether.

"Lorraine, we're trying to finish up here," Fulbright said with a slight rise at the end of his sentence and an arching of his eyebrows, plainly suggesting that she leave.

"Best to Mary, Mike," Lorraine whispered and cowered out of the office.

"Okay, Mullaney, I know when I'm being threatened," Fulbright snarled.

Mike slapped his hand to his chest and turned to Lizzie, feigning injury. "Oh, my! Threatened? Lizzie, did you hear a threat?"

Lizzie looked at Fulbright, saying no with a shake of her head, her now shorter tresses grazing her shoulders.

"All right, here's the deal," Fulbright offered to Mike. "I'll ease off, Lizzie, but there's no more talk about the dog in the dining room. And don't go putting any ideas into Amos's head."

"Oh, that's so nice of you, Howard," Mike said, while turning to Lizzie. "Didn't I tell you what a nice guy he is?"

"Oh, yes, Mike. Mr. Fulbright is everything you said he was."

"Although," Mike started again, causing Fulbright to look at him out of the corner of one eye, the other squinted closed. "Seems to me you've still got all those protesters over there. They are Evelyn's friends. Lizzie has no control over them. It's a free country. First Amendment and all that. Some of our residents took civics classes in school and know about that sort of thing."

"All right. Evelyn Martin gets her license back." Fulbright looked as if he'd swallowed something bitter.

He turned his attention back to Lizzie. "Now about the stolen property."

"Stolen property?"

By now Lizzie had become adept at playing the ingenue, raising both her delicate hands to her throat in mock offense, widening her eyes and turning her mouth into a cute O. She sensed Mike stifling a chuckle behind his paper. He was clearly enjoying this.

"The golf cart!"

This time Mike lowered his paper with a decided crumple. Lizzie looked from Fulbright to the Machete.

"Lizzie, do you know anything about a stolen golf cart?" Mike asked, as one might ask a five-year-old where the candy in the candy dish had gone.

She again shook her head.

"Howard, you're not missing any golf carts, are you?" Mike asked in the most solicitous way. "I'm sure the residents' council would be pretty upset if they caught wind of Wren Haven's assets being mismanaged. You know, like mysteriously disappearing. Howard, you haven't got weak inventory controls, have you?"

Fulbright pointed at Lizzie. "That thing you've been toting Evelyn Martin around in!"

Finally, Lizzie felt caught. *What's the expression? The jig's up?* There was no denying that she'd been driving something around, and if she couldn't account for it, she wasn't sure that Mike's witty suggestion that the residents' council would hang Fulbright would work. Mike looked as if he was readying a comeback, but she surmised there was a risk, as well. She pretended to a penitent bow of her head but below the visual edge of the desk where Fulbright could not see, she made a sharp horizontal gesture to Mike for silence. Thankfully, Mike had enough peripheral vision to catch it.

"Silas needs a cart," she said evenly, this time sincerely.

"Who's Silas?" Fulbright demanded.

Do not reach across that desk and strangle this jerk. Yes, it's a crime that Silas is his longest serving employee—and proud of it—and that this jerk doesn't even know his name. That's what makes him a jerk.

Lizzie just held her temper and looked up, addressing Fulbright directly. "Silas. He's part of the original staff and has been working here longer than any of your other employees. Silas is part of the gardening crew now and he enjoys his job, but he's got a bad knee. I can't even guess how old he is. And the gardening tools he has to lug around are heavy. Silas could use the cart."

Fulbright ran a finger over his lips, considering this suggestion.

Lizzie played her card. "If Evelyn gets her scooter license back, I won't be needing the golf cart anymore."

Mike addressed Fulbright with a particularly annoying smile.

"Guess that makes up your inventory, Howard."

"Oh, shut up, Mullaney. Okay. Silas gets the cart. I'll take care of it tomorrow. Get out of here, both of you."

They both stood. Mike looked like he might have been revving up for a parting shot, but Lizzie took a half step forward and preempted him by dipping a little curtsey and saying in her best little girl voice, "Nice to have met you, Mr. Fulbright."

As soon as the elevator door closed on them, they both sputtered a laugh. Mike slapped Lizzie on the back.

"You were great! Did you practice that curtsey?" They both laughed again.

"Now tell me, Lizzie," he said, much more seriously, "have you ever considered law school?"

chapter 48

Lizzie came back into the apartment from the Wren Haven library to find Mimi in the living room, a photo album open on her lap. Her eyes looked somewhat red, and she held a damp tissue in her left hand.

Lizzie had seen this album before, and knew it well, in fact. She knew it held photos of herself from a young age, and photos of Jane from a young age. Why was Mimi torturing herself with the photo album? Obviously, those pictures still brought her to tears. As they would her. So, no, she wouldn't go look over her shoulder at it, since she didn't want to look at it and start tearing up too, especially now that things had been going somewhat better. She didn't want to see the pictures of Mom and Dad getting married. Mom and Dad bringing her home from the hospital. Mom and Dad with her after the third-grade school play when she'd played a woodland fairy.

Mimi seemed not to have heard Lizzie come in and was a tad surprised to notice her. She cleared her throat.

"Oh Lizzie, would you run down to the pharmacy for me? I need some more of those eye drops. Larry, the pharmacist, knows what to give you. Have him put it on my account."

"Sure," Lizzie said, glad to have an excuse to leave the apartment and avoid the photo album. She didn't think Mimi needed eye drops. They were probably an excuse to get her out of the apartment to give her a couple more minutes of privacy to recover from yet another session of sobbing that she thought Lizzie didn't know about. Lizzie sighed as she walked to the pharmacy. *It's okay, Mimi. I miss them, too.*

She picked up her pace, picturing the blue and yellow eye drop box to divert her thoughts before she, too, felt given to tears.

Waiting for Larry to work up the computerized tab, Lizzie was thumbing the magazine rack when she heard something like a soft crash. Looking behind her, Lizzie saw Harriet Wilson standing amid a heap of tissue boxes. Lizzie took a few quick steps over to her.

"Oh, I'm okay, Lizzie," Harriet said. "Just a little embarrassed. I was reaching over this box here." She pointed to a large box on the floor, open and full of cough syrup bottles. Above it was a half-empty shelf awaiting restocking. "And I pulled this whole mess down around me."

"No harm done," Lizzie said. "I'll take care of this."

Harriet took the vitamins she had been reaching for and sheepishly moved over toward the cash register. Lizzie restacked the dozen or so boxes of tissues on the shelf, then pulled the carton of cough syrup boxes closer. She began filling in the cough syrup shelf when Larry came over to her and handed her the eye drops. Lizzie put them in her pocket before continuing to restock the shelves.

"Thanks, Lizzie," he said, "I'll get this finished up."

But Lizzie kept neatly piling the syrup boxes for another minute, the two of them working side by side until the carton was empty. Both stood, Larry grabbing the now-empty carton from the floor. Lizzie looked around and noticed that some other shelves were partially empty, and a couple were dusty.

"Larry," she said tentatively, "suppose you could use some help around here?"

"Geez, I don't know, Lizzie," he replied, kind of sucking air in through his teeth and looking out from under raised eyebrows in the way people do when they want to give you a thanks-but-no-thanks answer. "You're not sixteen yet, are you? There's a state employment law."

Lizzie held up her hand to end his discomfort. "Sure. I understand. Just thought I'd ask." She patted the pocket with the eye drops and asked, "You need me to sign something?"

He nodded, and they both went back to the pharmacy counter. She signed, took Mimi's copy of the receipt, and pushed the other back across to Larry. He reached for it absent-mindedly, seeming to be lost in thought about something.

"I wonder, Lizzie . . ." He hesitated before continuing, "I wonder if you would mind doing a favor for Mrs. Fernandez."

Lizzie shrugged. "Sure. What?" She had met Lydia Fernandez once or twice and could picture her.

"Well, she's had a prescription sitting here for a week. I don't know whether she's forgotten about it or has just had difficulty getting over here for it. Her back acts up occasionally, you know."

Lizzie nodded, certain that Larry ought not to be telling her about Lydia Fernandez's back problem.

He reached to a rack behind the counter and seemed to fumble with something. He handed her a white bag, stapled at the top.

"You suppose you could run her prescription over to her? She's all the way over in the far building."

Lizzie looked at the address and said, "Sure."

"Let me know how you make out," Larry said. "I'll call and let her know you're on your way over."

Lizzie shrugged and left, Mimi's eye drops in her pocket and Lydia Fernandez's prescription bag in her hand. Dormant for the last month or so, Lizzie's cynicism began to awaken. Let him know how I make out? That sounded suspiciously like "report back." Delivering one little white bag to a senior citizen wasn't exactly rocket science. What did he think she was going to do, start a black market for Tylenol?

Lydia Fernandez was an older version of Rosa. Her hair was thick, wavy, and still a lustrous black, the shots of silver looking like a deliberate highlight.

"Madre de Dios! Lizzie, come in. I forgot all about this prescription. I would have missed it when I ran out," she said, reaching for the white bag in Lizzie's hand.

"Here it is," Lizzie said, handing it to her, then turning to go.

Lydia grabbed her hand and virtually dragged her into her apartment, which was tastefully furnished in cream and peach.

"I must be subconsciously rebelling against my doctor." She seemed to be searching for something. "Doesn't surprise me. My patients used to rebel against me too."

"You're a doctor?"

"Yes, practicing many years before I retired," she said, stepping over to the breakfast bar. "Ah, here!" she said to herself as she grabbed her wallet. "Oncologist," she added, as she pressed a couple of dollars into Lizzie's hand. "Thank you so much," she said with one of those flashing white smiles Lizzie had seen on Rosa so often.

"No, that's not necessary."

"Lizzie, you walked all the way over here and it was a very nice thing for you to do. I insist!" she said with an index finger in the air and a note of finality in her voice.

Feeling a bit irritated, Lizzie returned to the pharmacy.

"Mission accomplished," she said as neutrally as she could manage and held out the dollar bills.

Larry folded her fingers back around the notes and said, "That's yours."

Lizzie, dumbfounded for the moment, recalled the session with Fulbright. Although she and Machete Mike had had a good laugh over the episode, she had no wish to repeat it.

"Larry, I know that there's a rule about not tipping here at Wren Haven."

"Correction," he said with an air of authority. "There is no tipping of Wren Haven employees," the last word emphasized. He grinned.

"Well, thank you very much!" Lizzie said, her earlier uncharitable thought of Larry dissipated.

"Now," he said, handing her several more bags. "How would you like to do some favors for a few more residents?"

"Why not?"

Some tipped and some didn't. Some were cheerful and some miserable. Some invited her in for a soft drink and sometimes she said yes if she thought they'd be interesting to chat with for a few minutes, and some she declined. But for the rest of that summer, Lizzie made a point of stopping by the pharmacy once a day and, inevitably, she was too busy to go to Shelly's beach house for a week.

Skipping Shelly's invitation in favor of making runs for the Wren Haven Pharmacy yielded another unexpected benefit. Lizzie now found it wise to visit the Wren Haven branch of RealBank to open an account for herself, one with a very handy ATM card.

chapter 49

A FEW DAYS FURTHER INTO JULY, LIZZIE WAS MUNCHING her cornflakes when Mimi surprised her with, "Herb's suggested we go to the state park for a hike. Would you like to ask Rod along and come with us?"

"Rod's gone."

"Oh?"

Lizzie was reading the section of the *Wren Haven News* that Mimi had finished.

"Summer session before regular classes start. He left two days before my classes were over." It had been short and sweet. She didn't expect anything more, and it wasn't. Mentally, she gave a shrug and went back to reading.

Still, the awkward invitation to tag along on the hike hung in the air. A moment later, rescue came when she answered Mimi's landline and found the call was for her. It was Lydia Fernandez, asking if Lizzie could come over to give her a hand. Lizzie could not imagine what Lydia wanted but, forty minutes later, showered and dressed, she went anyway. A trip over to the furthest building in the complex was always a chance to stretch her legs and break into a jog if the indoor corridors were empty. Today she chose to go by the outside paths instead of using the skybridge, the scene of the notorious collision and possible defective construction. That route would be more welcome in the winter months.

"Lizzie, my back is killing me," Lydia told her as soon as she arrived.

Someday I'm going to decorate an apartment just like this, Lizzie thought, then realized she should give her attention to Lydia.

"What can I do for you?"

"I have a suitcase and some boxes that should go up on the upper shelf of my closet, and with my back, I can't manage it."

They walked into the bedroom, and Lydia flicked her wrist toward the corner.

"That suitcase has been sitting in the corner since my last cruise and I am sick of looking at it. Do you think you can lift it up?"

"Sure."

Unpacked, the suitcase was light, and after a few quick hefts and shoves, Lizzie had not only it, but several cardboard boxes neatly positioned in Lydia's closet.

Lizzie was a little less surprised this time when Lydia gave her a few folded bills, saying, "I insist!" before Lizzie could protest.

A few days later Winnie called, wondering if Lizzie could sew a couple of missing buttons back on some blouses, and stitch up a hem that had come loose from a favorite dress. It was one of those warm, lazy summer afternoons when getting a breeze on Winnie's patio and passing a needle back and forth was about all one might feel like doing anyway.

If there was one word to describe Winnie, it would be *demure*. Slight of frame, she was soft spoken and wore her silver-blonde hair in an old-fashioned pageboy. Winnie watched Lizzie's patient, graceful stitching and said, "I can't see to thread a needle anymore."

So, Lizzie took care to select the perfectly matching thread from Winnie's sewing basket and stitched neat secure stitches. These were the stitches her mother had taught her when she had tried to make a dress for a favorite doll long ago.

While Lizzie stitched, Winnie chatted, and Lizzie was glad to be distracted from the memory of the sewing lesson. Winnie spoke about her family, her late husband and, surprisingly, about an early career as an army nurse. Winnie had been stationed in Vietnam and had survived persistent rain, high humidity, and the occasional typhoon. She talked about running low on medical supplies and triaging in the dark. Lizzie had nothing to contribute to the conversation, so she continued sewing and listening to Winnie's experiences. She tried to picture this petite woman in army fatigues and couldn't.

"Oh, Lizzie, you're doing such a perfect job," Winnie commented. More quietly, she added, "I like to look nice, and I can't go around with missing buttons."

"Absolutely," Lizzie agreed.

"You know," Winnie went on, "some people, when they get older and can't see as well as they used to, don't care for their clothes properly."

Lizzie nodded, encouraging Winnie to continue.

"You see them with stains down the front of their clothes because they can't see well enough to realize that they've spilled something."

Lizzie pitied this fact of life; she'd seen it herself once or twice in her months at Wren Haven.

Winnie hung her head slightly and with a touch of embarrassment asked, "Lizzie, if you ever see me with a stain on my clothes, you'll tell me, won't you? I'd want you to tell me."

A memory flashed by. She found herself back in the car with her mother, foregoing the chance to reach out and be reassuring—an opportunity she'd never have again. Lizzie tamped down the pang of regret. Lizzie reached out and touched Winnie's arm.

"Of course!" she said. Then added, "Will you teach me to play golf?"

At that, Winnie brightened. "You bet! Got to have our seer understand the game!"

On that lighter note, Lizzie prepared to leave. And when Winnie slipped a ten into her palm, Lizzie suppressed a moment of guilt because she'd learned enough about pride to realize that handing the money back would hurt, and that's the last thing she wanted to do to this sweet lady—this sweet lady who had once worn army fatigues and dressed wounds in near darkness and who now just wanted to know she was dressed nicely when she went to dinner.

chapter 50

"Greg!" Lizzie panted as she banged on what she hoped was Gregory Cox's door. The four-and-a-half corridor sprint had winded her more than she thought it would. "Greg!"

The door opened to a surprised Greg, who seemed even more surprised when Lizzie grabbed his wrist and yanked him into the hallway, sending the documents he had in hand flurrying to the floor in all directions.

"Come on! Hurry!"

Greg trotted after her.

"Is there some emergency?"

"Yes, it's an emergency and I know you can tell if there's a real danger. You're an architect, right?"

"Yes. Just renewed my licenses."

"Well, hurry!"

"Since when is an architect needed for an emergency? Especially here at Wren Haven."

Halfway down the corridor, Lizzie slowed, bent, braced her palms on her knees, and tilted her head up at Greg. By now, they were both a bit out of breath.

"It's Helen Cameron, the woman who just moved in next to Mimi."

"Lizzie, if she's having a heart attack, we ought to call security. They're trained in CPR."

Lizzie gulped another breath. "It's not a heart attack. It may be a mental break, but I don't think it's a heart attack." She took another couple of deep breaths. "Mimi and I were having breakfast when we heard a crash. Loud. Then another crash. A smaller one. We both ran next door. Helen's door was unlocked. Greg, she's pulling the place apart. She's got a chainsaw. I'm afraid she's going to wreck something. Like maybe she'll saw right through to Mimi's apartment and into my bedroom. Mimi's with her now, trying to keep her from doing more damage."

Greg jerked his head back and blinked behind his glasses.

"You've left Mimi alone with a madwoman with a power saw?"

Lizzie, still panting, nodded.

"Okay, okay. But ease up. I'm not as young as you are."

A minute later, they were in Helen's apartment. Helen, a slight woman with reddish hair, stood in the middle of a pile of rubble—freshly painted sheetrock, by the look of it—wearing overalls and safety goggles. Bed sheets covered everything, including several of what looked to be large pieces of furniture and brand-new carpeting. Mimi was speaking in soothing tones with her arms extended in an effort to fend off Helen's periodic jabs with the saw, made more threatening with the revs that accompanied each thrust.

Lizzie tiptoed into Helen's line of vision, followed by Greg.

"Helen, this is one of our Wren Haven neighbors, Gregory Cox. He's here to help."

Helen peered through her goggles. "Great. You can help by getting some of this mess cleared away and getting these busybodies out of my apartment."

Greg sidled in Helen's direction, fishing with his left hand for the wall outlet behind him. Finding it, he pulled the plug on the power saw.

"Nice to meet you, Helen. What have you got going on here?"

"I don't like it."

"You don't like what, Helen?"

"This apartment. I don't like it."

Lizzie hung back as Greg surveyed the remaining standard walls, freshly repainted as per Wren Haven policy before a new resident moved in.

"What don't you like about it?"

"I don't like it. I want one of those open-plan designs. A more modern style. I want some sunlight in my kitchen."

Lizzie moved over to Mimi's side, watching Greg.

He stepped over to what had been a wall, now reduced to rubble, running his hand up the remaining side wall and looking up into the ceiling area where the top of the dividing wall had been.

"Well, this would certainly do the trick. Fortunately, I don't think you've hit any load-bearing walls. But you can't just demolish the place."

"Sure I can. I read what it said on the Wren Haven website. It says residents can decorate their homes to reflect their personal style. My personal style is sunlight. I'm decorating my home."

Greg seemed to choose his words carefully, his voice calm and respectful. "I see your point, but I think decorating means more like paint and wallpaper, not reconfiguring floor plans."

Helen stamped one foot and hung her head like a scolded child.

Lizzie clasped her hands behind her neck, elbows meeting in front. Now what had she done? She'd stuck her nose in again and had gotten Greg mixed up in this when, according to him, Helen had done no actual harm. She'd just been trying to make herself more at home. And now she looked crushed and embarrassed in front of her new neighbors.

"Helen," Mimi asked, "why did you choose this apartment if you don't like it?"

That's a reasonable question, Lizzie thought.

Helen crumpled onto the floor in her overalls, pushing the goggles up onto her forehead. She rubbed an eye with her white-dusted fingers before replying.

"I didn't. I didn't choose it." She seemed a little out of breath.

Lizzie sat down on the floor next to her.

"I didn't choose it and I don't want to be here at all. My sons put me here. My two darling sons."

There was something not so darling about the way she said *darling*.

"The sons I fed at my breast and nursed through their childhood illnesses and sent to the best schools. Those sons."

There was a sledgehammer in the corner, and Helen was eyeing it.

Lizzie put her shoulder between Helen and the line of sight to the sledgehammer.

"They put you here?"

"They said they thought I wouldn't eat properly if I lived alone."

They might not be totally wrong, considering how the overalls hung on her bony shoulders, thought Lizzie.

"My husband died two weeks ago. Then on Wednesday my sons showed up at my house and told me I was moving here. The moving van arrived the next day."

The grief, the anger, the frustration, the resentment of her sons taking over her life without even consulting her—it was all there in Helen's voice. No wonder she wanted to smash something with the sledgehammer.

Being plunked down at Wren Haven with no say in the matter was something Lizzie, of all people, could relate to. At the time, she didn't have a sledgehammer to swing but had done her own swinging with the gin bottle. She hoped her recollection wasn't causing her to color from chagrin.

Still on the floor, Helen rested her elbows on her knees and rubbed her temples. She and I are not so very different, Lizzie thought, both of us landing here at Wren Haven through no decision of our own. Poor Helen. From the sound of it, she probably wasn't on good terms with her closest family members. Yep, she knew what that was like, didn't she? By now, the sons could have sold her house out from under their mother, regardless of whether the sons thought they were just doing what they thought was in their mother's best interest. Helen was neither crazy nor dangerous.

The same thought seemed to have hit Mimi and Greg, as Lizzie saw them exchange a surprised glance.

Greg squatted down. "I'm an architect. Do you want me to give you a hand? I don't think you'll need construction permits, but you'll definitely need to submit a written plan to the Wren Haven management. I'm sure they'll want to have properly licensed contractors finish the work you've started. It won't hurt to have some drawings as well. There's got to be a way around this without getting you thrown out of Wren Haven."

"Thrown out? They could throw me out? Where would I go?"

Everyone looked to the side or at the floor. Lizzie certainly didn't have an answer to that question, and it seemed the others didn't either.

Standing, Greg took charge. "We'll do everything we can to keep it from coming to that." He scanned the room with the sheeted floor, wall fragments, and dust everywhere.

"Do you ladies think you could get this room in better shape while I chat with Alice? I know she handled a variety of legal matters while she was practicing. Let's hope real estate and construction were two of them. I can draft an opinion and ask my colleagues at Aquatecture to produce some drawings, but Alice will have to do the heavy lifting with the Wren Haven documents to see how many regulations have been violated. And keep Helen out of Fulbright's clutches."

Helen looked alarmed.

Greg spoke to Helen again. "Do you have any other remodeling ideas? Do you like your bathroom? Are all the kitchen appliances fine?"

Helen nodded. "Yes."

"Well, that's good," he said. "Is there anything else you don't like?"

Helen folded her arms on her knees, put her head down on them, and began to cry. A moment later she swiped at her eyes and the white plaster powder smeared on her cheeks. Mimi handed her a tissue from her pocket. Lizzie lightly stroked her back.

"It's okay," Lizzie whispered. "What else don't you like?"

"It's just . . ." Helen blew her nose. "The whole place feels so claustrophobic. So . . . so closed in." Helen's shoulders shuddered as she sobbed.

Lizzie felt the coals of guilt smoldering in her stomach. Interior walls were one thing, but she didn't know how Greg could possibly fix the square footage of the apartment. This was her fault. She'd pulled him into Helen's problem and maybe it would cause him to be embarrassed if he couldn't satisfy her.

With her usual calmness, Mimi looked around at the sheeted furniture, running her hands over the back of what was apparently a large, upholstered chair.

"Did you have a large house? Big living room? Big dining room?"

"Yes," Helen said. "It was a lovely home. Spacious rooms that they don't build anymore. We raised our children there. It was a shock to be forced to leave."

"Well, that's part of the problem," Mimi said, injecting some practicality into the conversation. "Your furniture is out of proportion to the space."

"Out of proportion?" The last of Helen's tears fell from her lashes. She stood and walked around the compact living room, her sneakered feet kicking up little puffs of dust.

"Sure," Mimi went on in the same easy drawl she had used to tell Lizzie that Wren Haven had a well-equipped computer center.

"It's just a matter of adapting to your new surroundings. It's called downsizing. Didn't your sons help you with that?"

Helen shook her head with a blank, disoriented look on her face, then seemed to brighten a bit.

"New furniture!" she said with an unmistakable lift in her voice. "I should get new furniture!"

Greg joined the more cheerful line of conversation.

"Do you have a favorite color?"

"Yellow. I like yellow."

"Yellow! I like yellow too. Why don't you come over to visit me this afternoon? You can meet my wife, Beth. I'm sure she'd like to help you pick out some yellow paint. And furniture. She's got a golden touch with interior decorating; a natural talent."

He addressed himself to Lizzie and Mimi in a lower tone. "I saw a dumpster out back. Let's keep this quiet until I can chat with Alice."

Definitely, Lizzie thought, as Greg departed. Fulbright would have a field day with this situation, especially if he found out she had any part of it. And Helen might not come out of it unscathed. With this chainsaw action, he could probably declare her of questionable mental competence and get her sent to the assisted living section, at minimum.

Lizzie popped up and stood at Helen's shoulder, offering her a hand up.

"C'mon, Helen. Mimi and I will help you gather up these sheets and all . . . this," she said with a wave toward the crumbled Sheetrock. "And then you can get showered."

Lizzie brushed her jeans with something of an overblown motion and attempted a lighter tone with, "We're all going to need a shower. Later this afternoon we'll take you over to the Coxes and you can meet Beth."

"Right," Mimi said, already gathering up the corners of one sheet. Undoubtedly attempting some optimism, she said, "It won't take long to get acquainted here. You already know Lizzie and me.

And now you've met Greg. This afternoon you'll meet Beth. And wait until you see the Coxes' apartment. Their place is gorgeous. Beth is just the right one to talk to."

"And drapes! I should have new drapes!"

As Helen perked up with a more upbeat line of thinking, Lizzie breathed a sigh of relief. She had one less thing to feel she'd messed up, thanks to Greg. And probably thanks to Alice, Beth, and Mimi as well. There was just one niggling question that she had to ask. "Helen, where did you get the chainsaw and the sledgehammer?"

Helen's earlier feistiness returned, this time with a cheesy grin.

"I stole 'em! I watched those maintenance men and followed one of them to their tool shed, and —"

"Stop!" Lizzie shouted as the image of Fulbright returned. With raised palms, she turned her head away and said, "I don't want to know. I can't know any more of this." She rolled her eyes and joined Mimi in cleaning up the floor.

A week later, Lizzie allowed herself a moment of satisfaction when she saw a contractor's van parked outside Helen's patio door.

For the remainder of the summer and into the fall, she would occasionally meet Beth heading toward Helen's apartment, usually laden with wallpaper or fabric samples. She could sometimes hear excited snippets of conversation escaping from Helen's front door into the hall. Hearing the sounds of two friends having a ball with the project would always be a cheerful moment for Lizzie, despite whatever else might have happened in the course of a single day.

chapter 51

A S EVERYONE AT HER TABLE WAS FINISHING UP DINNER one evening, it surprised Lizzie to feel a tap on her shoulder. She looked up and saw Angelina Lacroix.

"Madame Lacroix! *Bon soir! Ca va bien?*"

"*Oui*, Lizzie. *Et vous?*"

"I am well, thank you."

Aside from Madame's coming to her aid last February, the only thing Lizzie knew of her was what Mimi had shared one lazy Saturday over BLT sandwiches. Mimi liked Madame but said nobody remembered when or why Madame Lacroix had made Wren Haven her home. Some would say Madame had moved to Wren Haven after a romantic break with a well-known European fashion designer. Others would say she had once owned an upscale label but had mismanaged it and needed to sell it for a pittance. The more scornful types carped that she was no one special but only thought herself so. However, as far as Lizzie was concerned, none of this mattered.

While some spoke negatively about her behind her back, Mimi believed her methods only resulted in positive outcomes. Lizzie had to agree. Madame would keep a sharp eye out for a well-dressed resident, male or female, approach them in the dining hall or in one of Wren Haven's many corridors, and the dialog would proceed along the lines of, "Why, Nadine, how well you look! Losing all that weight has done wonders for you!"

"What? What are you talking about? I haven't lost any weight."

"Of course you have! Look at how this suit is hanging on you. You have all this room back here," she'd say, grabbing some fabric on the back of the outfit where, of course, the hapless Nadine could not see. "The fabric of this suit is beautiful. It must be altered. Wearing it like this does you no favors."

"Altered? This suit is so old I wouldn't think about putting any money into it."

"No? Well then, you can donate it to the Surprise Shoppe. Come see me tomorrow."

"What? I was going to wear this to my garden club luncheon next week."

"Don't worry. I have something much better for you—a beautiful silk dress with a matching jacket. Ooh, la la! And on sale! A much better color for you, anyway."

And so, Nadine would feel terrific in her beautiful new silk dress and Mme. Lacroix would replenish her inventory all in one fell swoop with the Fellowship Fund increasing its treasury to boot. The most amazing thing was that Nadine would look much better in her new frock, as would the next owner of Nadine's suit.

But this evening, something else was on Madame's mind.

"Lizzie, I have a favor to ask. You know it's fall preview season."

Fall previews? Lizzie needed a moment to adjust. Did she mean previews like in the fashion industry? Well, this was Madame Lacroix, so, yeah, probably so.

"Uh, what can I do for you?" Lizzie winced, hoping she wasn't inadvertently volunteering to reorganize that huge warehouse of a shop. Or maybe retag the merchandise.

"Our annual fashion show is coming up, and this year I want a fresh look. So, I wondered if you would be one of our models."

Not what Lizzie had expected. It was so far removed from anything she would volunteer to do. Was she supposed to wear the old-lady clothes from the Surprise Shoppe? In public? She scrambled for an excuse. Since it was August, she couldn't plead the need to study or an upcoming class trip.

Mimi perked up with raised eyebrows and short nods toward Lizzie.

As a delaying tactic, Lizzie reached for her water glass and took a sip. Then a new notion struck. So what if it was uncool? Who would know? This was Wren Haven and only the residents would be attending. It might make Mimi happy or proud or whatever. Lizzie looked up to face Madame Lacroix—whose expression was so hopeful—and the presupposed uncoolness gave way to poignant gratitude at the memory of Madame Lacroix's extreme kindness when . . . well, last February. "Of course, I will."

By now most of their tablemates had left, so as graciously as possible, Lizzie said, "Won't you have a seat? You can tell me what you need me to do."

Mimi seemed eager to be party to the conversation, leaning forward, one elbow on the table supporting her chin on her palm. One might have expected Mac to depart when the conversation turned to a fashion show, but he remained at the table, listening with his hands folded in his lap.

"Thank you, Lizzie. I am so glad you will do it. Adding a younger edge could bring more energy to the show. You know we have some stylish residents here."

Sure, stylish after you've gotten through with them, Lizzie thought with genuine admiration.

"And I usually have about a dozen and a half models, but this year," Madame said with a note of dismay, "Julie Jackson went to live with her daughter. Myrna Smith moved to live someplace else. LuLu Harris is going to be on a cruise, and Joyce Thompson is gone. So, it seems the right time to refresh the total show, and you are the first one I've asked."

"I'm sure it will be splendid as always," Mimi chimed in. "Lizzie, it's always an afternoon tea along with the fashion show. Very elegant."

Madame was going on about her energized new vision and Lizzie took it all in, meanwhile surveying the dining hall. She leaned back in her chair and put her hands in the front pockets of her jeans. The memory of Tamika on the bus hit her with a pang of chagrin. She'd acted like a know-it-all, yet again inviting a near disaster by saying the wrong thing and doing the wrong thing. Should she put her nose into someone else's business this time? Sometimes people appreciated the help, and sometimes they didn't. She remembered the vibration of Tamika kicking the seat in front of her. Should she help? After all, it was Madame's show. But she seemed like she was having a bit of a time pulling it together. Madame had been super nice, so perhaps she'd just offer.

"I know where you can get a lot of young models."

Madame Lacroix leaned forward, clearly surprised and interested in whatever Lizzie might suggest.

"Oui?"

Lizzie pointedly looked at Tamika.

Madame's gaze swung toward Tamika, who was clearing tables. Then Lizzie nodded toward several of the other younger staff.

"Brilliant!" Madame Lacroix seemed pleased. "Our theme this year will be Style at Any Age! And I'll coordinate colors. I'll choose a color for one of the younger models, then the same color in a different outfit for one of the residents, and they will both walk out together."

Lizzie regarded Madame Lacroix and restrained a smile. One could practically hear her thoughts. She seemed already lost on the catwalk.

Mimi interrupted the reverie. "Who will you get to announce? Joyce used to announce all your shows, but she's gone."

By this time, Lizzie had learned that "gone" did not mean a trip to the store. Gone meant gone to the Great Beyond. Nobody at the table flinched at the reference.

"*Oui,* another problem. And she had such a beautiful voice." Madame sighed. "I asked Rosalie Glassman if she had any ideas, but she said no, since their work is on the manufacturing side of the garment industry."

Amid the chatter of tea, fashion, and models, Mac had a suggestion.

"You could ask Amos. He used to be a radio announcer and was pretty famous in his region."

Mac craned his neck and scanned the dining hall.

"In fact, I see him over there, seated near the far wall."

It wasn't difficult to identify the large man who bore a striking resemblance to James Earl Jones.

"Would you like me to introduce you?"

With that, Mac took Madame off to recruit Amos.

chapter 52

A WEEK AND A HALF LATER, MADAME LACROIX CALLED A rehearsal. Amos seemed like a fish out of water and felt like one. He was either uncharacteristically stumbling over his words or nearly falling asleep. At the rehearsal break, he slumped down onto a chair with his elbows on his knees, head in hands.

I spent a forty-year career building a reputation, he thought. Am I supposed to destroy it in a single afternoon at a retirement community? There's my professional image to consider. This show is stultifying, and what makes it even worse is nobody realizes—or maybe nobody cares—how bad it is.

Finally, he pulled Madame Lacroix aside.

"Angie, this is deadly. Didn't you say you wanted a higher energy level? I've got nothing to work with—not even a proper microphone."

Her expression betrayed her anxiety; she looked like she hadn't slept much in recent days. Her fretting voice was somewhere between an accusation and a plea. "You have better ideas?"

Amos shifted his considerable weight to one foot, put one hand on his hip and threw the other hand out to the side. "Don't these fashion shows usually have some kind of musical accompaniment?"

"Oh, *bien sur*. The nice man from the audio-visual department always pipes in *Moon River* or *Blue Danube*."

"I hate to tell you this, Angie, but if you want more energy, something that says youthfulness, that music is not going to cut it."

Angie looked close to tears. "No? No youth? No energy?" A clunking noise from across the room diverted her attention. Past the racks of the selected outfits a few models practiced their twirls, at which she raised her fingers to her temples and gave a small shake of her head.

Amos put a gentle hand on her shoulder. "Angie?"

She turned to face Amos again. "Bad microphone?"

Amos sighed. He could feel her despair and felt sorry for sounding harsh. He nearly put his arm around her shoulder, but instead said, "Look, Angie, do you want me to see what I can do about the music and lighting?" He surveyed the Great Hall and envisioned the runway. "I can take that much off your hands."

She pressed her palm to her heart and closed her eyes. "Oh, Amos, that would be wonderful."

That much I think I can do, Amos thought. As the harried Angie dashed off to rescue another catastrophe in the making, he pulled out his cell and hit the phone icon.

chapter 53

THE UPDATED THEME HAD SPARKED ENTHUSIASM AMONG the Wren Haven residents, and the Style at Any Age fashion show sold out.

The food service staff had arranged cocktail tables in the Great Hall to allow the models to float through in a serpentine route. Strains of *Moon River* were already wafting through the speakers. Sylvia Pawling had overseen placement of the pink linen tablecloths, napkins, and fresh flowers. The afternoon elegance of delicate, crustless cucumber sandwiches was accompanied by pots of tea and plates of cookies. The event was ready to begin.

Lizzie took her place in the lineup, disheartened to realize Madame had partnered her with Janna Duff. Lizzie winced. Why Janna? That old battleax! Didn't Janna know that no one likes an old sour . . . A sudden feeling of deep guilt welled up inside her gut. She felt flushed and wondered if her cheeks were scarlet. The physical reaction was one thing; her memories, appearing like a silent movie, were quite another. She remembered packing her suitcase to visit Mimi, when she had deliberately tried to dampen her mother's good cheer with insolence. Then came the memory of mouthing off to Mimi. From somewhere in her subconscious the phrase "casting stones" came to her. Lizzie's guilt surged in waves with each recollection. Ashamed, she flinched when Janna touched her shoulder.

"Lizzie, you look fabulous! Of course, I think we all do. And look how well-matched you and I are. I've always loved the color lavender. Don't you?" Janna gleefully tapped her fingertips together. Her eyes were wide, surrounded by perfectly applied mascara.

This Janna was sweet and upbeat, smiling, complimentary, and ready to do her part for a good cause. Could this even be the same person? Lizzie blinked and then felt even more repentant about the mean-spirited thoughts she'd had of Janna a moment earlier.

Janna looked Lizzie up and down and said, "Let me fix your collar. It needs to be straightened a bit."

Lizzie let her fix her collar, smooth her skirt, and brush her hair away from her face.

At the end of the lineup, Lizzie spotted Albert, the accountant. He was the show's finale, all by himself, and boy, did he look sharp. He wore a forest green sport coat, a brown fedora, and carried a brass-headed ebony walking stick. Gone was the gray complexion under a wrinkled brow. Albert looked thrilled, excitedly hopping from foot to foot in anticipation.

A week ago, Amos had told Madame Lacroix he'd take care of the audio-visuals and he absolutely did. He'd enlisted his nephew, a computer wizard extraordinaire and part-time DJ. Relieved at having turned over this aspect of the event to Amos, Madame could give her full attention to clothes, models, hair, and makeup.

Precisely at 2:00 p.m., the lights in the Great Hall went out, and the room pitched into blackness. In the cafeteria, which served as the show's backstage, Lizzie heard Madame react in a dry-throated panic.

"What's happening? What's wrong? Did we just have a power failure? Amos is supposed to be taking care of all this! Amos!"

No one heard her last cry due to the high-decibel hyena howl leading into the 1963 pop hit *Wipe Out*. In the next moment, a blinding flash of white light and the twang of guitars filled the open space.

The first two models, the sedate Winnie, and a friend of Tamika's looked at each other with understandable shock and shrugged. Winnie exclaimed, "Go with it."

Style at Any Age was an incontrovertible hit. The models of all ages effortlessly bopped through the designated route to the music's thumps, while Amos's commentary punctuated the occasional strobe bursts. Still in the lineup, Lizzie could hear clapping—not polite patter, but enthusiastic smacks in time with the music. And there was at least one very distinct "Whoop!" from somewhere at the far side of the Great Hall.

Winnie wowed the crowd with a vigorous shimmy during the drum solo, and Albert was the perfect choice to end the show. He executed a graceful pirouette and tipped his hat in perfect time with the spotlight snapping off.

Madame Lacroix appeared pleasantly shocked when Amos dragged her out from backstage at the end of the show, and the audience gave her a standing ovation.

Tamika and Lizzie, both slightly out of breath, hung on each other in exhausted laughter. This had been so much fun that Lizzie felt foolish about nearly foregoing Madame Lacroix's invitation that evening in the dining hall. It had been three times as much fun as any basketball game, and it was definitely more fun than hanging out with Shelly.

"C'mon, Tamika, let's take one more pass down the runway. It looks the audience wants a closer look at some of the outfits." Tamika grabbed Lizzie's hand and they jogged out.

A few days later, Lizzie ran into Albert in the hallway. "I saw you in the fashion show, Albert. You looked great!"

"Oh, it was so much fun," he said, evidently happy to take a minute to relive the show instead of returning to his solitary day-to-day job. "And it was such a success that Madame has had to extend the Surprise Shoppe's hours."

"Madame Lacroix seemed pleased."

Albert's face became as illuminated as it had been on the runway.

"She should be. Between the door receipts and additional Shoppe sales, the show broke all previous records for raising money for the Fellowship Fund."

Albert's remark jolted Lizzie's memory of the show's fun to its more serious purpose: to raise money for residents who might outlive their assets and to provide scholarships for those who served at dinner and rode on the bus with her. Students like Tamika. Suddenly, coolness had a new definition and the guilt that had visited her gut from time to time was supplanted with a glow of satisfaction.

But the best part, Lizzie had to admit, was the after-show conversation she overheard between Amos and Madame Lacroix—something about teaming up and taking the show on the road. Lizzie wondered if it might become a new business venture.

chapter 54

Lizzie rode over to Henry's on the bike he had given her and rapped on his patio slider.

"C'mon in, Lizzie," she heard from the other side of the glass.

The door slid open easily, unlike Mimi's door. She made a mental note to call maintenance to get Mimi's door fixed.

Henry tossed her a bottle of water, saying, "Sorry to hold us up. Got a phone call I needed to take."

"Anything wrong? We can reschedule, if . . ."

"Nah, just one of my old buddies wondering whether I remembered something from a big case. Something from long ago."

Lizzie looked around. She had never been inside Henry's apartment. There were photographs everywhere, on the shelves, on the coffee table, and on every surface, it seemed. Many were of Henry and an attractive woman, no doubt the recently-departed Cathy. There were several photos of Henry in a blue uniform.

"You were a cop?"

"New York's finest!"

"And this is you in uniform?"

Henry grinned. "Yeah, for a lot of years. Retired as a detective, first grade."

Lizzie gazed at several framed newspaper articles on the wall. The headlines were impressive: Major Drug Bust. Bomb Defused. Plot Averted.

Lizzie liked Henry. She couldn't picture him carrying or firing a gun. She recoiled at the possibility that he had a gun in the apartment and stepped back out into the sunlit patio to divert her thoughts.

She was anxious to get started on this beautiful bike-riding day. There wouldn't be too many more days like this before school started in September.

The bicycle had been a tremendous gift. For Henry, his generosity surely released another reminder of Cathy, but to Lizzie, it was an unexpected boon of freedom. She would occasionally ride alone to escape the Wren Haven property, though she was much too far away to meet up with Shelly or anyone else from school.

Today's ride would last only for an hour since Henry had a doctor's appointment to get back for. "Ready, Henry?" she called.

chapter 55

THE FRESH MORNING AIR HAD DONE BOTH HENRY and Lizzie good, getting the blood circulating. They separated at the fork to their respective buildings. Lizzie headed toward Mimi's building but didn't feel like calling it quits yet. She turned herself around and rode toward the main Wren Haven entrance.

There was a roadside vegetable stand a couple of miles away and she would occasionally ride there and bring back a surprise for Mimi of fresh strawberries or blueberries or whatever was just harvested and bursting with the flavor one couldn't get from supermarket fare. So, with the general intent of seeing what was on offer on a beautiful August day Lizzie pedaled leisurely along the paved but not well-traveled road.

A beat-up pickup truck barreled down the road, grazing Lizzie's sleeve and clipping her front tire. She swerved, trying to regain her balance, but still catapulted a couple of feet into a drainage ditch.

Pain radiated through her shoulder.

An attempt to stand produced momentary dizziness and another shooting pain. Finally levering the bike off her hip, she noticed the basket now hung by only one clamp. Blood dripped from an unidentified location, tracing a path down her leg.

The sun in her eyes became a shadow as the silhouette of a young man appeared above her.

With an angry fling of his arm and a scowl of his mouth, he yelled, "What are you doing riding a bicycle in the middle of the road?"

"What am *I* doing? What are *you* doing running me off the road and into a ditch?" Lizzie shot back.

"You were riding down the middle of the road!"

"I was not! If I had been in the middle of the road, I wouldn't have been forced into this ditch!"

Lizzie's logic seemed to get through to him. He reached down to give her a hand up that turned into more of a yank that felt resentful.

"Arrr!" she cried, nearing tears but pushing through the pain to get herself upright.

"Well, you look like you can stand. That probably means nothing's broken."

He glanced back at his truck, now parked a few feet down the road.

"You probably demolished your bike."

"You're the one who was driving like a maniac, probably over the speed limit!"

"I was going to say," he drew the last word out into sarcasm, "leave your bike and if you can walk to the truck, I'll give you a ride to wherever you're going."

He looked at the truck again and gave a condescending grunt. "Never mind. I'll back up for you."

Lizzie stared at the bike. A short-lived gift from Henry! But as she took a step, she realized that tending to the blood and the pain was more important than her bike and more important than being angry at the jerk. She had to be grateful for the ride. Had he not stopped, she might have been stuck there for hours; one more annoyance of not having a damned cell phone.

Lizzie had just shut the passenger door when the idiot driver jackrabbited ahead.

"I live the other way."

"Yeah, well, I've got a delivery to make, and you've made me late, so you're just going to have to wait until I drop off the goods," he spouted, jerking his thumb back toward the bed of the pickup.

Lizzie wanted to make a suitable retort, but checked herself with the reminder that he was taking her back to Wren Haven. One delivery stop didn't have to be such a big deal, she thought, also belatedly wishing he wouldn't kidnap or kill her.

It turned out he was delivering produce to the vegetable stand that had been her destination. But between his running her off the road and his snide attacks, she had lost all interest in any blueberries. Instead, she sat in the cab, sullen and impatient. She could rotate her shoulder somewhat well, and felt grateful for that, at least. There was a box of tissues, dented and discarded, on the floor. She grabbed a few and dabbed at the scrapes and punctures on her calf, stinging her skin and sparking a cynical thought: Who knew how long these tissues had been knocking around this filthy truck? She'd probably get some kind of flesh-eating disease.

Lizzie counted a dozen crates he had unloaded, and she grew increasingly irritated at seeing him chit-chat with the woman minding the fruit stand. He surely had no regard for time. Now he seemed to be sampling the merchandise. She didn't enjoy being dependent on another person like this, especially one like him, a total jerk.

"Okay. Where to?" he demanded as he jumped in and banged the driver's side door shut.

Lizzie gave him directions without looking at him. Her elbow on the door rim, she rested her head on the heel of her hand, and occasionally wiped her leg with a tissue.

He gave a derisive snort as she directed him up the long drive.

"You live at Wren Haven? The old folks' home?"

She didn't even want to respond to such a snarky remark, maintaining her sullen silence.

"Just pull up over here," she said as they approached Mimi's patio door. Descending the cab with a new set of pains, she turned to face him.

"Thank you," she forced herself to say, as she slammed the door shut and limped toward Mimi's patio door.

The next day, a sharp rap on the glass patio door startled both Lizzie and Mimi. This never happened unless it was a security check or someone they expected to arrive by car. Still limping, Lizzie could make out the same silhouette she had seen standing above her the day before. What did he want?

She yanked the glass door open.

He stood with his weight on one foot, hand on his hip. He was not smiling and said only, "I brought your bike back."

"Really?" That was unexpected.

"Yeah, turns out it wasn't all that banged up." He went to the bed of the truck and lifted it out. "I took it for a spin this morning and it's fine. The basket came loose, but I just tightened up the clamp, and it's holding all right."

"Well, thank you," Lizzie said sweetly, meaning it. "I can't tell you how much I appreciate this."

She took the bike, rolled it back and forth to the extent the cement square of the patio would allow, and decided that, indeed, it did not appear damaged. She put down the kickstand and set the bike at the side of the patio. As the guy wiped his forehead, she realized the August sun was scorching.

"Would you like something to drink?"

He nodded.

"Well, have a seat," she offered, gesturing to the patio chairs.

Two minutes later, Lizzie came back with two tall glasses of iced tea.

"What's your name?"

"David."

"I'm Lizzie. I live here with my grandmother."

She took the chair opposite him.

He took a couple of swallows. "Look, I've really got to apologize for yesterday."

Lizzie could feel the flames of annoyance rekindling, but she reminded herself to be gracious and accept his apology.

"I was in the worst mood ever," he said. "And it was probably over something that will seem stupid a year from now."

"Oh?"

"Yeah, it was just over beach day."

"Beach day?"

He took another couple of swallows.

"It's a tradition with the upcoming seniors. Before the start of classes, a lot of kids go to the beach, sort of like an end-of-summer ritual, before the big push with senior year and college applications and all that."

Lizzie nodded, anticipating an explanation for why she had been forced into a ditch and now had bruises on her right leg.

"Anyway, it's next week."

The thoughts in her head increased to an exasperated yell. What on earth could the connection be between his beach day and my bicycle?

He pitched forward to put his elbows on his knees, then dipped his head and looked off to the left where the hedges and flowers were in full summer bloom.

Lizzie waited. Could he be embarrassed about something? She had felt guilty and embarrassed many times in her life; no eye contact looked like a symptom.

His voice was much softer now.

"Yeah. It happened yesterday, about an hour before I drove down that road." He looked down again. "My girlfriend broke up with me." He took a breath before continuing. "So that screws up beach day. And I'd had to beg my boss to rearrange my work schedule to get coverage so I could get the day off and . . ." He shook his head at the futility of his dashed plans.

What could she say to that?

"Yeah," he whispered, almost to himself. Without looking at Lizzie, he drank the rest of his iced tea. "I know it's no excuse." He finished by raising his eyes toward Lizzie, "But that's what happened. And I'm sorry you got hurt."

He glanced at the bandage covering the injury on her right leg and the bruise that was peeking out from beneath it, grimacing and sucking air through pursed lips.

"And I'm sorry I was such a jerk to you. You didn't deserve that. You didn't deserve to get the brunt of my anger for my girlfriend's breaking up with me. I'm really sorry."

Lizzie saw his vulnerability and didn't want to make him feel worse.

Giving him a serene smile, she said, "I'll live."

David drained the last drops from his glass.

"How long were you going with her?"

"Year and a half."

He studied the patio ceiling for a moment before continuing. A definite note of disgust entered his voice.

"The one thing that kept me going all summer with this horrible job running around with the blueberries was Sarah." He looked at Lizzie. "That's her name, Sarah. So, Sarah and the beach day coming up." He took a breath. "Now Sarah's gone and beach day? Well, I guess I'll just skip it and spend the day with the blueberries."

David stood. "Sorry again. I didn't mean to dump all this on you. Thanks for the iced tea."

"I'll do it," Lizzie said flatly.

"Excuse me?"

"I'll do it. I'll go with you. To beach day. Pretend to be your girlfriend."

David blinked and looked a bit disoriented.

"She'll be there? Sarah? At the beach?"

"Probably."

"Will she be there with anyone else?"

David rubbed his lips with his thumb, looking down. "I don't know. Maybe. Possibly."

Lizzie leaned back in her chair, her thoughts smug. She hadn't spent the best years of her life creating Miss Coolness for nothing.

"Then you need to go. Show up. Like you're moving on. With or without her. And like you're not going to let her defeat you."

David looked amazed. "You'd do that? After what I did to you?"

He gestured to the bandage.

"Why not? It's just one day out of my life." Knowing she could get off the property for a day delighted her. It would keep her mind off the reason she lived at Wren Haven. Despite whose fault the accident was, it was thoughtful of him to retrieve her bike, ensure its functionality, repair the basket, and deliver it to Wren Haven. And a nice guy like this shouldn't have to suffer on account of a girlfriend who clearly didn't deserve him. Miss Coolness was back in action.

chapter 56

Lizzie had examined her swimsuit and judged it to be in good enough shape for beach day. The worst wound had healed enough that she didn't need the bandages. David stood at the top of the sand drift, surveying the beach from behind his mirrored sunglasses.

Lizzie put her sunglasses on as well. "Which one?"

"I'm looking." David continued scanning for another few seconds. "Okay. Over to the left. Blue two-piece suit. There are a few big towels together and there are like four, no, five, kids over there. She's the blonde."

Lizzie scanned right and then left, as if trying to find a place on the beach for them, and then she paid attention to the area David indicated.

"Okay. Got her."

A half-hour later, settled at mid-beach, Lizzie kept watch, propped on her elbow when the reviled Sarah pranced toward them, evidently heading for the snack bar or restroom. Lizzie nailed the timing.

"Daaavey, let me put some more lotion on you. I don't want you getting burned."

When they judged Sarah was out of earshot, they both snickered behind their hands.

"Did you practice that?" David asked, deeply appreciative.

Lizzie rolled back and lay sunward.

"Comes naturally," she quipped and enjoyed a moment of smugness.

It turned out to be a good day. David introduced her to his friends, an unexpected benefit because his school was conveniently closer to Wren Haven than hers.

And he was undeniably a new friend. He had put Mimi's phone number in his cell phone contacts and she had written his number down for whenever she got her cell working again.

chapter 57

AS RELUCTANT AS LIZZIE WAS TO ADMIT IT, THE DAYS OF THE August calendar were now in double digits. Summer would wind down in a few weeks. If she was serious about trying out for the swim team, she needed to get some practice time in.

Delivering prescriptions and hanging with James could only consume so many hours, and she'd already devoured the best of the thrillers in the Wren Haven library. No more excuses.

She suited up in the locker room, gasping under the freezing cold shower, and then made her way out to the pool. The tile cold beneath her bare feet, Lizzie draped her towel over one of the lounge chairs surrounding the pool and looked around. She smiled, realizing she had the Olympic-size pool all to herself.

Just then, a stalwart-looking woman approached from the small side office.

"Hi, I'm Marge Perry. I'm the swim manager and run the cardio exercise program."

"Hello, I'm Lizzie Olsen." Lizzie shook her hand.

"Oh, so you're Mimi Kidder's granddaughter. Mimi said you might try out for the swim team this year. I guess that's why you're here."

News travels fast around here, Lizzie thought. She acknowledged the manager's question with a nod and said, "I know I've got to improve my time."

"Well, I'd be happy to give you a hand with that. Go ahead. Let's see what you've got."

So, with goggles in place, Lizzie made an okay dive into the deep end. After the first couple of laps, she pushed her goggles back and rubbed the remaining chlorinated drops of water from her eyes.

"You need more even pacing, Lizzie. Strong and steady. Go again.

After another couple of laps, Lizzie hauled herself up onto the pool's edge. The chlorine that had seeped under her goggles made Marge's advancing figure hazy.

Marge asked, "How'd you feel out there?"

"Like I need to do better?"

"I'd say that's accurate. But don't worry. It's within the realm of the possible. Remember that and you'll be fine." Marge gave the air a forceful poke. "Tomorrow. 3:00."

Marge walked off toward her side office.

So, every day, six days a week, Lizzie reported to the pool at 3:00 and Marge put her through her paces. As the new school year drew nearer, Lizzie grew stronger.

chapter 58

With a tad more confidence, both physically and mentally, Lizzie began her junior year. The bank account she opened over the summer now held a decent amount of money from the small tasks she did for Wren Haven residents. At the risk of pride, Lizzie realized she had enough financial control to buy a gorgeous pair of deep mulberry corduroys, a coordinating sweater, and a fresh pair of jeans for the new school year. Altogether, she entered the high school building with a bit more stride in her step and her chin raised.

On the first Thursday of the new year, Lizzie leaned against the glass case displaying all the athletic awards the school had won over the years. Half-listening to Shelly's latest chit-chat, something in the trophy case caught her eye.

"Shel, talk to you tomorrow," Lizzie said as her way of dismissal.

On the left side of the first shelf of the trophy case she saw a small, framed newspaper article. It was yellowing and had a headline declaring, "Local Girl Makes Olympic Swim Team." The first paragraph read, "Recent graduate Margaret Nelson learned yesterday that she has earned a place on the US Olympic swim team." Lizzie didn't read the rest of the story, more intrigued by the accompanying photograph. Unmistakably, the picture was of a much younger, smiling Marge. Who could have foreseen that she'd have a bona fide Olympic athlete to coach her at the Wren Haven pool? Incredible.

Lizzie signed up for Spanish—so much easier than French—and was eager to tackle accounting. She wound up sitting next to Jeffrey Snyder in history class. They exchanged comments and quips and built a friendship.

After the summer hiatus, she enjoyed getting reacquainted with Rosa. She still pulled up to the front of the school with her characteristic swoosh. But, contrary to when they had started this routine last winter, whenever Lizzie felt one of the guys checking her out, she looked back. She even allowed herself to coin a new phrase: Enhanced Coolness. Who could have predicted it would be Mimi who would create the Enhanced Coolness derived from finding Rosa for her to ride with?

According to Rosa, Luisa had graduated from beauty school and had landed an excellent job at an upscale salon. She was building her own clientele and had hopes of becoming the acting manager when the current manager went on maternity leave in a few months.

"Good for her," Lizzie said sincerely. "I'm happy for her." Then, thinking back, she asked, "Does she still have the same hair as when I met her?"

"Oh, no, long gone. Where she work now, she have professional image to maintain, you know."

Lizzie mentally echoed the comment, her thoughts exactly.

"Now her hair all black. She look more like me." Rosa flashed one of her bright white smiles.

Returning to the routine of riding the Wren Haven bus in the afternoon, Lizzie stopped by George's customary lair in the lobby.

"How's the new school year treating you, cutie pie?"

"Fine, so far. But I miss the summer already." Changing the subject, she added, "Janna was my partner for the fashion show."

"I know. I saw you both. And you both did an amazing job."

"You were there? I didn't see you. Of course, there was a crowd of people, a big audience."

"Of course I was there! I had to see Janna in the show, didn't I?" George smiled from ear to ear, obviously proud of Janna.

Lizzie was a tad perplexed. The first time she had met—if you could call it that—Janna, it hadn't been a cordial encounter. Based on George's apparent eagerness to leave his apartment—evidenced by the stack of papers at his feet—Lizzie assumed George's life with a dragon was pure misery.

Searching for her most diplomatic vocabulary, Lizzie said, "It surprised me to see her taking part. She didn't strike me as the type for that sort of event."

"Are you kidding? Neatness, precision, timing? That's her comfort zone!"

She must have looked confused because George added, "She's OCD, you know."

"OCD?"

George nodded, pushing out his lower lip and slipping into medical man mode. "Obsessive-compulsive disorder."

Taking in Lizzie's pitying look, he added, "Oh, it's okay. She's only mildly affected." He grinned. "And there's an upside. Haven't you ever noticed how my shirts are always perfectly ironed? As long as I don't drive her crazy with my newspapers," he gestured to his usual morass of newsprint, "we get along fine. She's my gal!" he finished with another grin.

Lizzie walked a little more slowly than usual to Mimi's. It was clear now why Janna had been upset when George started showing her his old documents and it explained her fussing over her before the show. Lizzie had misjudged someone before, but this was the first time she consciously acknowledged doing so. She'd have to remember that.

* * *

September's start would have been satisfactory if not for one small thing. It was so small that Lizzie questioned whether her imagination was running wild. It had happened the day Mimi had taken her back-to-school shopping, the day she had found the fabulous corduroy pants. Mimi hadn't filled the entire tank at the gas station.

"Just twenty dollars' worth, please."

The statement held no significance. But later that day, there was something else. They had been in the women's wear department of the mall's largest department store when Lizzie had noticed the sale sign.

"Look, Mimi, all the swimwear is on sale. Didn't you say you needed a new suit for water aerobics?"

"Oh, no, dear. The one I have is fine."

Once again, Lizzie had given little thought to it, but there had been no offer of a snack before they left the mall. And Mimi had just canceled her subscription to that *People* magazine she seemed to like so much. It felt like that night after the barbeque long ago when she pieced together her parents' financial situation. Each incident in isolation was inconsequential but taken together, they gave Lizzie an uneasy suspicion.

chapter 59

Getting ready for Sunday brunch, Lizzie grabbed her messenger bag, the one big enough to hold her laptop.

"Planning to grab a handful of cookies from the dining hall, dear?" Mimi asked.

"Maybe I'll go over to the library afterward," seemed an adequate answer.

Lizzie scanned the brunch crowd for Mac. Happy to spot him, she waved him down to join their table.

Ten minutes later, Lizzie suggested, "Mac, care for a game of pool after brunch?"

"Sure. Why not?"

Mac was finishing faster than the others, so Lizzie matched his pace to leave with him.

Apart from the buffet brunch, Sundays tended to be quiet at Wren Haven, popular for both on-campus and off-campus family visits. The wing devoted to activities reflected the quietude.

As they walked down one corridor, Mac remarked, "We'll probably have to take the dust cover off the pool table and look for where they keep the chalk for the cues."

A half minute later, Lizzie ducked into the craft room they were passing. Mac followed her with a quizzical look on his face.

"It's okay. I don't really want a game of pool."

"No?"

"No." Lizzie pulled a couple of chairs over to a card table and flung her bag on the surface. "Have a seat."

Lizzie pulled her laptop out and fired it up.

While waiting for it to boot, she said, "Mac, you told me you were a finance guy."

"Yes, I was for many years."

"I need you to help me." Lizzie took a moment to open a document and then swung the screen toward Mac. "Can you tell me whether Mimi is poor?"

Mac took his glasses out of his breast pocket and put them on, scrunched his brow, and then looked at the screen. When what he was seeing dawned on him, he immediately pushed it away.

"Lizzie, this is Mimi's bank statement. It's a very personal thing. I shouldn't be seeing this."

"Mac, I'm worried. Mimi's been clipping coupons more often than usual. She's canceled her favorite magazine subscription. She makes sure I have everything I need, but I don't think she's bought so much as a lipstick for herself since I can't remember when."

"Still, Lizzie . . ." He turned his head to the side with a distasteful grimace.

"Mac, if she needs cash, I've got some. I opened a bank account over the summer. There's something in the way she's been acting, and I can't put my finger on it. But it feels uncomfortable, and this is the only way I can think of to see if I'm right."

"Have you asked her? Have you thought of just saying, 'Mimi, are we in financial straits?'"

Lizzie's shoulders dropped.

"And what do you think she'd say? 'Why yes, Lizzie, I was just scraping by until you came to live with me and now I'm bankrupt.'"

"Right. I see what you mean. Still, Lizzie, I don't think . . ." He paused and rubbed the back of his neck. "You know, invasion of privacy?"

"You sound like Mike."

"Do I? The way you just said it, I'm not sure if that's good or bad."

"I'm just worried, Mac."

He folded his arms and shook his head.

"You know, Lizzie, Mimi's pretty sharp. Don't you think she's got a grip on her finances?"

She cut him off with, "I think there is some more money I could get," not going into the sale of her parents' house. "And I'm almost sixteen. I could get a job after school."

Mac made a calming motion with his hand and pulled the laptop closer.

"Lizzie, I'm sure it's nothing, but if it will put your mind at ease, I'll take a look."

He adjusted his glasses and gave her another glance.

"Mind you, this is not right, and I don't feel good about it."

"Thanks, Mac." A sigh of relief escaped as she leaned her forehead on her fingertips, her elbow on the table.

He read for several minutes.

"Well, I give you credit for raising a red flag," Mac said. "She had an overdraft this past month." He read some more. "She's got an overdraft line set up at the bank so everything's fine, or will be if . . ."

Mac worked, thinking out loud. "Well, I can see some automatic transfers coming in, probably some pension payments and Social Security." His observations faded to softer murmurings. "And I know what it costs to live here, so some of these debits make sense." He glanced at Lizzie. "What's this line item for another bank? Do you know?"

"Credit card."

"Okay."

Mac continued reading the numbers on the page from one line item to the next.

"Well, this is curious. Certain transfers would usually be considered normal, such as internet, cable, electric, and other basic utilities."

"So?"

"Utilities are all covered in Wren Haven's monthly maintenance fee. She shouldn't be paying them twice. Do you have her prior months statements?"

Lizzie nodded and showed him the tabs she had organized.

"Let's see if there's a pattern. The expenses in question show up in August, then in July, but not before then. Mimi doesn't own any other property, does she? Something she would have bought this past spring?"

"No, not that I'm aware of."

"Does Mimi make other payments electronically or by check?"

"By check. That much I know. Anytime she writes a check, she leaves me a note about who it was to, how much, and the date. I enter it into the computer software I set up for her."

"Well, here's one that is not a check. It's an electronic transfer, and it looks like some kind of subscription, a fairly expensive one, to Scientific Survey."

Mac looked at Lizzie for confirmation.

"Is she receiving a new magazine or an electronic subscription of some sort?"

"No, that doesn't sound right." Lizzie stood and began pacing. "In fact, she canceled her favorite magazine. That's part of what got me worried. And there was another newspaper that she used to get but, now that you mention it, I haven't seen that one around for a while, either."

"Let's see. *Scientific Survey* also starts showing up over the summer. Let's go back a little further. Oh, now this is interesting. Here's another electronic payment, not to *Scientific Survey* but to Scientific Membership, back in June to the tune of $1,950. That could easily be what kicked her into this credit cycle."

Mac returned to his scrutinizing.

"Well, one good thing is the credit card transfers don't seem to have had a major bump up in recent months. Lizzie, monitor this one; see whether it goes up substantially on future statements."

Mac closed the laptop and sat back, looking at the lid. "When the bank statements come in, does Mimi look them over?"

"No, not since I got the computer program running for her. Now she just hands me the statements when they come in and I reconcile them to the bank downloads."

Mac raised his eyebrows with a slow intake of breath.

"Mimi said her eyes were failing, so she was happy for me to take over reconciling the bank statements. She'd been doing them by hand, and I half think that she just didn't want the challenge of learning something new. When I download from the bank, the computer program automatically fills in any missing entries."

"Do you remember when the last bank statement came in?"

"A couple days ago." Lizzie tilted her head back to stare at the ceiling, recalling the scene. "It was after school, so late afternoon. Mimi brought the mail in with her after her book club meeting. She shuffled through the stack of mail, then opened the bank envelope, glanced at the statement, shook her head, and handed it to me."

"So you don't think she went through all the line items to see whether there was anything out of the ordinary?"

"No, she just took it out of the envelope and looked at it quickly."

"She could have just glimpsed the bottom line?"

Lizzie nodded, then shut her eyes, again recollecting the scene. "Yes, then she handed the statement to me. I think she made a comment like, 'Glad you're here to do this. It's tough for me to read this fine printing anymore.' I finished my homework, and after dinner I booted up my laptop and did the reconciliation."

Mac nodded. "Well, that fits. You're sure you haven't seen any *Scientific Survey* magazines around the apartment?"

"I'm positive."

"And you don't think she's getting something electronically, an electronic newsletter, for example?"

"No. She hardly touches either of our computers."

Mac remained silent for a bit, then said, "Well, there's something absolutely not right about keeping Mimi out of the loop on something that is essentially her business, her private business. On the other hand, there is something not quite right about troubling her with something that we—you and I—don't even know is a problem. We only think there might be a problem." He stared at the laptop in contemplation, then said, "Let me have a word with Henry."

As Lizzie snuggled under the covers that night, she could already feel herself falling asleep. Mac giving her a hand with the banking issue was such a deep relief that she felt lighter; light enough that she might start floating up to the ceiling. Thanking Mac for his help seemed utterly inadequate, since she wouldn't even have known where to start in analyzing bank statements. She quietly chuckled over her naivete last April. She had thought all it would take to survive was riding her bike to the supermarket. Thank goodness for a friend like Mac. On that note of comfort, she drifted into a deep sleep.

chapter 60

"Pants or skirt?" Mimi held one of each up at waist height.

Lizzie looked up from where she lay stomach-down across Mimi's bed, flipping through a back issue of *People*.

"The skirt is nice, but I think the blouse would look better with pants. But for pants, I think you want a real black and those are closer to a charcoal gray."

Mimi pulled another pair out of the closet. "How about these?"

Lizzie scrutinized. "They look a little long. Are you going to wear them with heels or flats? You could try the black patent spikes."

"Heavens, no, I couldn't wear those!"

With one bounce, Lizzie swung herself off the bed and over to the closet. Squinting a bit, she reached in and pulled out a third pair of pants. She made a note to call the maintenance department to get an LED light in Mimi's closet.

"Here. Try these. I bet they'll be perfect. They look like a much better cut." She scanned the shoe rack. "And try these pumps. These heels are only, like, an inch."

Lizzie held the pants and shoes up to Mimi's waist to compare them to the black and white print blouse she wore. "Red-carpet worthy!" Miss Coolness strikes again.

"Thank you, darling. I think you're quite right."

"Where are you going?"

"Out to dinner with Herb. There's a new restaurant in town that we've been wanting to try." Mimi was still assessing the outfit in her full-length mirror. "You can manage dinner in the dining hall on your own, can't you?"

"Sure. No problem."

Lizzie went to the desk and opened her laptop, looked over her shoulder to make sure that Mimi was still in her own bedroom, then emailed Mac: Herb is taking Mimi out to dinner this evening. She opened her geometry book next to the computer, glancing every few minutes at incoming email. She hoped he had his cell phone on.

A couple of minutes later, she got a reply: Okay, I'll tell Henry.

Herb and Mimi waved to Mac and Henry as they departed the Wren Haven lobby for their evening out. Two-and-a-half minutes later, Lizzie opened the door to Mimi's apartment.

"C'mon in, guys."

Henry and Mac gave each other a quick look and a nod.

Henry asked, "Where does Mimi keep her checkbook? And where do you keep your laptop?"

"Both in here." Lizzie ushered them into her sofa bedroom, which she was glad to have remembered to tidy up.

Henry sat at the desk, opening the drawers. He handed Mac the checkbook with its paper register.

Two minutes later, Henry made a one-word statement, "Bingo."

He held up Mimi's tattered address book. One page under the P tab contained a list of cryptic lines in three different handwritings. The last entry in a rounded hand stood out in clear blue ink, unlike the prior lines, some of which were in pencil and some in ink, many looking rather faded.

Henry held the page open. "Lizzie, did you write this?"

Lizzie stepped over to Henry, looked over his shoulder and nodded. "Yes, the last one. That's the password to the RealBank account."

"And the others?"

"The ones above are Mimi's entries. The ones at the top, the ones looking pretty faded, would be my grandfather's handwriting."

Henry had a couple of small gadgets he planted so no one would notice them: one inside the desk lamp Herb had given Lizzie and the other above the door jamb.

Their work was done.

chapter 61

A WEEK LATER, HENRY CAUGHT UP WITH MAC AT THE mailboxes.

"Morning, Mac," Henry said casually as he inserted his key into his box.

"Morning, Henry," Mac said equally casually without looking up from the junk mail he was sorting through. In a lower voice, Mac asked, "Find anything?"

Henry glanced over his shoulder at the handful of residents milling around.

"Walk with me. Let's go outside."

The two set out on the gravel path toward the jogging route, empty this late in the morning.

"Not a blessed thing, Mac."

Mac stopped short and, with a half-turn toward Henry, dropped his shoulders and exhaled in defeat.

"Nothing?"

They continued walking, hearing the crunch of the gravel beneath their feet.

"No, nothing. And I watched I can't tell you how many hours of nanny-cam. There were a couple of possibilities, but they fizzled out."

"Is that right?"

"Yeah, a couple of maintenance guys came in to fix a curtain rod in that room, but they came and went without touching anything on the desk. The next day, a man in a fire department uniform entered, but he was only there for an inspection. He just looked around quickly and left. My best candidate was the housekeeper. She would know the apartment well, have the confidence of the homeowner, and she seemed to do her work when both Mimi and Lizzie were out of the apartment."

At this, Mac gawped at Henry. "Marietta?" With a lighter tone, Mac quipped, "It's always the maid, right?"

"No," Henry said, "actually not. It's usually someone with regular access to the victim's finances." He stopped walking and looked intently at Mac to make sure he had his attention. "Usually someone like Lizzie."

Mac's jaw dropped. "Lizzie? No, I can't believe that."

Henry, still circumspect, watched Mac make a little circle, fairly stomping on the gravel.

Henry watched Mac's every minute move, his thoughts informed by decades of carrying the gold shield. Forget friendship—objectively, he was probably the smartest guy he'd ever met and he knew Lizzie better than anyone else at Wren Haven. Maybe even better than Mimi. If the suggestion that Lizzie could be the guilty party at all rang true to him, this was when it would show.

"For God's sake, Henry, Lizzie's the one who brought this mess to our attention."

"It wouldn't be the first time the culprit put himself—or herself—in the center of the investigation, intending to appear innocent to deflect attention from themselves."

Mac kicked at the gravel.

Henry watched Mac for another moment and detected not a flicker of misgiving from him.

"Fortunately, Mac, I agree with you. Unless something to the contrary comes to light, I think we can rule her out."

Mac gave a sigh of relief and nodded as they resumed walking. "And you're sure it wasn't Marietta?"

"No dice. She didn't open any of the drawers, and the only thing she did with the laptop was lift it up to dust underneath."

"Can't say I'm disappointed, Henry, because Marietta cleans my apartment too."

They made their way back to the lobby.

"Where do we go from here?"

Henry chafed his hands against the fall air and then put them in his pockets as they walked.

"Well, I went to visit Emma Jeffries at the bank. You know her?"

"Sure. Gracious lady. Sharp too."

"She took it rather well, considering."

"Considering what?"

"Well, considering I had no factual evidence to give her, she reminded me she's bound by client confidentiality regulations. That means we couldn't have a conversation about this. All I could do was point her in the right direction and tell her where to look. I suggested she review all the entries you flagged."

"That's it? I thought for sure you could make some phone calls to your detective buddies like I see on TV."

Henry gave a one-shouldered shrug and a frown.

"Well, I did. I had a friendly chat with a few old friends. What I learned was if we want to take official action, we'll need a subpoena." Henry's lower lip jutted out and he gave a short shake of his head. "Given that there's only a few thousand dollars at stake . . . well, you can see it's a matter of proportion."

Henry looked down and slowly shook his head as they walked. "The bigger issue is not getting Mimi upset over something we don't even know for a fact has occurred. We only suspect foul play."

Mac kicked a few stones on the walkway. "And how could I possibly tell Mimi we even know as much as we do? What would I say? 'Your granddaughter roped me into snooping around in your personal finances. And then I pulled a couple of other people in on it and now half of Wren Haven thinks you're not competent enough to look after your own affairs.'"

Mac looked up at the sky and let a breath escape before turning to Henry in exasperation. "So, Henry, not a blessed thing is going to happen? Someone is going to continue helping themselves to Mimi's assets?"

"I wouldn't be so sure, Mac."

For the first time, something like an impish smile curled Henry's lips.

"I said that Emma and I couldn't have a conversation, which is true. I spoke, and she listened. What I will tell you is that we were behind closed doors. She took notes. She treated me seriously. I think it helped she knew a bit about my prior life."

Mac nodded. "Oh, so back when you opened your own account she got you to talking about yourself, did she?"

"You got it, Mac. She's pretty shrewd. And, if you think about it, she's been running that branch like forever, which must mean it has a spotless record. I tell you what I'd be thinking if I were Emma Jeffries. First, I'd be thinking, 'I've had a couple of new hires in the last year. One of them always seems to be out sick or running five minutes late. And if a trail leads back to a member of my staff, it could tarnish any career prospects I might have. I'd much rather get credit for identifying and halting the fraud.' Second, I'd think, 'My branch is in a retirement community, and if there is any fraud going on, I want to prevent other customers from being victimized. I wouldn't want small dollar amounts turning into larger amounts that could draw the attention of others, including the press.'"

Mac nodded. "Makes sense. She's got a career risk, and the bank has a reputational risk."

"And if you know Emma, she can be pretty persuasive. I'd be willing to bet she's already turned it over to the bank's investigative unit along with some pretty forcefully expressed concerns. They're a national bank and have a sophisticated security operation. That much I found out from one of my old buddies who's now in private industry. He also mentioned the size of the initial transfer you identified, the $1,950 one, seemed deliberately chosen to fly under the radar of what could get tagged as suspicious. A bank employee might know what that threshold amount is."

Henry glanced in Mac's direction again. "If they're able to identify anything suspicious, they'll turn it over to law enforcement. That's the standard operating procedure."

Mac exhaled with relief. "I was worried I'd swatted a hornet's nest and possibly for no reason. But what was I going to do? Ignore fifteen-year-old Lizzie who was reaching out to me? Let Mimi's accounts get depleted and see the two of them impoverished?"

"I think the bank will take it from here. Rest easy. You've done everything you can."

"Do you still have those cameras in there?"

"I told Lizzie how to disengage them, and she's already given them back to me.

"I appreciate everything you've done, Hank. I'm sure Lizzie does too."

"You're the one who spotted something fishy, Mac. And it took you, what? Ten minutes?"

Mac threw his head back and laughed.

"Well, maybe fifteen."

chapter 62

"It's getting cold," Lizzie said as she got ready to meet Rosa one morning.

"Yes," Mimi said without looking up from her copy of the *Wren Haven News*. "The leaves are turning."

"Mimi," Lizzie ventured. How could she do this without getting into another fight? She had to admit the last one was her fault. "I'm going to need my winter clothes, at least my wool sweaters and the heavier coat I usually wear to school in the winter. I also need my boots."

Mimi peered over the top of her reading glasses. "You know that everything is stored away."

Lizzie nodded. "Yes."

"Okay. Saturday, then."

Lizzie gave Mimi a quick kiss and left.

* * *

The first Saturday in October was a beautiful fall day with colorful trees and a clear blue sky when spectacular color from every tree and a deep sky-blue sky would usually make one feel uplifted and glad to be alive—unless one were on the way to reopen a wound that had slowly been healing for the last eight months.

As the storage unit's chrome door slid up with a clatter, Mimi lightly touched Lizzie's forearm. Lizzie had prepared herself for a rush of pain. However, at first glance her only sensation was, oddly, a familial comfort from seeing the fabric of the living room sofa, her stuffed rabbit sitting on the chair at her father's desk, the dining room table with its chairs turned upside down, and a tattered picnic basket. Familiar, and family-related, but out of context.

She saw wardrobe boxes labeled *Clothes*, and she began to open them. One was from her own closet, along with a few smaller boxes. Together, Lizzie and Mimi gathered the clothing items Lizzie wanted, and they loaded them into Mimi's car.

"Do you want this ottoman?" Lizzie asked. "It's larger than the one you have."

Mimi looked it over, used her foot to push it on its casters, and then said, "No, dear, I don't think so. It would take up more floor space and I'm used to the one I have."

Lizzie continued rummaging around, running her hands over one thing and another, and then she lifted a lamp.

"Edith was saying at dinner last night that she had broken a lamp and needed another one. She could have this one."

"Nice thought, honey," was Mimi's vague and unenthusiastic reply. Lizzie replaced it where it had been.

They continued looking at various items, considering possible uses for everything from throw rugs to potato mashers.

Then Lizzie squatted in front of the dresser that had been hers. She was at eye level with a gash that had been there forever, an accidental dent from when she and Shelly had been fooling around with roller skates a few years ago. The bottom drawer had always been hard to open. She wriggled it open after a few tries, pawed through the junk inside, then shoved it shut. She contemplated taking the dresser with them but wondered if it made sense to even haul it to Wren Haven. No, the bedroom furniture her parents had bought her when she was eleven would not be making the trip.

Finally, Mimi went to a corner and lifted a small box. This had to be her parents' ashes.

"Maybe we should take this?" Mimi sounded frail. "I put it here because at the time . . . "

Mimi lightly rubbed the cardboard surface. Then she held the box against her chest, staring at the cement floor.

Lizzie put her arm around Mimi's shoulders. Mimi seemed a half-inch smaller, somehow, and was close to tears.

"The funeral home called and asked me to come and collect . . . collect this."

Hold it together, Lizzie, she told herself. You can be the grown-up. This had to have been difficult. Not only had Mimi had to drive . . . how far? To where? To identify the . . . the bodies. She'd had to decide on the cremations, organize the viewing, visit the church, and then collect the ashes. By herself. Driving again to the funeral home, by herself, while Lizzie was sitting comfortably in English class or hanging out with Shelly. "You did what you had to do, Mimi," Lizzie said while gently rubbing Mimi's upper arm. "You did great. Couldn't have done better." Lizzie gave her an extra little side hug. Say it, she told herself. Say what you're thinking or someday you will regret that you didn't, and you'll lie in bed at night and . . . "I appreciate how you shielded me from so much."

Mimi leaned into Lizzie's shoulder and cried. Lizzie kept her arm around Mimi. *Hold it together, Lizzie,* she thought.

The tears eventually stopped, but Mimi held the box even tighter.

Lizzie's thoughts were clear and deliberate. Mimi shouldn't have to do everything. She could do this. She could make a decision. "We can take them," she said.

She stroked her grandmother's hair, now more of an all-over

silver than when Lizzie had first moved in with her.

"Don't you have a storage locker at Wren Haven?" Lizzie asked. Mimi nodded.

"Okay. We can keep them there until we get things sorted out." Lizzie gently pried the box from Mimi's hands. "You need to drive. I can hold them."

Mimi exhaled. She closed her eyes for a moment and then smiled at Lizzie. Her steps toward the car were almost visibly lighter. Lizzie hid her emotions but not because she was brave. They had both known they would have to face this day and confront so many reminders. The tears were gone, or at least suppressed, for the remainder of the afternoon.

They did celebrate one discovery: a small, framed photograph of Lizzie with her parents when she was three years old. Jane had kept it on her dresser. Mimi slipped the picture into the pocket of her sweater.

At the end of the day, besides the ashes and her clothes, there was little else Lizzie could rationalize hauling back to Wren Haven. She did tuck one semi-nice watercolor under her arm in a last-minute decision. Lizzie trusted that whatever pieces of jewelry Mimi had taken were likely the only valuable ones there were, and they were safe in Mimi's jewelry box. A chest of silver existed somewhere, passed down from her father's family, but they had yet to discover its whereabouts.

Two minutes into the return trip home, Lizzie asked, "Mimi, as long as we're down this way, would you mind making an extra stop?"

"No, of course not."

"Okay. At the next light, make a right."

Another minute later, Lizzie asked, "Can you see it? The red sign. There's a bank on the right. I have an account there I need to close."

chapter 63

THE RIDE TOWARD WREN HAVEN WAS SOLEMN UNTIL Mimi broke the silence.

"You'll never guess what happened yesterday," she remarked, while giving Lizzie the first optimistic look of the day.

"What?"

"The bank called. It was Mrs. Jeffries. Do you know her?"

"Sure, she's the one who opened my account for me over the summer."

"She was very pleasant and mentioned some irregularities in my account and said they would transfer all my money into a new account. She also mentioned you would need to change your login credentials."

Relief shot through Lizzie at this news. Had she been alone, she would have let out a whoop of joy. As it was, she silently thanked Mac, Henry, and Mrs. Jeffries for sparing her grandmother from insufficiency and humiliation.

"That is excellent news," Lizzie responded, trying for a neutral tone.

"It sure is. Feel like stopping at that nice ice cream place up the road?"

Whether it was due to dealing with the storage locker ordeal or closing her bank account, Lizzie experienced a sense of resolution. They were quiet and less sad as they sat across from each other eating ice cream sundaes. It felt nice to decompress a little after the stress they had both just been through. Although it had not felt incredibly stressful as they sorted through the detritus of lost lives, at some level, apprehension and loss were colliding just below the surface for both of them.

Lizzie took her time eating the ice cream. Today she was intensely aware of the deliciousness of the melting vanilla and the smooth, round shape of the spoon, conducive to a more relaxed rumination.

"Does it cost a lot to maintain that storage locker?" Lizzie asked.

"Not a lot but, yes, there is a monthly fee."

It made little sense to Lizzie to hold on to all that stuff until she graduated college, especially her childhood bedroom furniture. And all the items her parents had collected over the years? No, she wouldn't want any of that, either.

They were both contemplative for a stretch until Mimi spoke again. "It really is all yours, dear. Do you have any thoughts about what you'd like to do with it? Do you want to try eBay?"

"Think we could make much?"

Mimi looked down at her dish and played with the whipped cream, seeming to consider her answer before speaking.

"In all honesty, no, I don't think so."

"Hmm. That's what I think too."

Twenty minutes later Mimi put the heat on in the car.

"Maybe all that stuff doesn't have to go to waste," Lizzie said.

"Because?" Mimi responded, trying to make a left-hand turn

while she had the light.

"We could donate it all to the Surprise Shoppe. Madame Lacroix can hold an auction."

Mimi raised her eyebrows, giving Lizzie a humorous frown-smile. "Oh, yes, I can just see this. Madame dragging the boxes around, breaking a fingernail. Herb plugging the blender in to see whether it works."

Lizzie slapped her thighs and let a laugh escape as she realized the absurdity of the scene.

"Or how about Amos sitting on one of the living room chairs and it collapsing underneath him?"

Their laughter was effortless as they headed toward home.

In the end, practicality won out. There were people who did this sort of work for a living. Besides, Lizzie had exams to pass, and Mimi preferred water aerobics to dealing with eBay.

Lizzie hung the watercolor above the sofa bed. On the nights when she couldn't sleep and felt her world falling apart, she imagined her parents comforting her with an invisible shield. Like a celestial vacuum, the top of the watercolor frame sucked in any sadness or frustration. Seconds later an invisible blanket would unfurl from the bottom of the frame and gently drift down to cover her. Then she would sleep.

chapter 64

LIZZIE AWOKE EARLY FOR IT BEING A SATURDAY. EVEN more unusually, she awoke restless. Restless for what, she didn't know. Just restless, as if a frisson of electricity was dancing across her shoulders. She dressed in jeans and a light sweater, perfect for an unpredictable October day that hinted at spring instead of fall.

She poured milk into her bowl of cornflakes, listening to its fresh crackling in the quiet apartment. Mimi still slept. Lizzie pulled a spoon out of the silverware drawer but did not sit to eat. Instead, holding the bowl, she walked barefoot toward the sliding glass door and stared out at the parking lot. She ate, standing up, after noticing some movement in the distance. Was that Silas in his golf cart? Maybe. It disappeared around the corner of another Wren Haven building. No one was in the playground over to the left, just visible beyond the rise in the fading grass. A flock of geese flew above, headed south for the winter. She continued to gaze, allowing the pinkish cast of the rising sun, the quiet surroundings, and the regular geometry of the Wren Haven buildings to hypnotize her.

She stowed her dish and spoon in the dishwasher, brushed her teeth, and wondered what this current of energy was that was making her itch to do something. She picked up the phone and called Henry.

"Henry? It's Lizzie. I didn't get you up too early, did I? Good. I thought you might be up. Feel like a ride?"

Bicycling so early on a Saturday morning was perfect. She'd be able to work off whatever this idle energy was. Soon the temperature would drop and bicycling would be a less attractive proposition.

They rode side by side.

"Henry, I never thanked you for everything you did about the banking problem. It was nice of you to spend all that time and I wouldn't have known where to start."

"Eh, it's not a closed case yet, but at least you don't need to worry about anything else at this point." He quickly glanced at Lizzie. "Mac mentioned you were worried about having to dip into your savings or maybe get a job. I don't think you need to worry about that anymore. That's the important thing. Just concentrate on your grades. It won't be long before you need to think about college."

He emphasized the last word with a grin and raised eyebrows.

Henry always had some alternative route to introduce her to, and today was no exception. A half hour after exiting the Wren Haven grounds, they crested a hill and, both out of breath, put their bikes to the side and rested in a beautiful clearing with an incredible view.

"We're on state property here," Henry explained.

"It's beautiful."

"Mmm-hmm," Henry murmured, nodding. "Over to the south," he said with an expansive sweep of his arm, "is the original Whitely farm."

"Whitely?"

"Yup, the family who first settled this area with some sustainable commerce. I think the property is still being farmed. At least it looks that way from here. Apples, I think."

Lizzie leaned back on her palms, glad to stretch her legs out after the ride. She wondered if that's where David's blueberries came from.

They sat on the grass, taking it all in, the sharp pine scent a cleanser for nasal passages and lungs. Lizzie looked more closely at the immediate space. The drying grass prickled her palms and the morning breeze made her still warm cheeks tingle.

Henry tried more small talk. Lizzie just stared into the distance.

"Got something on your mind?"

She didn't respond at once, wondering how much was proper to share. But Henry was a friend and who else would she tell? She changed to a cross-legged position, now shoulder to shoulder with him.

"It's nothing all that important," she said, still taking in the rocks, the trees, and the drying wildflowers. "I was thinking this might be as good a place as any for . . . "

Henry waited for her to finish her thought.

"We—Mimi and I—we have my parents' ashes. Right now, they're just in Mimi's Wren Haven storage locker and it seems we ought to do something with them."

As she spoke, Lizzie knew why something felt different this morning. What was different was that, however awkward, however difficult this conversation was, today she was not upset. She wasn't sniffling and weeping.

"Isn't that what people are supposed to do? Scatter the ashes someplace? I have a friend whose grandfather passed away. He used to be a sailor, so her family took a boat trip and scattered his ashes in the water."

She gazed upward at the blue sky, framed by the pine needles. A few of the needles were catching the glint of the sun.

Henry brought her attention back down to earth. "Was there someplace special to your parents?"

Like the city of Paris? No. The woods where we spent that rain-soaked vacation week? Definitely not. The house with the dripping faucet and the garden where nothing seemed to grow? She didn't think so.

"Not that I know of. That's why I was thinking . . . Anyway, if ash scattering is something I should take care of, then I guess I have to find . . ." there was a slight waver in her voice that she hoped Henry wouldn't hear. But, of course, he did and gave her a moment to gather herself.

"Not everyone scatters the ashes, Lizzie."

"No? It's not, like, a responsibility?"

"No, it's not. A ritual like that is to comfort the living or to honor wishes expressed by the deceased, but it's not a law, or any kind of social expectation."

"No?"

"No, certainly not." He paused and chewed his lower lip for a moment. "Since your parents were so young, I'm guessing they hadn't expressed anything related to their passing."

"No, not that I know of. Mimi arranged everything."

Henry nodded, and there was another silent moment between them.

"Then what do people do?" Lizzie asked. "They can't just keep the cardboard box in a storage locker forever," she said, a touch of her old cynicism creeping back in.

Henry took his time in responding. "Well, with no expression from the decedents, it really depends on the wishes of the family." He looked at her and said, "And you're family. You and Mimi."

Lizzie nodded, dry-eyed.

"You'd need a permit but scattering them here would be perfectly fine. This is a beautiful spot and if you think that would make you feel good, why not?" He paused before rounding out his advice. "But some people can't bear the thought of distributing the ashes; they feel like they are throwing away or rejecting their loved ones. That's why many people keep the ashes."

"Keep them? Are you kidding?"

"I guess it's a lot less common today, but sometimes people get a nice urn—the funeral home can help with that—and just keep the ashes on a shelf somewhere."

"Like a knickknack?"

"Yes. And some of those urns are quite beautiful works of art. They look like they belong in a museum."

Lizzie was so stunned she couldn't say anything.

Henry looked out toward the old Whitely property.

"Some people just take the box of ashes and bury it somewhere. I have an aunt who did that when my uncle died. They had both loved gardening and had done some gorgeous landscaping together, so it was right for them." He thought some more and turned in Lizzie's direction. "But another option is a columbarium."

"A what?"

"It's a formal place, usually at a traditional cemetery, with walls of small niches, above ground, for sealing in the ashes. And, just like a graveyard, family can visit whenever they want. That's what I did when Cathy . . . " Now it was Henry who needed to take a moment and clear his throat. "You know I lost my wife not long ago."

Yes, she knew and understood this moment. They sat together in silence for another couple of minutes.

Henry took the conversation in a different direction. "It was Cathy's idea to move to Wren Haven. I'd had a good career as a cop and retired a good deal earlier than most people. Cathy too." He turned to Lizzie with a small smile. "She trained the police dogs. Loved her job."

Henry looked toward the Whitely property again.

"So, we were both free—no more work, no kids."

At this, he smiled in the rueful way people do when recollecting a bittersweet time. "To tell you the truth, the way Cathy used to talk about the dogs, I think she thought they were her kids."

He was silent for a minute, then gave a slow wag of his head.

"So anyway, we had a long runway ahead of us, or so we thought.

Then Cathy got diagnosed. We thought it would make sense to have a simplified living situation, so we checked into Wren Haven." Henry spoke slowly. "Now that I think about it, though, although she let me think it was a joint decision, she was the real driver behind our move here." He paused, then said, "And she'd always be dragging me to one activity or another, introducing me around, getting me to volunteer for things. I think she knew her time was more limited than she let on and wanted to make sure I wasn't alone." He pressed the heel of his hand to his eye.

A bunch of kids ran by on the trail behind them. Henry waited until they were out of earshot before continuing, this time a bit more brightly.

"And it worked! I've got plenty of friends to go places with, nice people to join for dinner, and even a bike-riding chum!"

At this, Lizzie gave him the smile of a friend and a light pat on the shoulder.

chapter 65

It ended just as it had started, with an uncharacteristic action from the usually predictable Mimi.

One afternoon, Lizzie arrived home from school and threw her jacket and books onto the sofa bed. She was pleased with herself for having made it a habit to tidy up before rushing off to school in the morning.

Hanging on the louvered door of the closet was a chic black pantsuit.

"Mimi," she called, "what's this?" She turned to Mimi, who leaned against the doorjamb.

"Like it?"

"Well, it's beautiful, of course, but it looks a little small for you."

"I got a call from the Surprise Shoppe this afternoon. Madame Lacroix just had this come in and thought it might be your size."

Lizzie brushed her fingertips over the lightweight wool. Although knowing next to nothing about high-end garments, it took all of another thirty seconds to realize that the seams, cut, and construction were like nothing she had ever seen—and in a good way. The label was unmistakable. A distinctive string was wrapped around the middle button, suggesting the lack of a tag.

Mimi gave the string a little tug. "Looks brand new."

"It's from the Surprise Shoppe?"

"That's why it's called the Surprise Shoppe!"

"But this must have cost—"

"Don't worry about it. Madame said few customers would wear such a small size, so she just charged the same as anything else she had on her rack. Go ahead. Slip it on."

Almost afraid to take the jacket from the hanger, Lizzie gently held it aloft for a moment and then slipped one arm in, then the other. It fit perfectly. Of course it would if Madame said it would. As she turned to look at herself in the mirror, Lizzie ignored her saucer eyes and open mouth, taking in the dramatic asymmetric closure and tapered waist.

"For me?" she said again in disbelief.

Mimi gave a modest shrug and a small smile. "A little present. For no reason."

At that point Lizzie let herself relax and savor the beautiful ensemble, not only over the unexpected addition to her wardrobe but because she could now truly believe Mimi was no longer overly concerned with her bank balance. Whatever Emma Jeffries—and Mac and Henry—had done behind the scenes had put Mimi at ease.

chapter 66

"Hey, Mimi," Lizzie called as she did her usual after-school whiz-through Mimi's front door.

"Hey, yourself," Mimi replied from the kitchen table.

Lizzie found Mimi with papers, pencils, cookbooks, and other paraphernalia spread before her.

"What are you working on?"

"Planning Thanksgiving dinner."

"Won't there be a nice dinner in the dining hall?"

"Of course there will."

But Lizzie had been at Wren Haven long enough to surmise what Mimi wasn't saying: that Thanksgiving dinner in the dining room would be dreadful. The food would definitely be extra special, but for a holiday such as Easter or Thanksgiving, the dining room would be mostly empty with a significant proportion of the populace having decamped for relatives' homes. Those remaining would be like the kids who ate lunch alone in the school cafeteria, feeling like they were wearing a sign around their necks reading *Loser*.

Mimi continued her upbeat planning. "But Thanksgiving is a family holiday. Home-roasted turkey. All the trimmings." A beat of silence; two beats. "And I just thought since this will be the first holiday since . . . "

Of course. Lizzie didn't want to think about it, frankly.

"I always used to go to your house, but now that you are here," Mimi said, "I thought we could try rounding up some of the family and invite them over."

"What family?" Lizzie asked, bewildered.

"Yes, I know," Mimi responded. "You don't have any siblings and mine are long gone. I was the baby of my family, you know."

Lizzie slipped her coat off, slung it over the back of the other kitchen chair, and sat down.

"No, I didn't know."

"I had an older brother, Arnold—we called him Arnie—and my sister, Mae. But they were ten and twelve years older than me, so I grew up almost like you, like an only child. And I'm not having much luck," she said, tapping the handwritten phone directory on the table, the one Henry had leafed through. "I've crossed off lots of names and addresses of friends and distant family. Mae had a daughter, but I've just found out that she and her family have moved and now live halfway across the country."

Lizzie blinked at the revelation of having relatives she'd never met.

"Then I thought of Mrs. Perkins. I don't know if you'd remember her. She was a widow and my neighbor before I moved here. Gracious woman. And she's still got the same phone number. But it turns out that Mrs. Perkins is now Mrs. Santelli! Last April, she married a widower with a large family, so they'll be spending Thanksgiving with them. But there is one more and I'm glad you're home because I've got a project for you. Your father's brother, Stanley."

Immediately, Lizzie felt numb, followed by a trace of the lightheadedness she had experienced the morning she had awoken late and Mimi's eyes had been pink and glassy. She said nothing.

"I haven't heard anything about him for a few years now, so I imagine you haven't heard from him either."

Mimi began to stack all the papers and books together. "I don't have any contact information for him, so I thought you could try tracking him down on the internet. You're so much more facile than I am about all this social media stuff."

"Lizzie? Did you hear me?"

Lizzie swallowed and nodded.

Mimi's humor faded with a distinct note of disappointment. "I thought you'd be pleased."

Lizzie stayed silent. "It's just . . ." How could she express her revulsion over Stanley's cornering her, the smell of his hot alcoholic breath in her face, his attempt to shove his hands . . . "I may spend Thanksgiving with Shelly."

She hadn't spoken to Shelly in months, but she bet she could wangle an invitation for Thanksgiving dinner out of her, especially knowing Shelly didn't like any of her relatives.

"Nonsense. You and I are still a family. Small, yes, but I can still roast a turkey."

Lizzie interrupted her with a fling of her wrist, a jerk of her chin, and the short temper that had receded in the spring.

"Go right ahead and invite him if you want, but I won't be here." She stared at her knees, her elbows pressed to her sides, as she bit the inside of her cheek.

For a good twenty seconds, Mimi sat with her mouth open at this reaction. She stared at the blank kitchen wall as if running scenarios in her mind. Then she clasped her hand to her mouth, pressing her eyes shut. When she opened her eyes, she touched Lizzie's arm.

"Lizzie, did your Uncle Stanley hurt you?"

Hurt? What constitutes hurt? She'd been twelve! This wasn't something anyone would want to discuss with a grandmother.

Lizzie stayed silent for a long stretch, before saying, "No, not hurt."

Thankfully, Stanley had been drunk enough and Lizzie strong enough, even at twelve, to squirm away to the safety of her father's arm. Her voice was scratchy with embarrassment as she repeated, "No."

"Ah," sighed Mimi. She stared at the ceiling for a few seconds before again facing her granddaughter.

"Lizzie, honey, I'm so sorry. I didn't know."

Now the wave of guilt came. Lizzie looked at the books and papers on the kitchen table. Mimi had been copying recipes out of the cookbooks. She'd been making phone calls and shopping lists, probably for hours.

Obviously, Mimi wanted to make the holiday special for her. But now all Lizzie could do was put her elbows on the table and her hands on top of her bowed head, embarrassed and guilty over the whole episode. Embarrassed by Stanley, guilty over her outburst, guilty about lying to Mimi about Shelly, and guilty over rejecting Mimi's well-intentioned holiday plans. It was all compounded by Mimi's palpable disappointment as she absently flipped the pages of her worn address book.

A half minute into wallowing in self-criticism, Lizzie had a genuine light-bulb moment.

"What about Herb? We could invite Herb! I heard him say at dinner the other night he wished he had an excuse to not spend Thanksgiving with his wild grandsons. And besides," Lizzie said, now with a mischievous twinkle, "Herb is almost family."

Mimi chuckled and even blushed a little. "Right you are, Lizzie, right you are."

"And Mac. Could we invite Mac?"

"We could invite your whole golfing foursome if you'd like to," Mimi agreed with a rise in her voice. Then, through a half laugh, she said, "It'll be like one of those sappy Thanksgiving movies."

Lizzie joined the joke, her voice at a happier pitch than the angry tone of her reaction to the specter of Stanley. "One where everyone gives thanks with the unconventional, unrelated friends as they gather for a big family dinner."

The two of them went on like this, throwing in bits of silliness.

Lizzie thought to herself how she must be aging too soon if she was finishing Mimi's sentences. But a laugh always felt good, and this scenario was definitely preferable to Thanksgiving with Shelly.

chapter 67

THANKSGIVING MORNING PROMISED A BEAUTIFUL FALL DAY with sun filtering through the remaining leaves on the trees. Lizzie slipped into her scuffs and rubbed her eyes as she shuffled out to the kitchen. The turkey was already in the oven, the sweet potatoes scrubbed and ready to go in later, and the napkins, china, and crystal sparkled on the dining room table. Mimi must have been up quite early.

"Good morning, angel," Mimi greeted her from behind her paper.

Lizzie yawned with a blurred "mmm" as she set the cornflakes and milk on the table. The two of them sat silently, Lizzie crunching and Mimi leafing through yesterday's *Wren Haven News* and occasionally taking a sip of coffee. It was a quiet day: no groundskeepers out mowing or raking, no maintenance staff vacuuming the hall carpet.

Lizzie read the back page of Mimi's paper. The lull in her

crunching caught Mimi's attention.

"How're ya doing, honey?"

"Okay."

"What are you looking at?"

Mimi turned the paper so she could see what Lizzie had been reading.

"Just the ad for Disney World. Mom and Dad said we could go sometime, but that was a long time ago."

Lizzie took another spoonful, contemplative. This felt right. She could finally talk about her Mom and Dad in the past tense.

"After a while, I just grew tired of asking."

She finished the dregs of her cereal, rinsed her bowl and put it in the dishwasher, then headed for the shower.

chapter 68

"I invited Silas," Lizzie called as she combed her wet hair.

"You've got fifteen minutes," Mimi called back.

"What?" Lizzie stepped out of the bathroom, wrapped in a towel, comb at mid-stroke, astonished to see Mimi whizzing around the apartment with her coat on.

"You've got exactly fifteen minutes to pack a bag. Don't forget your swimsuit."

"Mimi, what?"

Mimi seemed elated.

"I don't understand what's going on."

Mimi gave her the biggest smile Lizzie had ever seen from her.

"I called the number on the ad, and we can just make the last flight if we hurry. We're going to Disney World!"

"But what about Thanksgiving dinner? And I have to pack."

"Oh, don't worry about anything. They're all adults. They can help themselves without our hovering around. And packing? It's Florida! Bathing suit, underwear, t-shirts, and shorts. Done."

Lizzie stared at Mimi.

"Well, don't just stand there. Get dressed!"

Fourteen-and-a-half minutes later, bags in hand, Mimi locked the patio door as they exited toward the car park.

"Mimi, you're locking the door. How will they get in?"

Mimi did a Lizzie imitation by rolling her eyes and drooping her shoulders. "Lizzie, Rosa is a security guard. She's got a master key."

As they headed toward the car, Lizzie giggled.

"What's so funny?"

Lizzie looked at Mimi. "You invited Rosa?"

"Sure."

Lizzie giggled again. "I invited James."

They both giggled together.

Cruising toward Wren Haven's main gate, they passed Silas on the restored golf cart. It looked like he had a white bakery box on the seat beside him. When he recognized Mimi's car, he raised his hand to wave as he watched them ride past him.

Mimi saluted him with a huge, slow wave and then gave Lizzie a quick glance, looking delighted.

Lizzie reached out and grasped Mimi's hand on the descending arc of Mimi's wave to Silas. "We're going to have the best time ever!"

epilogue

Mimi was right. The guests at 218 Wren Haven baked the potatoes and served themselves. They had a grand time speculating as to Mimi and Lizzie's absence. The only clue was a cryptic note saying, "We skipped town for the weekend. Have a nice Thanksgiving without us."

No one realized James was also absent.

Henry's ten-minute visit to Emma Jeffries at the bank had set some bigger wheels in motion, as he'd suspected it would. The payments to utility companies from Mimi's account were not for services at Wren Haven but at 585 Appleton Street, six miles away. The Appleton Street address was also the residence of James Heathwood. Scientific Survey was a nonexistent entity whose president was also James Heathwood. When the court assigned the irascible Judge Conroy to hear the case, James won the lottery of luck. Conroy heard the case involving a foreign student who had bilked an American senior citizen out of a few thousand dollars, including James's sad story of how he had planned to return Mimi's money after finishing his PhD. Conroy counted the days until his upcoming retirement and weighed the potential of the case dragging on if he didn't dispatch it, so he swallowed a couple of antacid tablets and issued a ruling demanding repayment of funds with high interest within a year of graduation, along with community service teaching computer skills to inner-city children.

Wren Haven closed the computer center and turned it into a yoga studio. When Wren Haven originally opened, many residents were not computer literate, but few now needed basic instruction.

An article in the *Wren Haven News* stated, "Serena Patel will be the new technology concierge at Wren Haven. She will assist residents with setting up their smart TVs and other devices." Most thought this development was a definite step up. No one complained about closing the computer center.

That was until Madame Lacroix saw the article and stormed over to Howard Fulbright's office.

"Yoga studio gets beautiful space with enormous glass windows for sweaty workouts? Probably empty half the time? Yoga people can go to fitness center with lots of mats and ventilation. Surprise Shoppe needs much better visibility for residents to see new collections. Surprise Shoppe has tripled the hours it's open and tripled its contributions to the Fellowship Fund!"

However, the agreement had already been settled. As a concession, Fulbright agreed to give the Surprise Shoppe an even larger space near the craft rooms and cafeteria, which would have large windows and good foot traffic. He promised to renovate to Madame's specifications. With two proper dressing rooms and good lighting, Madame was satisfied.

On January 2 of the new year, Mac received a call from the pharmaceutical company he had worked for before retiring. Mac's self-description as a finance guy was modest. He had been the chief financial officer of one of the world's largest multinational corporations. His successor's risky transactions had caused trouble for both him and the company. They needed someone with a sterling reputation to take the reins for a half year while the board identified a replacement. Mac agreed and once again drove to the headquarters each weekday morning. He dove into rectifying the damage that had been done and relished reacquainting himself with his corporate surroundings with one exception: he couldn't get accustomed to the new casual dress code. His compromise—which he surprised himself by admitting was an improvement—was to don one of his impeccably tailored suits, minus a tie. Early in this new chapter, he had an idea that he was excited about. Although it would take a few months to gel, he thought he might institute an internship program for aspiring finance majors.

Amos never followed up on his idea for a traveling fashion show with Madame Lacroix because a much better opportunity came along. His nephew, the part-time DJ, found he was getting more bookings than he could handle. He had recently been promoted at his day job, and he persuaded Amos to take half the workload for a few nights a week. Amos and the voice that plumbed the depths of the earth were back in the spotlight again.

Tamika seemed to take a shine to merchandizing. Madame Lacroix arranged a summer internship for her at the Surprise Shoppe. After graduating, she got into a management trainee program with the retail chain that had successfully adapted to online shopping.

Lydia Fernandez found an ad for a spectacular month-long cruise for the spring and convinced Angelina Lacroix to travel with her. Following her success in upgrading the Surprise Shoppe, it was the perfect time for Madame to reconsider her isolation in the thrift shop operation, and she quickly agreed. It helped that the cruise schedule was such that she could also be in Milan during fashion week.

Saul and Rosalie Glassman succumbed to Madame Lacroix's appeal to take over management of the Surprise Shoppe while she travelled. As consistently proven, Madame Lacroix could be persuasive.

"I don't know, Angie," Rosalie had argued, "our expertise is in a different end of the industry."

Madame pointed out that she couldn't entrust the Surprise Shoppe to someone without a sense of style and the Glassmans were up on all the latest trends. She additionally thought Saul could improve the menswear section. The Surprise Shoppe entered a new era.

Helen Cameron's apartment had turned out astonishingly beautiful, which led her to hold an open house so she could meet more of her Wren Haven neighbors and also let them admire Beth Cox's interior design. A stroke of inspiration that could only be called brilliant hit Rosalie Glassman when she saw the result. With Madame out of the picture for at least a couple of months, Rosalie convinced Beth to take over the furniture section of the Surprise Shoppe. With Rosalie and Beth in a united front, they convinced Howard Fulbright to allocate at least as large a space to home furnishings as to apparel. After all, Beth had argued, furniture takes up more room than dresses and shirts. Fulbright found it hard to argue with that logic. Beth named the new enterprise Surprise Décor. Amos played master of ceremonies at its grand opening. The Fellowship Fund skyrocketed.

Henry, ever more entrenched in Wren Haven life, was voted secretary of its newly formed bicycle club, with which he rode Mondays and Thursdays.

RealBank recognized Emma Jeffries for her excellent customer service with a promotion to manage a larger branch.

Greta, one of Wren Haven's oldest, departed for the Great Beyond in January. Only a few close friends and family knew why she always wore long-sleeved sweaters: to hide her forearm with its numerical tattoo.

Not long thereafter, Snowball followed Greta to the Great Beyond. All of Charlie's Wren Haven friends helped him lay

Snowball to rest at the head of the walking trail. The next day, they all helped Charlie move into his new quarters at Wren Haven's assisted living residence.

George received an unexpected invitation. The Wren Haven librarian asked George if he would present a weekly current events roundup. Though he was at first skeptical of its value—after all, anyone could pick up as many of the newspapers in the lobby as they wanted—it proved to be quite popular. Many residents—Mimi was one—found it a struggle to manage the newsprint anymore and preferred in-person gatherings to sitting in front of a television or computer screen, so they appreciated George's weekly summaries. Sylvia Pawling assigned one of her newer staff to provide refreshments for the Wednesday afternoon meetings. Janna ensured the sessions started and ended punctually. She also ensured there were sufficient folding chairs, all meticulously arranged. Howard Fulbright even attended occasionally. Suitably impressed, he moved the event to the former Surprise Shoppe space, ordered the installation of better lighting, new carpeting and a fresh coat of paint.

Virginia kept her golfing championship, although she'd had to identify a substitute for Mac, at least through the following June. Carlos, a newcomer to Wren Haven, was rather good. She would have to watch her back if she wanted to hold on to her title.

Lizzie gave Winnie the television with the unused karaoke attachment. Winnie joined the line-dancing class and put a whole new spin on it to the delight of her classmates and even the instructor.

Luisa developed a loyal following and eventually opened her own salon. After opening her second salon, she hired Rosa to manage both; Luisa needed her time to scout locations for a third.

The Machete continued to relish tweaking Howard Fulbright. He studied building codes to write articles for the *Wren Haven News*, the latest challenging the water levels in Wren Haven's toilets.

Mimi and Herb furtively checked out any larger units at Wren Haven that came on the market. They were as giddy as teenagers, and planned a secret, two-year engagement so Lizzie could settle into college before they started their married life together.

Lizzie decided not to pursue her swim team ambition. After several recent experiences, Lizzie felt motivated to catch up in accounting, so she decided to spend more of her time in the library instead of at the pool. And besides, Albert was a cool guy who was happy to help her over any rough patches. She apologized to Marge, who had put so much time into coaching her. Fortunately, Marge did not make her feel guilty in the least.

There was one other event Lizzie would remember for many years. She would remember it with pride and self-assurance instead of the guilt, shame, and anger that had permeated so many of her earlier Wren Haven days. This memory was of the annual residents' council meeting. As usual, a near-capacity crowd had filled the auditorium. Mimi went, of course. She and Herb found seats next to Virginia. Mac was also there, as were Evelyn, Mike, and Alice. George and Janna arrived early. The Glassmans took front-row seats. Helen joined the Coxes.

In a mature act of contrition, after setting aside what she estimated she'd need for cell phone service and spending money for the next six years, Lizzie donated the proceeds from the sale of the storage locker contents to the Fellowship Fund. She had glided across the auditorium stage, handed the check to Howard Fulbright, and shook his hand. Everyone applauded. Lizzie hadn't worn the pink dress. Instead, she'd worn a chic black pantsuit, a distinctive onyx ring, and black patent-leather spikes. She towered over Fulbright. *Cool.*

Acknowledgments

My deepest gratitude goes to my husband, Frank, unfailingly supportive of all my professional endeavors.

Lizzie's journey to adulthood would have been less joyous without the encouragement of friends and family who lent their enthusiasm along the way, often clamoring to read her story.

Additionally, I wish to acknowledge Rev. Susan Sparks, Alice Mills, Laura Roth, Gregory Cox and Michael Petruzzi. Each generously contributed his or her professional knowledge to the research for this book.

Finally, I must thank Linda Stirling of The Publishing Circle, who recognized the potential of this story, whipping it into shape with patience, coaching, editing, publishing, and marketing.

About the Author

SKYLAR SLATE BEGAN WRITING CREATIVELY IN GRADE school, adapting children's stories into plays for her young friends to act in.

After earning a B. A. in English from Rutgers University, she spent the early years of her professional life in public relations and advertising. Pivoting to finance, she worked her way through New York University's Graduate School of Business Administration authoring a university newsletter.

During a forty-year career in finance, she gained some prominence in her field. In addition to writing extensive corporate memoranda and numerous speaking presentations, she has been published on a variety of institutional investing topics.

Coolness to the Wind is her first novel. It was inspired by spending extensive time with a family member who relocated to a retirement community similar to the fictional Wren Haven. The story is intended as a tribute to today's retirement alternatives, a dramatic leap from those of prior generations, as well as a recognition of the knowledge and experience of their residents.

Made in United States
North Haven, CT
30 August 2024